RAVEN

THE PIRATE PRINCESS

Year Three: Monsters of the Deep

Chapter Nine: The Black Fort

Written By: Jeremy Whitley

Pencils By:
(Pages 1-3, 10-19) Xenia Pamfil
(Pages 4-6, 20-24) Telênia Albuquerque

Inks By:
(Pages 1-3, 10-19) JB Fuller
(Pages 4-6, 20-24) Pocket Owl

Colors By:
(Pages 1-3, 10-19) Lexillo
(Pages 4-6, 20-24) Valentina Pinto

Lettered By: Alex Scherkenbach

Cover By: Telenia Albuquerque

Bryan Seaton: Publisher - Vito Delsante: Editor In Chief
Jason Martin: Publisher-Danger Zone
Chad Cicconi: Deck Swabber

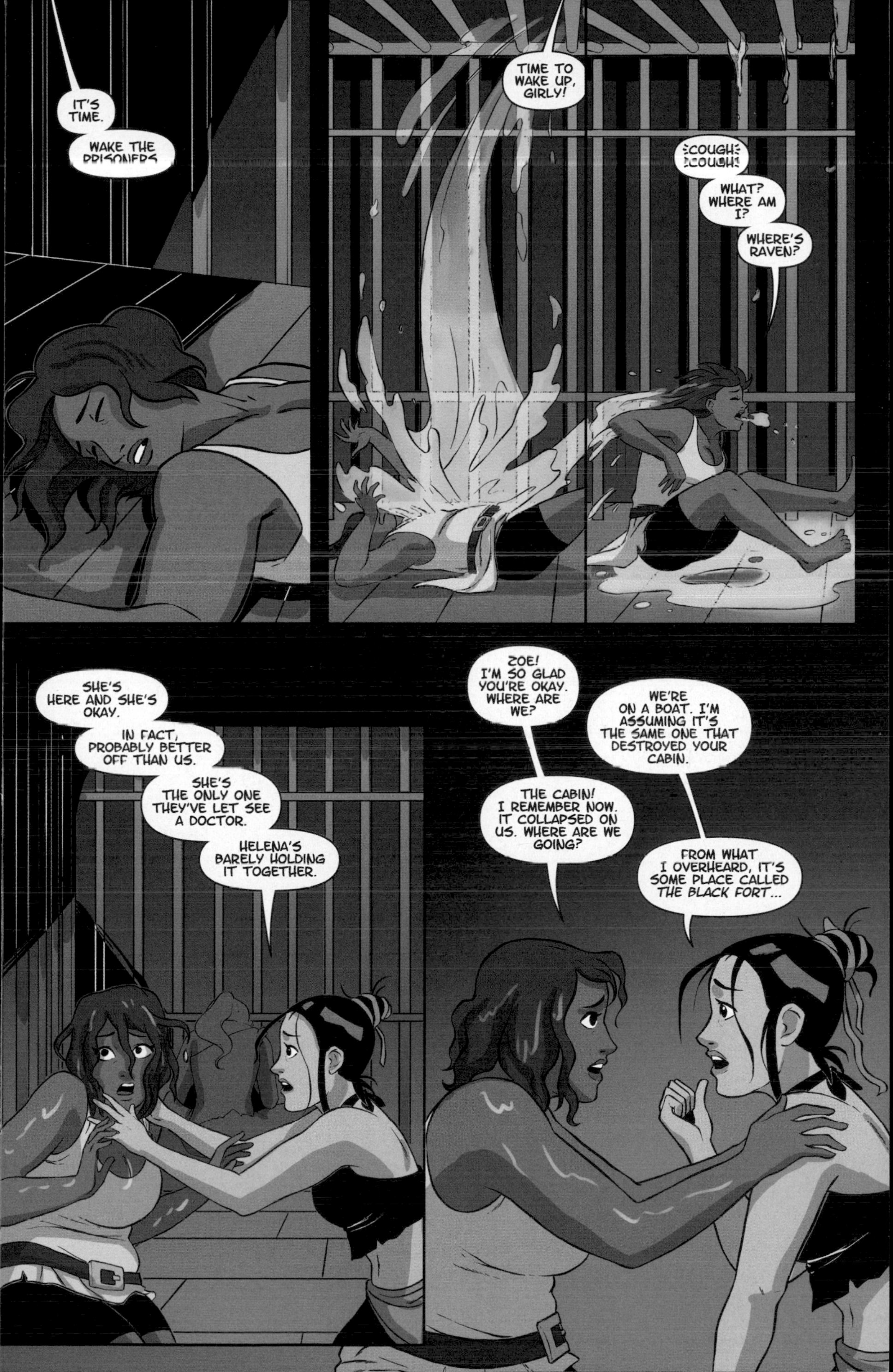
IT'S TIME.
WAKE THE PRISONERS.
TIME TO WAKE UP, GIRLY!
COUGH! COUGH!
WHAT? WHERE AM I?
WHERE'S RAVEN?
SHE'S HERE AND SHE'S OKAY.
IN FACT, PROBABLY BETTER OFF THAN US.
SHE'S THE ONLY ONE THEY'VE LET SEE A DOCTOR.
HELENA'S BARELY HOLDING IT TOGETHER.
ZOE! I'M SO GLAD YOU'RE OKAY. WHERE ARE WE?
WE'RE ON A BOAT. I'M ASSUMING IT'S THE SAME ONE THAT DESTROYED YOUR CABIN.
THE CABIN! I REMEMBER NOW. IT COLLAPSED ON US. WHERE ARE WE GOING?
FROM WHAT I OVERHEARD, IT'S SOME PLACE CALLED THE BLACK FORT...

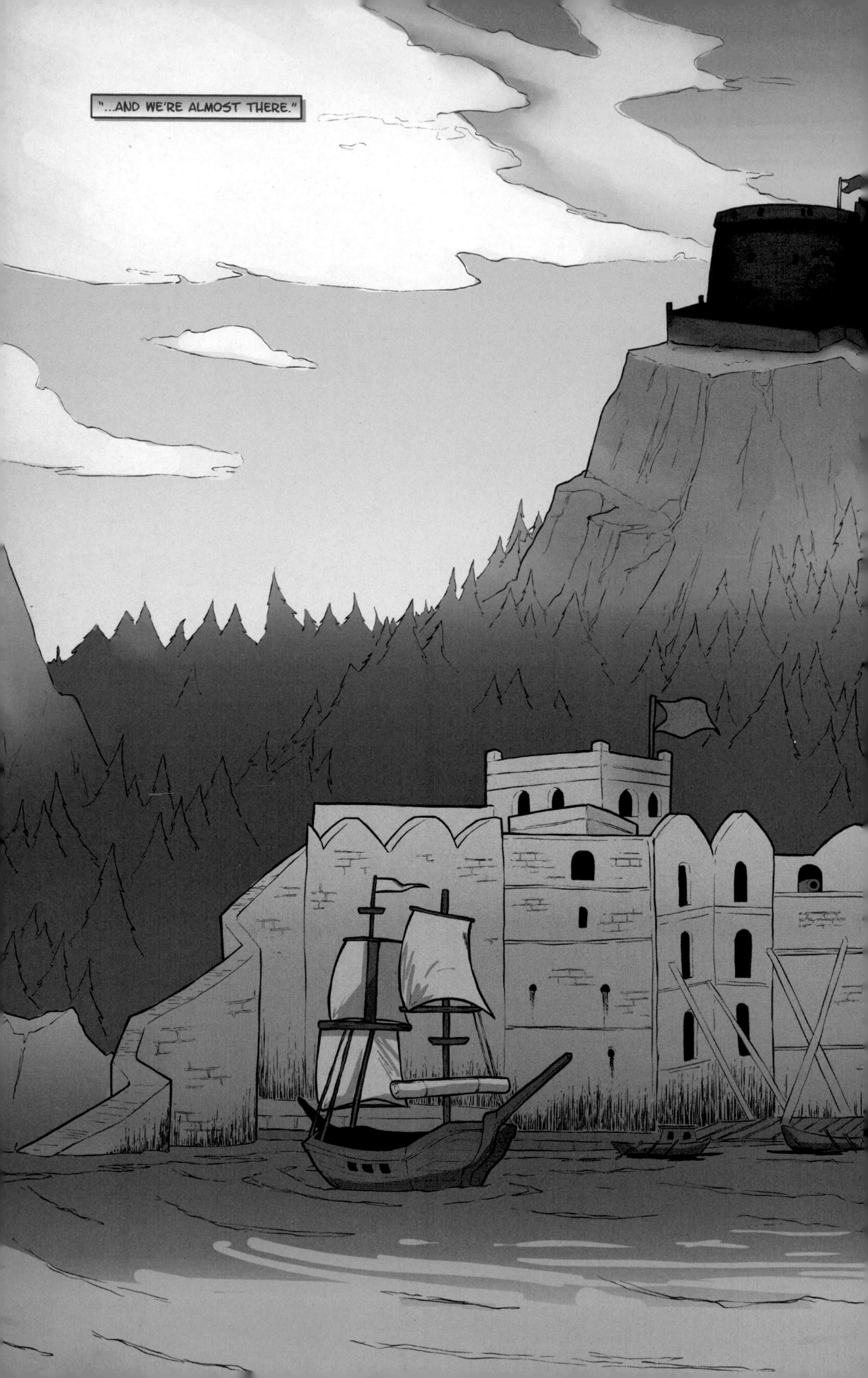
"...AND WE'RE ALMOST THERE."

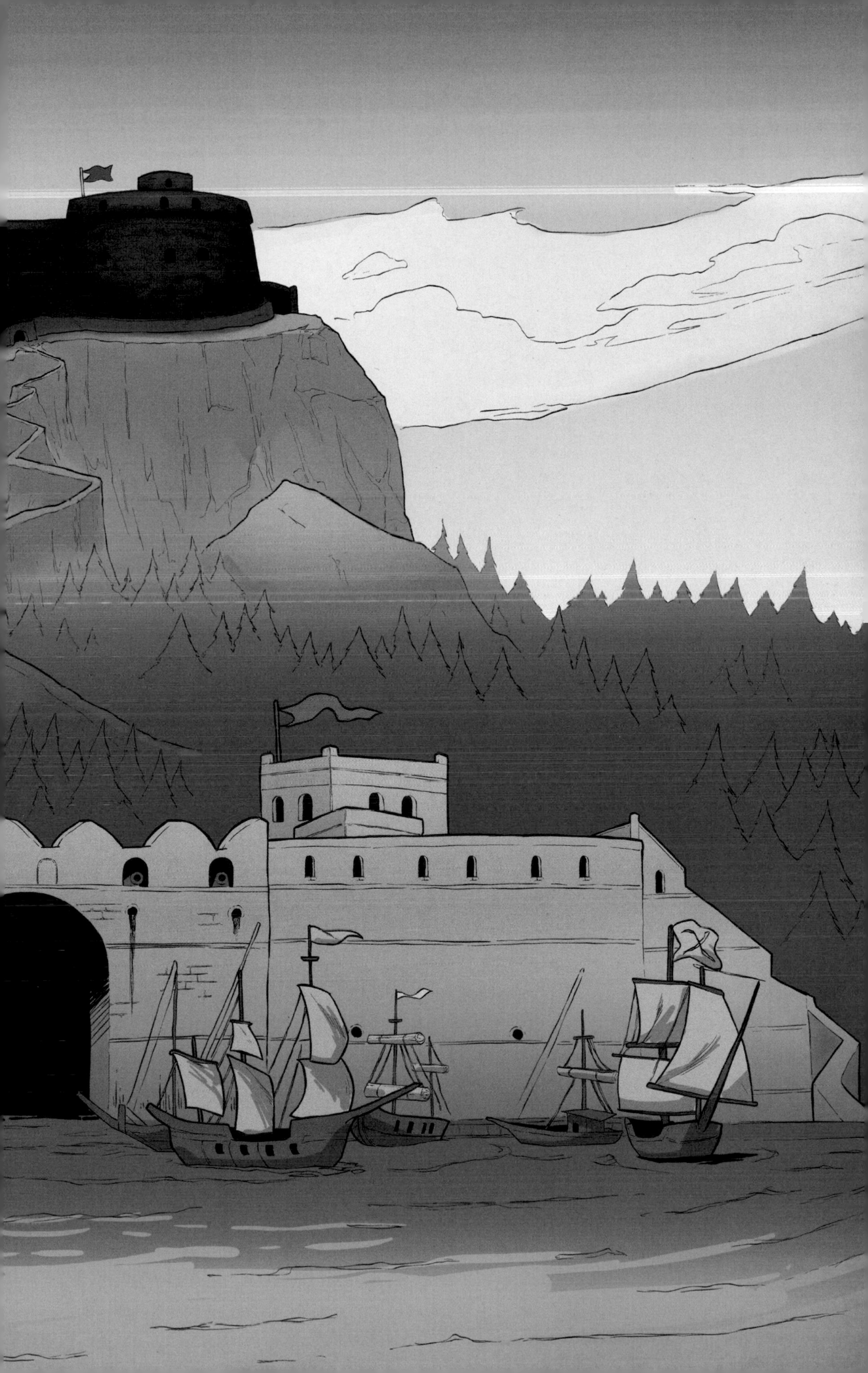

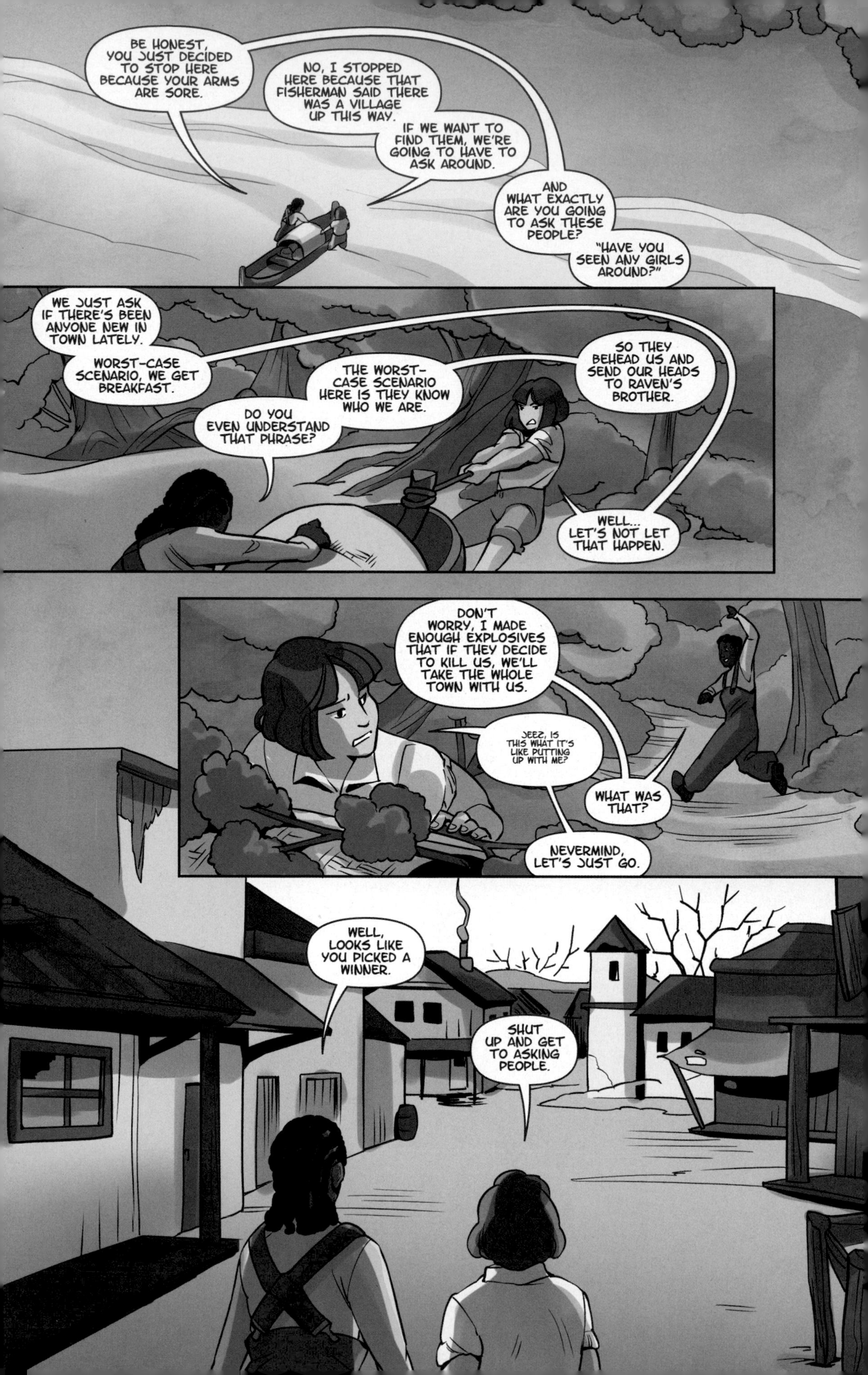
BE HONEST, YOU JUST DECIDED TO STOP HERE BECAUSE YOUR ARMS ARE SORE.
NO, I STOPPED HERE BECAUSE THAT FISHERMAN SAID THERE WAS A VILLAGE UP THIS WAY.
IF WE WANT TO FIND THEM, WE'RE GOING TO HAVE TO ASK AROUND.
AND WHAT EXACTLY ARE YOU GOING TO ASK THESE PEOPLE?
"HAVE YOU SEEN ANY GIRLS AROUND?"
WE JUST ASK IF THERE'S BEEN ANYONE NEW IN TOWN LATELY.
WORST-CASE SCENARIO, WE GET BREAKFAST.
THE WORST-CASE SCENARIO HERE IS THEY KNOW WHO WE ARE.
DO YOU EVEN UNDERSTAND THAT PHRASE?
SO THEY BEHEAD US AND SEND OUR HEADS TO RAVEN'S BROTHER.
WELL... LET'S NOT LET THAT HAPPEN.
DON'T WORRY, I MADE ENOUGH EXPLOSIVES THAT IF THEY DECIDE TO KILL US, WE'LL TAKE THE WHOLE TOWN WITH US.
JEEZ, IS THIS WHAT IT'S LIKE PUTTING UP WITH ME?
WHAT WAS THAT?
NEVERMIND, LET'S JUST GO.
WELL, LOOKS LIKE YOU PICKED A WINNER.
SHUT UP AND GET TO ASKING PEOPLE.

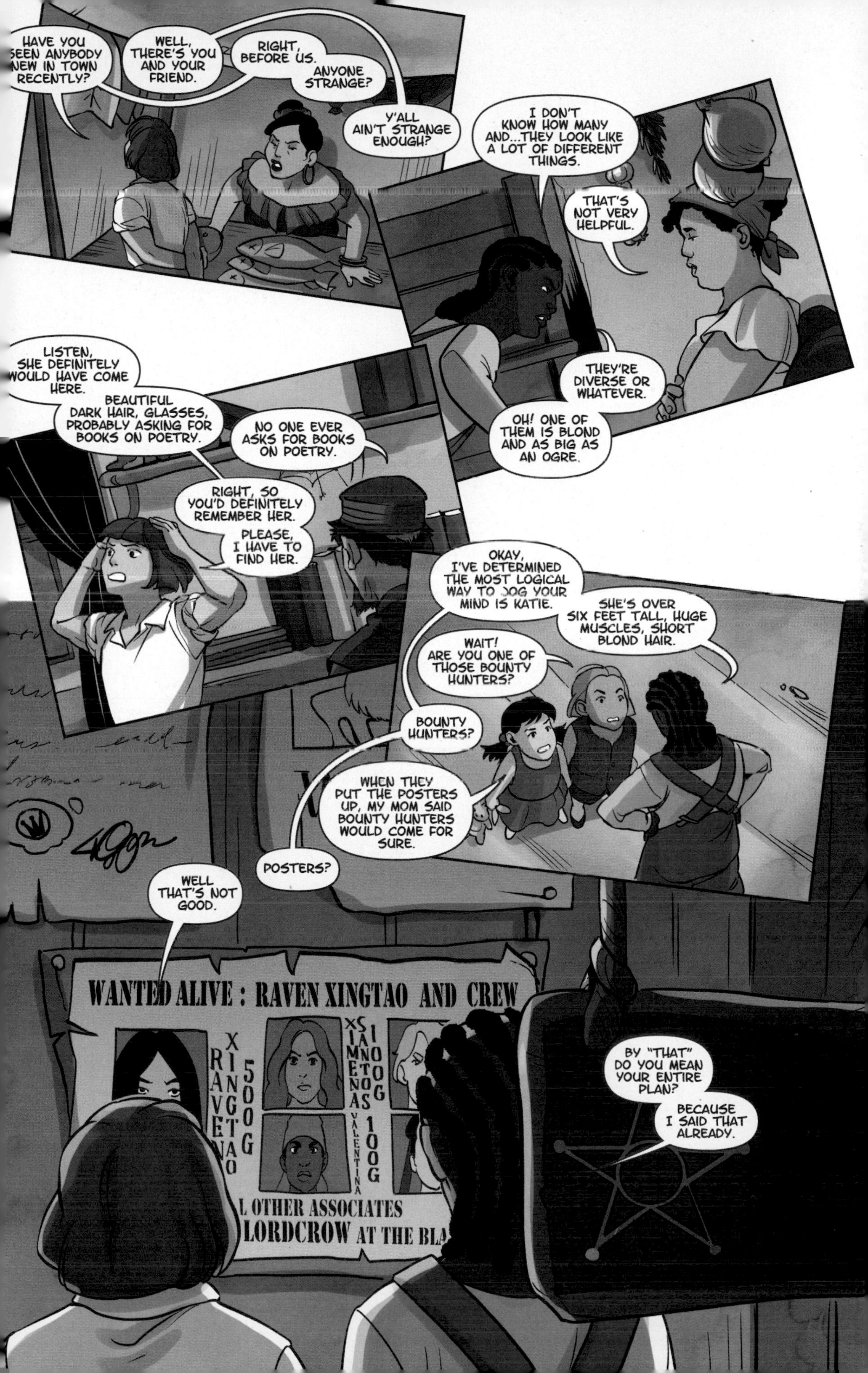
HAVE YOU SEEN ANYBODY NEW IN TOWN RECENTLY?
WELL, THERE'S YOU AND YOUR FRIEND.
RIGHT, BEFORE US.
ANYONE STRANGE?
Y'ALL AIN'T STRANGE ENOUGH?
I DON'T KNOW HOW MANY AND...THEY LOOK LIKE A LOT OF DIFFERENT THINGS.
THAT'S NOT VERY HELPFUL.
THEY'RE DIVERSE OR WHATEVER.
OH! ONE OF THEM IS BLOND AND AS BIG AS AN OGRE.
LISTEN, SHE DEFINITELY WOULD HAVE COME HERE.
BEAUTIFUL DARK HAIR, GLASSES, PROBABLY ASKING FOR BOOKS ON POETRY.
NO ONE EVER ASKS FOR BOOKS ON POETRY.
RIGHT, SO YOU'D DEFINITELY REMEMBER HER.
PLEASE, I HAVE TO FIND HER.
OKAY, I'VE DETERMINED THE MOST LOGICAL WAY TO JOG YOUR MIND IS KATIE.
SHE'S OVER SIX FEET TALL, HUGE MUSCLES, SHORT BLOND HAIR.
WAIT! ARE YOU ONE OF THOSE BOUNTY HUNTERS?
BOUNTY HUNTERS?
WHEN THEY PUT THE POSTERS UP, MY MOM SAID BOUNTY HUNTERS WOULD COME FOR SURE.
POSTERS?
WELL THAT'S NOT GOOD.
WANTED ALIVE : RAVEN XINGTAO AND CREW
RAVEN XINGTAO 500G
XIMENA SANTOS 100G
VALENTINA 100G
L OTHER ASSOCIATES
LORDCROW AT THE BLA
BY "THAT" DO YOU MEAN YOUR ENTIRE PLAN?
BECAUSE I SAID THAT ALREADY.

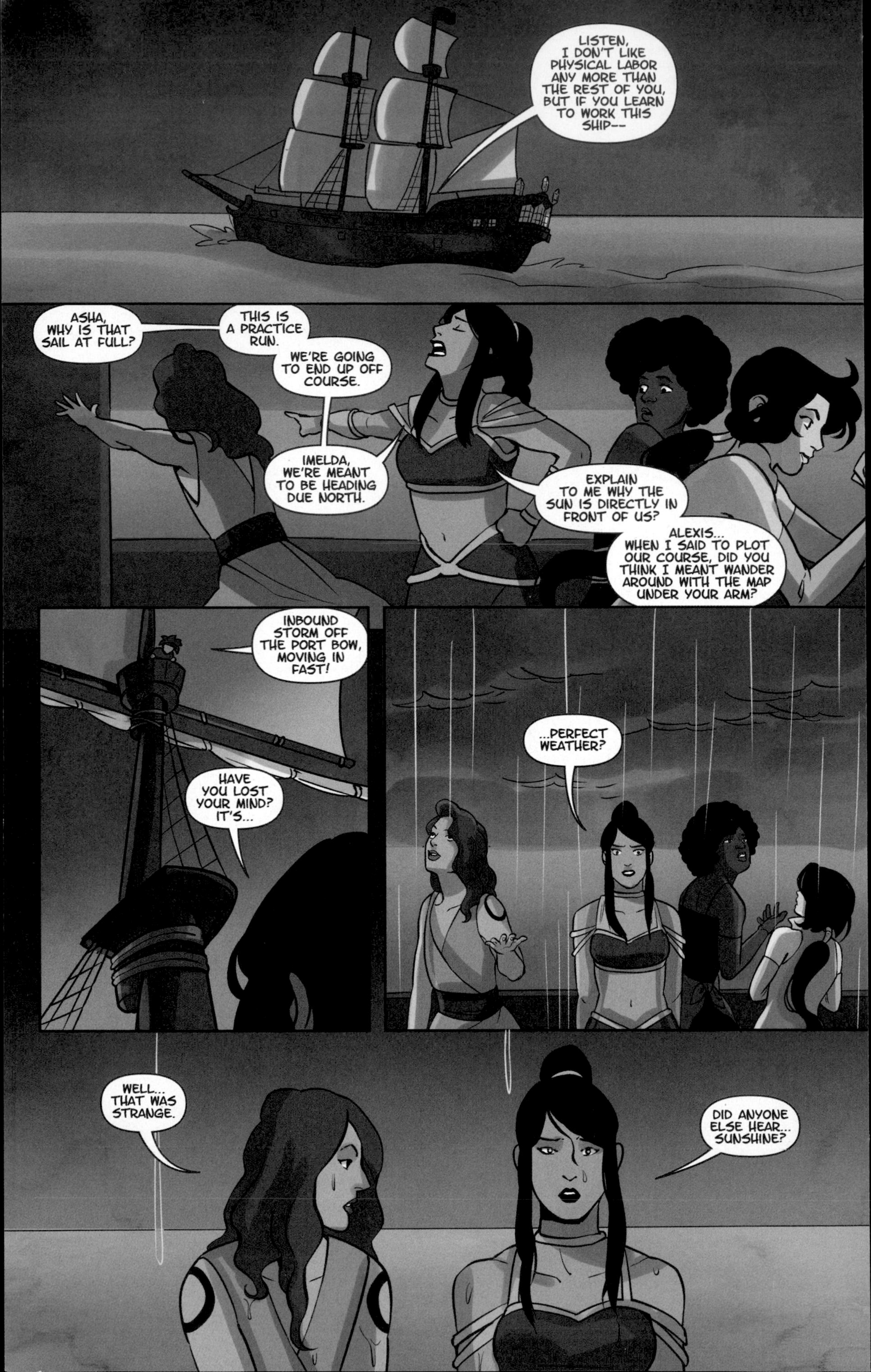
LISTEN, I DON'T LIKE PHYSICAL LABOR ANY MORE THAN THE REST OF YOU, BUT IF YOU LEARN TO WORK THIS SHIP--
ASHA, WHY IS THAT SAIL AT FULL?
THIS IS A PRACTICE RUN.
WE'RE GOING TO END UP OFF COURSE.
IMELDA, WE'RE MEANT TO BE HEADING DUE NORTH.
EXPLAIN TO ME WHY THE SUN IS DIRECTLY IN FRONT OF US?
ALEXIS... WHEN I SAID TO PLOT OUR COURSE, DID YOU THINK I MEANT WANDER AROUND WITH THE MAP UNDER YOUR ARM?
INBOUND STORM OFF THE PORT BOW, MOVING IN FAST!
HAVE YOU LOST YOUR MIND? IT'S...
...PERFECT WEATHER?
WELL... THAT WAS STRANGE.
DID ANYONE ELSE HEAR... SUNSHINE?

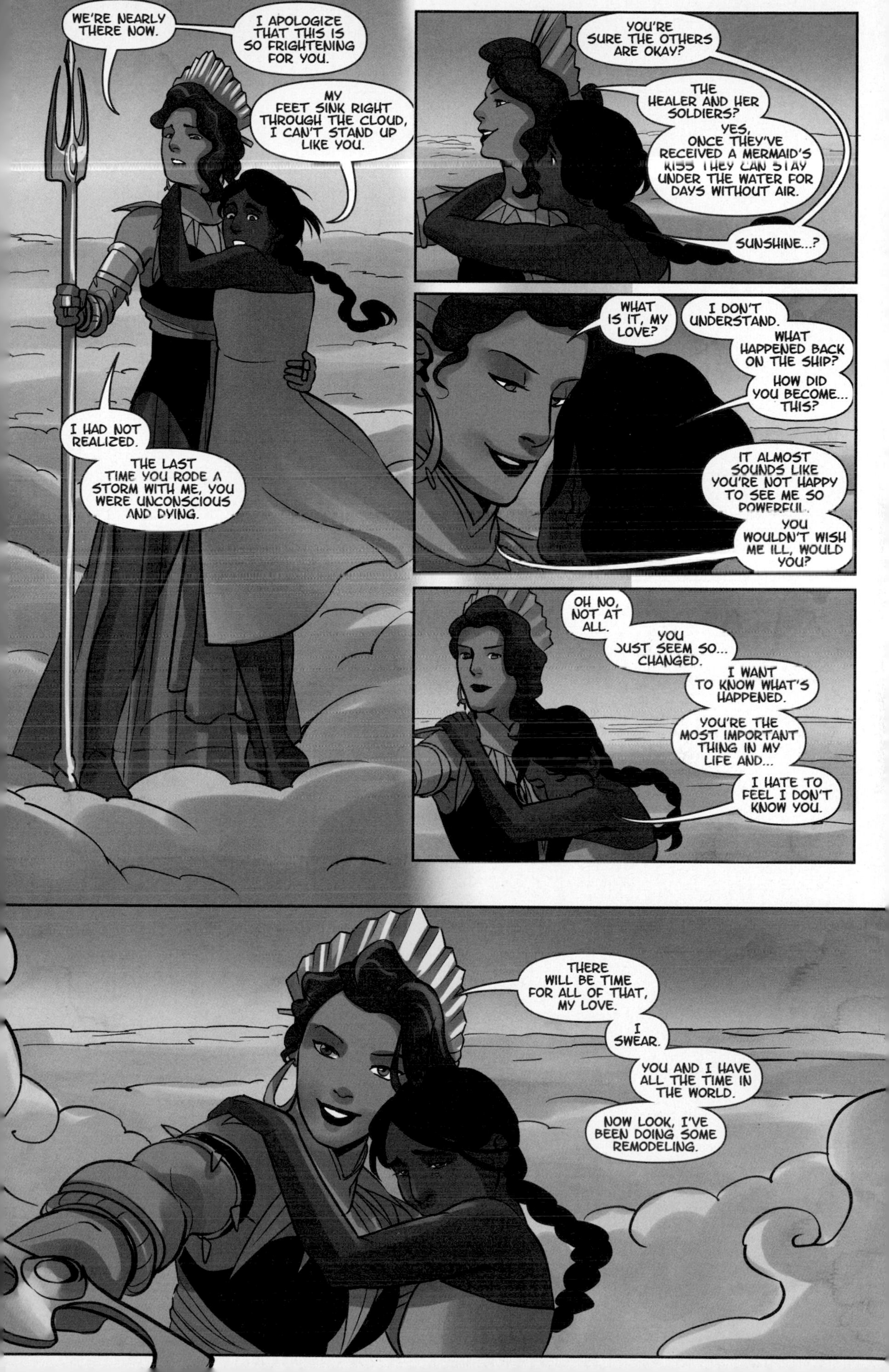
WE'RE NEARLY THERE NOW.
I APOLOGIZE THAT THIS IS SO FRIGHTENING FOR YOU.
MY FEET SINK RIGHT THROUGH THE CLOUD, I CAN'T STAND UP LIKE YOU.
I HAD NOT REALIZED.
THE LAST TIME YOU RODE A STORM WITH ME, YOU WERE UNCONSCIOUS AND DYING.
YOU'RE SURE THE OTHERS ARE OKAY?
THE HEALER AND HER SOLDIERS?
YES, ONCE THEY'VE RECEIVED A MERMAID'S KISS THEY CAN STAY UNDER THE WATER FOR DAYS WITHOUT AIR.
SUNSHINE...?
WHAT IS IT, MY LOVE?
I DON'T UNDERSTAND.
WHAT HAPPENED BACK ON THE SHIP?
HOW DID YOU BECOME... THIS?
IT ALMOST SOUNDS LIKE YOU'RE NOT HAPPY TO SEE ME SO POWERFUL.
YOU WOULDN'T WISH ME ILL, WOULD YOU?
OH NO, NOT AT ALL.
YOU JUST SEEM SO... CHANGED.
I WANT TO KNOW WHAT'S HAPPENED.
YOU'RE THE MOST IMPORTANT THING IN MY LIFE AND...
I HATE TO FEEL I DON'T KNOW YOU.
THERE WILL BE TIME FOR ALL OF THAT, MY LOVE.
I SWEAR.
YOU AND I HAVE ALL THE TIME IN THE WORLD.
NOW LOOK, I'VE BEEN DOING SOME REMODELING.

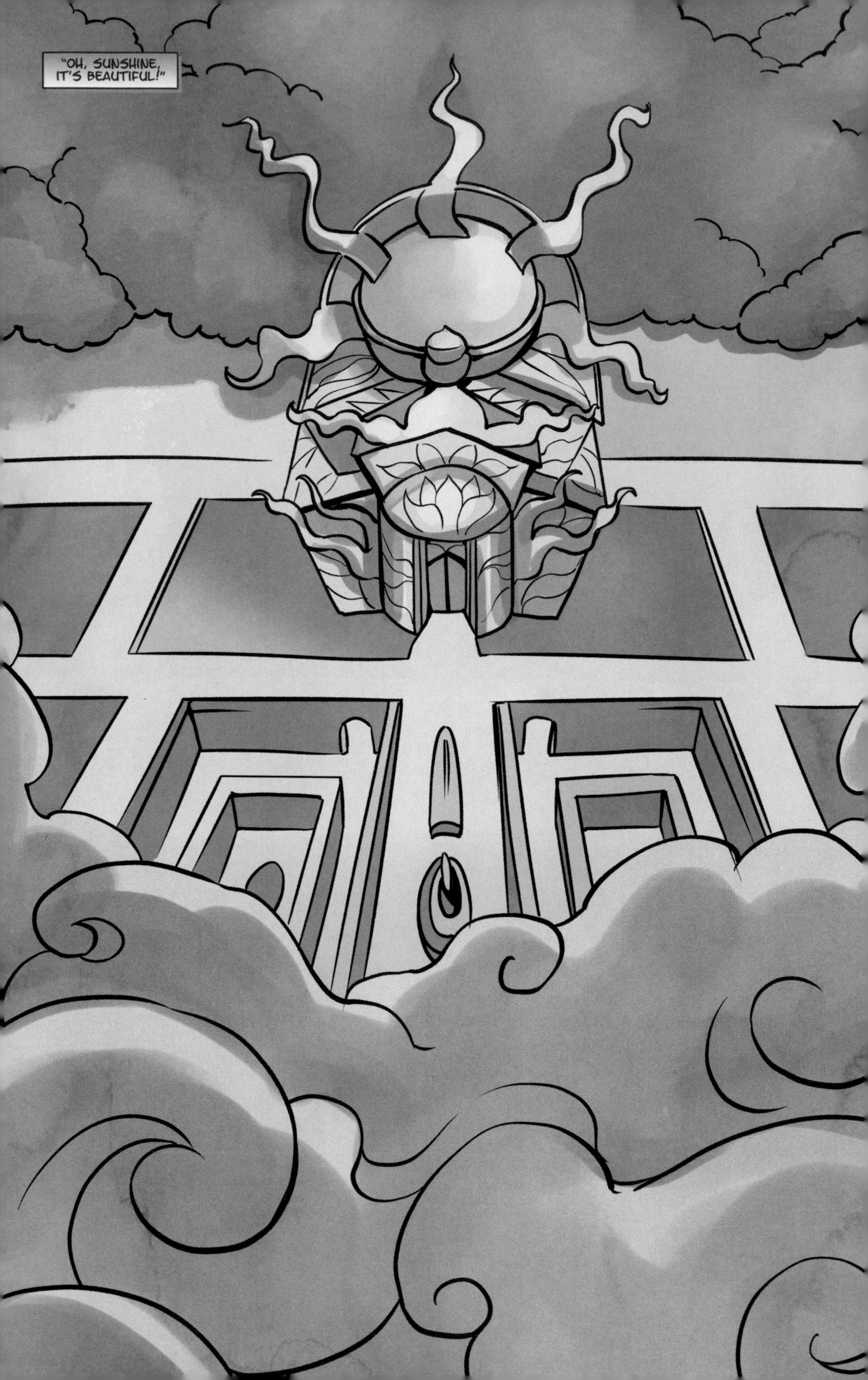
"OH, SUNSHINE, IT'S BEAUTIFUL!"

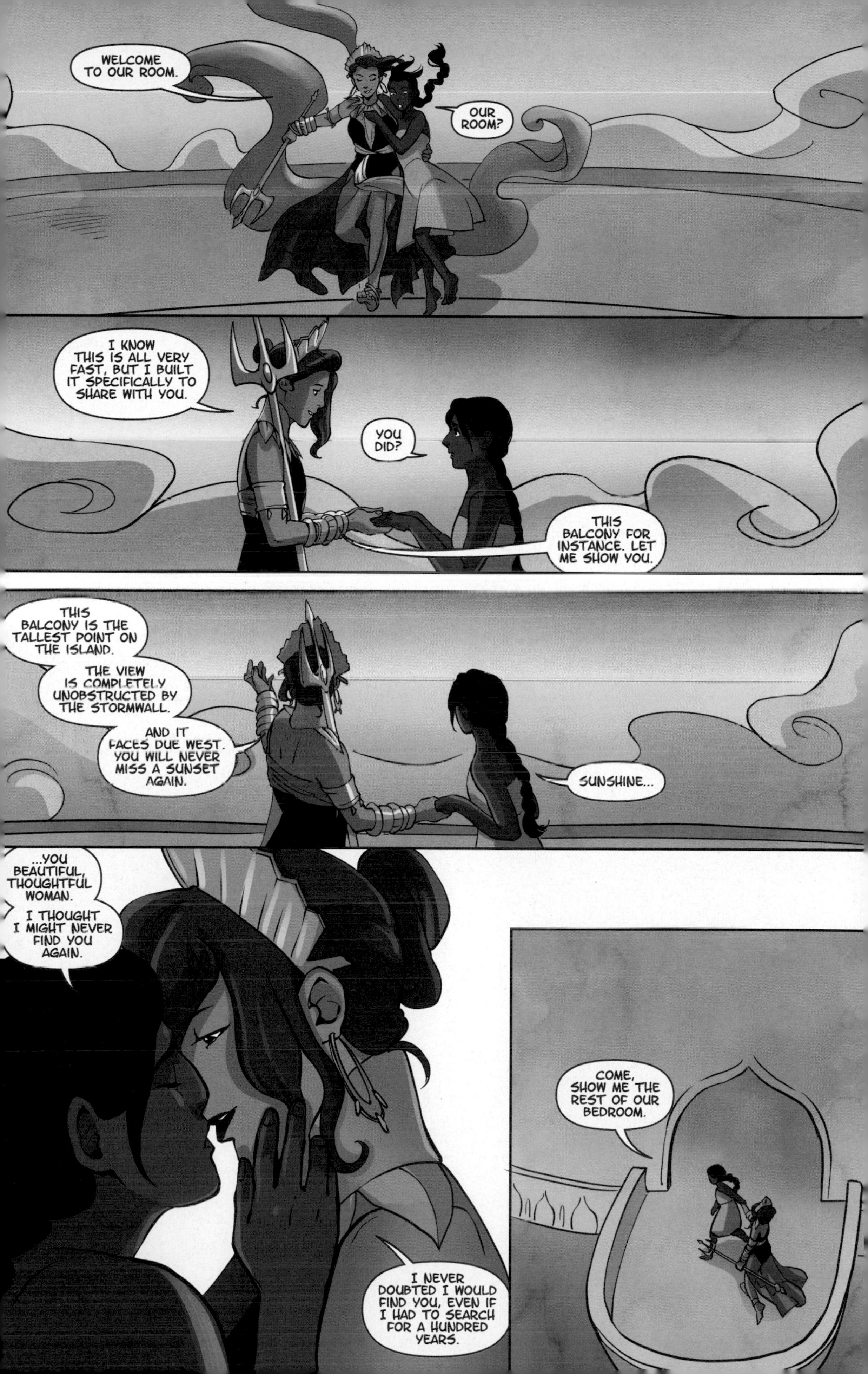
WELCOME TO OUR ROOM.
OUR ROOM?
I KNOW THIS IS ALL VERY FAST, BUT I BUILT IT SPECIFICALLY TO SHARE WITH YOU.
YOU DID?
THIS BALCONY FOR INSTANCE. LET ME SHOW YOU.
THIS BALCONY IS THE TALLEST POINT ON THE ISLAND.
THE VIEW IS COMPLETELY UNOBSTRUCTED BY THE STORMWALL.
AND IT FACES DUE WEST. YOU WILL NEVER MISS A SUNSET AGAIN.
SUNSHINE...
...YOU BEAUTIFUL, THOUGHTFUL WOMAN.
I THOUGHT I MIGHT NEVER FIND YOU AGAIN.
I NEVER DOUBTED I WOULD FIND YOU, EVEN IF I HAD TO SEARCH FOR A HUNDRED YEARS.
COME, SHOW ME THE REST OF OUR BEDROOM.

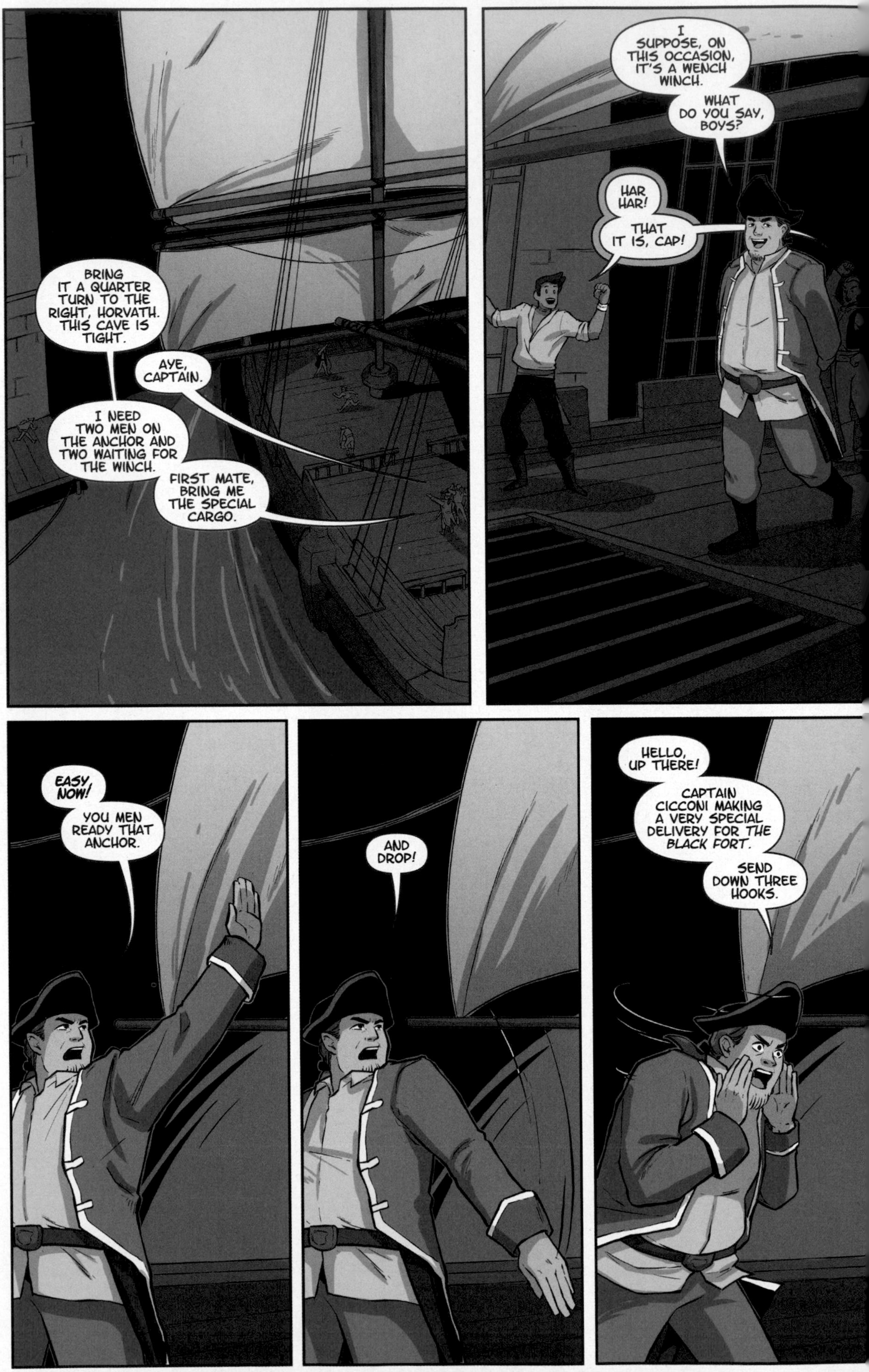

BRING IT A QUARTER TURN TO THE RIGHT, HORVATH. THIS CAVE IS TIGHT.
AYE, CAPTAIN.
I NEED TWO MEN ON THE ANCHOR AND TWO WAITING FOR THE WINCH.
FIRST MATE, BRING ME THE SPECIAL CARGO.
I SUPPOSE, ON THIS OCCASION, IT'S A WENCH WINCH.
WHAT DO YOU SAY, BOYS?
HAR HAR!
THAT IT IS, CAP!
EASY, NOW!
YOU MEN READY THAT ANCHOR.
AND DROP!
HELLO, UP THERE!
CAPTAIN CICCONI MAKING A VERY SPECIAL DELIVERY FOR *THE BLACK FORT*.
SEND DOWN THREE HOOKS.

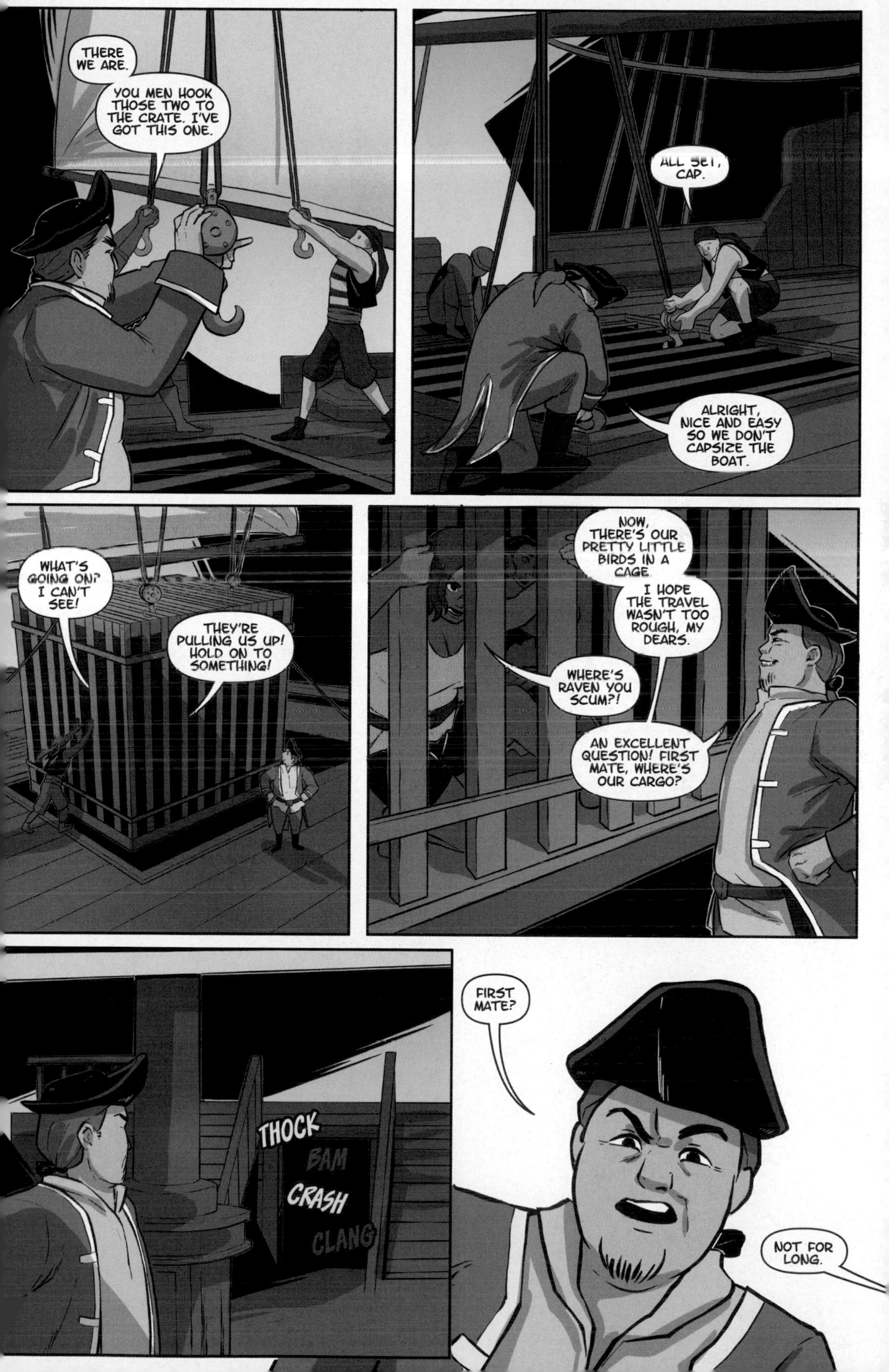
THERE WE ARE.
YOU MEN HOOK THOSE TWO TO THE CRATE. I'VE GOT THIS ONE.
ALL SET, CAP.
ALRIGHT, NICE AND EASY SO WE DON'T CAPSIZE THE BOAT.
WHAT'S GOING ON? I CAN'T SEE!
THEY'RE PULLING US UP! HOLD ON TO SOMETHING!
NOW, THERE'S OUR PRETTY LITTLE BIRDS IN A CAGE.
I HOPE THE TRAVEL WASN'T TOO ROUGH, MY DEARS.
WHERE'S RAVEN YOU SCUM?!
AN EXCELLENT QUESTION! FIRST MATE, WHERE'S OUR CARGO?
THOCK
BAM
CRASH
CLANG
FIRST MATE?
NOT FOR LONG.

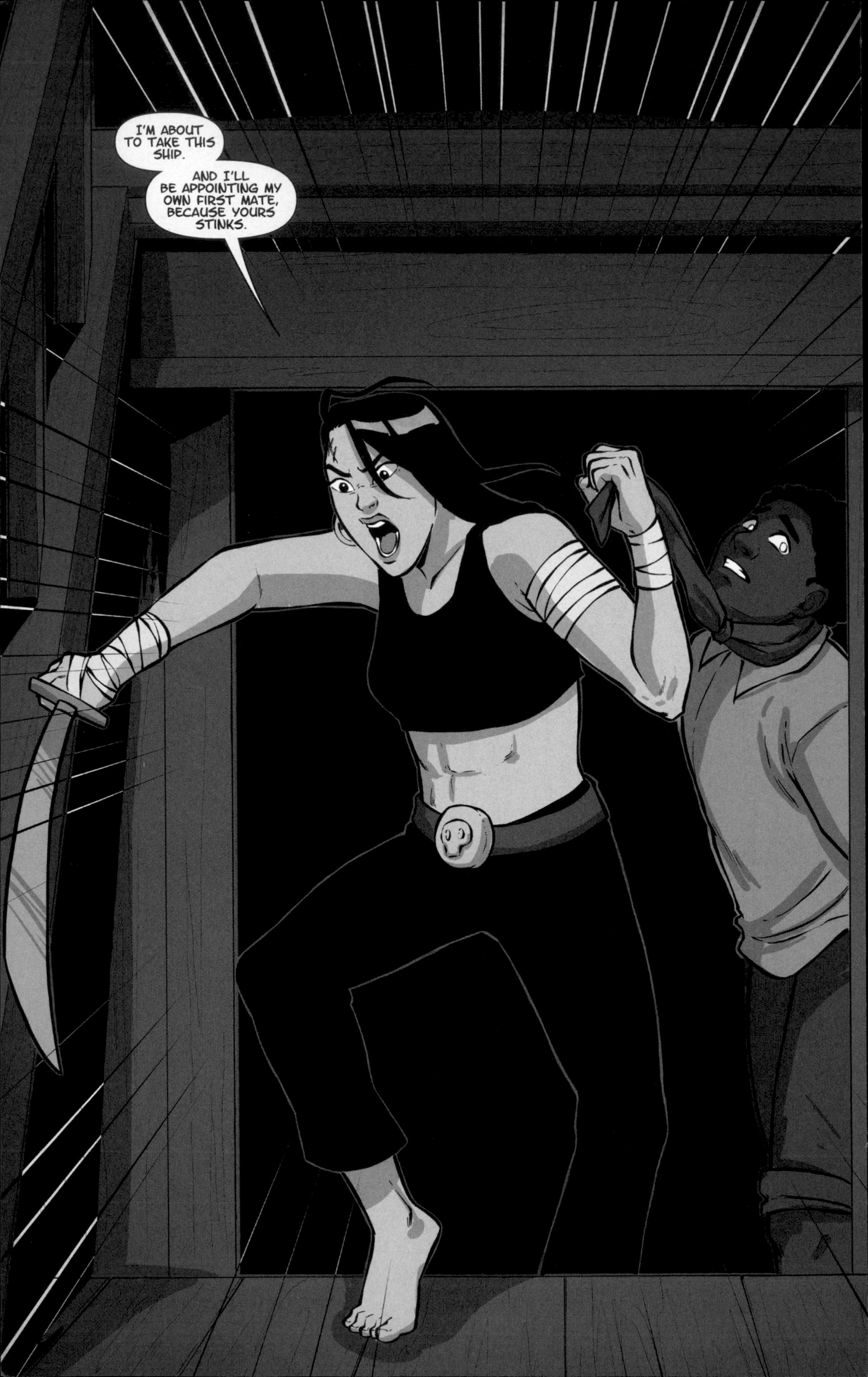
I'M ABOUT TO TAKE THIS SHIP.
AND I'LL BE APPOINTING MY OWN FIRST MATE, BECAUSE YOURS STINKS.

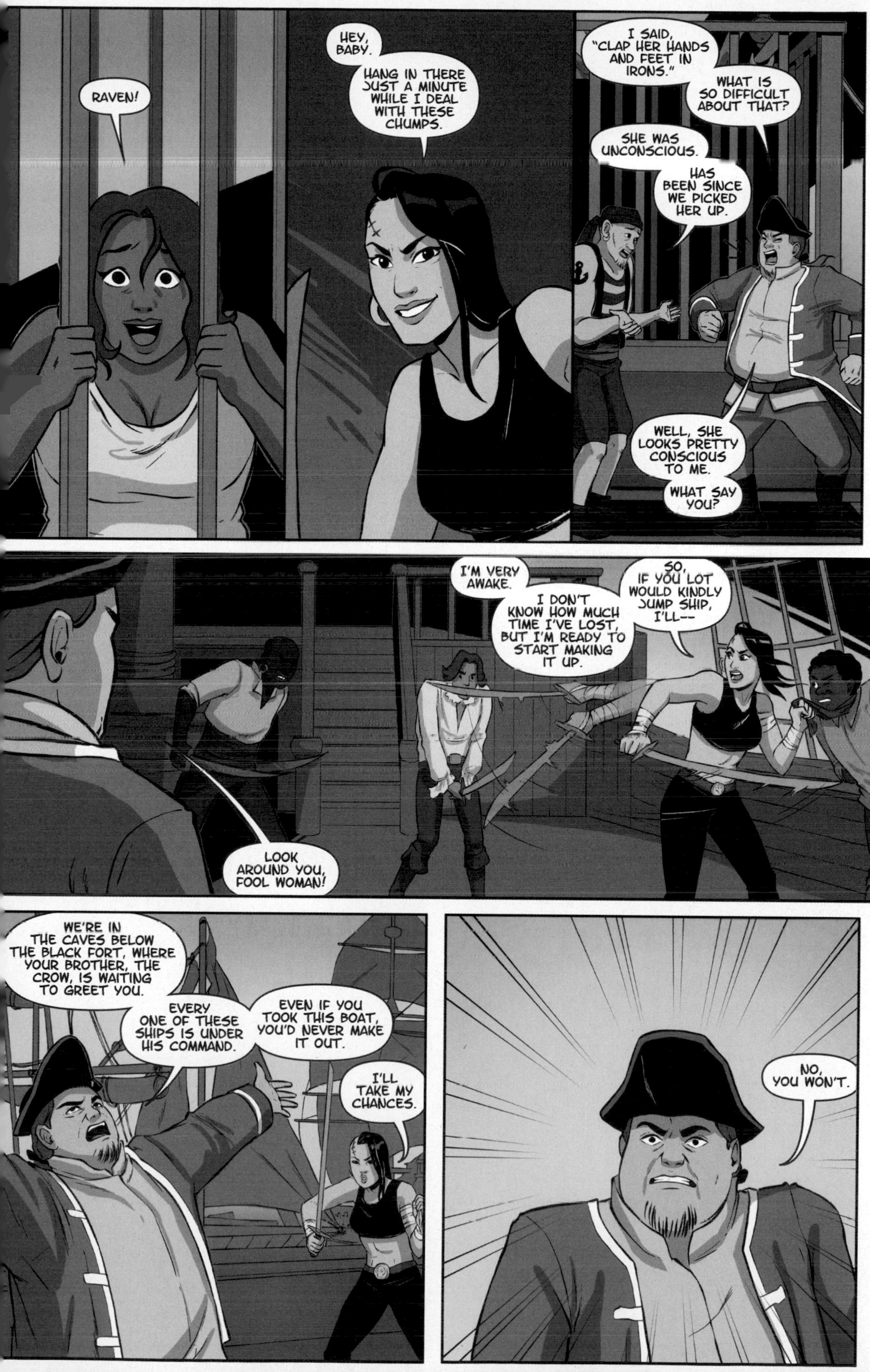
RAVEN!
HEY, BABY.
HANG IN THERE JUST A MINUTE WHILE I DEAL WITH THESE CHUMPS.
I SAID, "CLAP HER HANDS AND FEET IN IRONS."
WHAT IS SO DIFFICULT ABOUT THAT?
SHE WAS UNCONSCIOUS.
HAS BEEN SINCE WE PICKED HER UP.
WELL, SHE LOOKS PRETTY CONSCIOUS TO ME.
WHAT SAY YOU?
I'M VERY AWAKE.
I DON'T KNOW HOW MUCH TIME I'VE LOST, BUT I'M READY TO START MAKING IT UP.
SO, IF YOU LOT WOULD KINDLY JUMP SHIP, I'LL--
LOOK AROUND YOU, FOOL WOMAN!
WE'RE IN THE CAVES BELOW THE BLACK FORT, WHERE YOUR BROTHER, THE CROW, IS WAITING TO GREET YOU.
EVERY ONE OF THESE SHIPS IS UNDER HIS COMMAND.
EVEN IF YOU TOOK THIS BOAT, YOU'D NEVER MAKE IT OUT.
I'LL TAKE MY CHANCES.
NO, YOU WON'T.

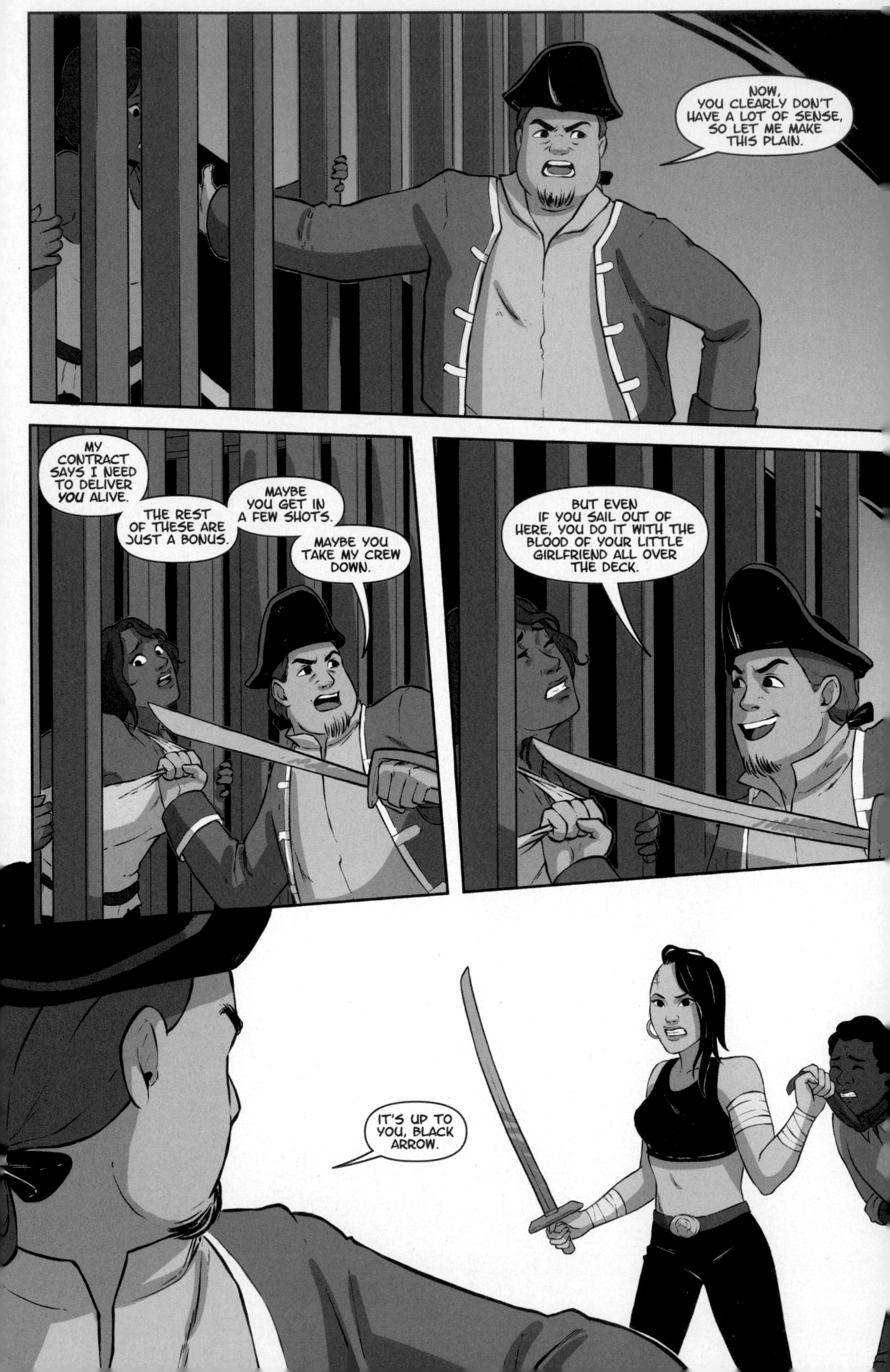
NOW, YOU CLEARLY DON'T HAVE A LOT OF SENSE, SO LET ME MAKE THIS PLAIN.
MY CONTRACT SAYS I NEED TO DELIVER *YOU* ALIVE.
THE REST OF THESE ARE JUST A BONUS.
MAYBE YOU GET IN A FEW SHOTS.
MAYBE YOU TAKE MY CREW DOWN.
BUT EVEN IF YOU SAIL OUT OF HERE, YOU DO IT WITH THE BLOOD OF YOUR LITTLE GIRLFRIEND ALL OVER THE DECK.
IT'S UP TO YOU, BLACK ARROW.

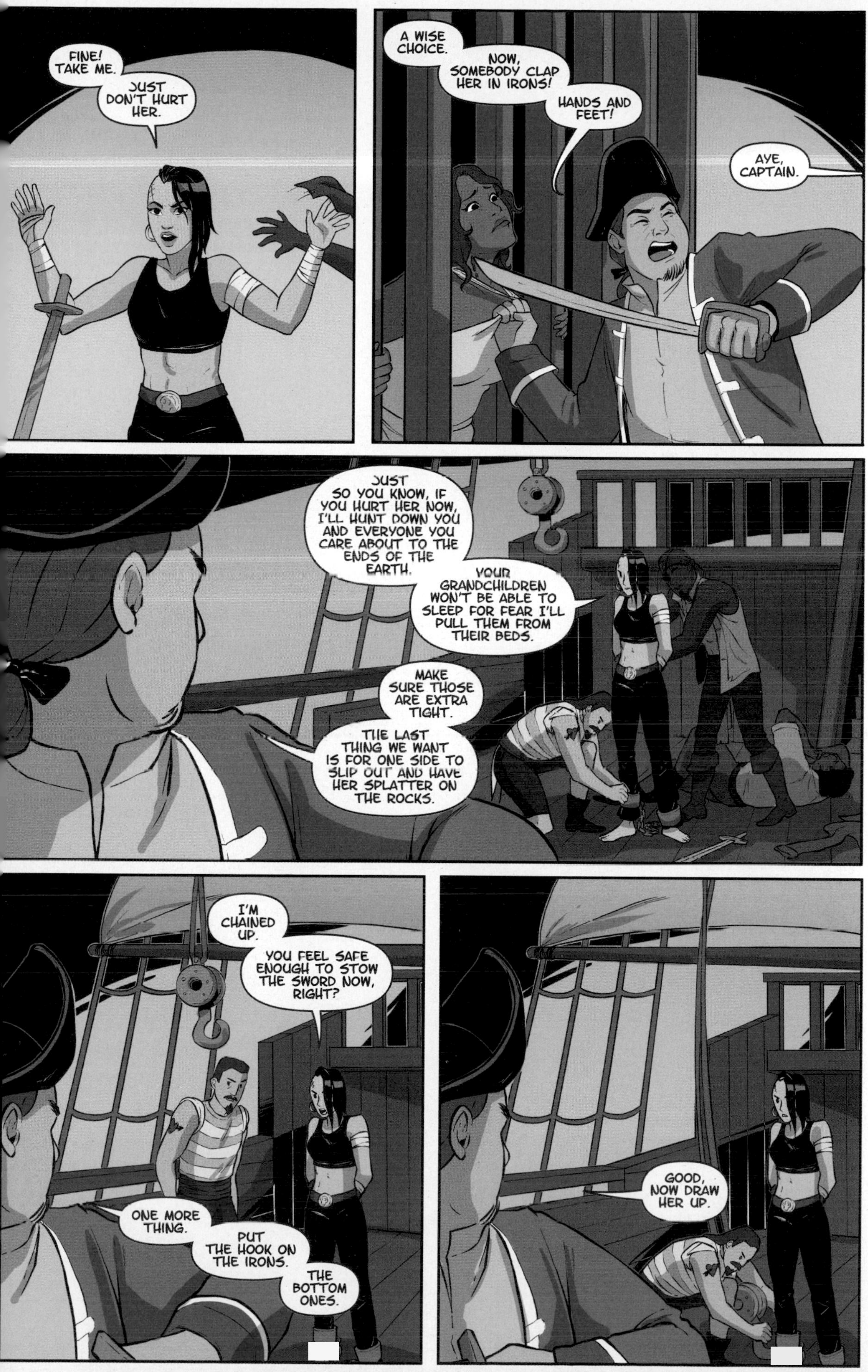
FINE! TAKE ME.
JUST DON'T HURT HER.
A WISE CHOICE.
NOW, SOMEBODY CLAP HER IN IRONS!
HANDS AND FEET!
AYE, CAPTAIN.
JUST SO YOU KNOW, IF YOU HURT HER NOW, I'LL HUNT DOWN YOU AND EVERYONE YOU CARE ABOUT TO THE ENDS OF THE EARTH.
YOUR GRANDCHILDREN WON'T BE ABLE TO SLEEP FOR FEAR I'LL PULL THEM FROM THEIR BEDS.
MAKE SURE THOSE ARE EXTRA TIGHT.
THE LAST THING WE WANT IS FOR ONE SIDE TO SLIP OUT AND HAVE HER SPLATTER ON THE ROCKS.
I'M CHAINED UP.
YOU FEEL SAFE ENOUGH TO STOW THE SWORD NOW, RIGHT?
ONE MORE THING.
PUT THE HOOK ON THE IRONS.
THE BOTTOM ONES.
GOOD, NOW DRAW HER UP.

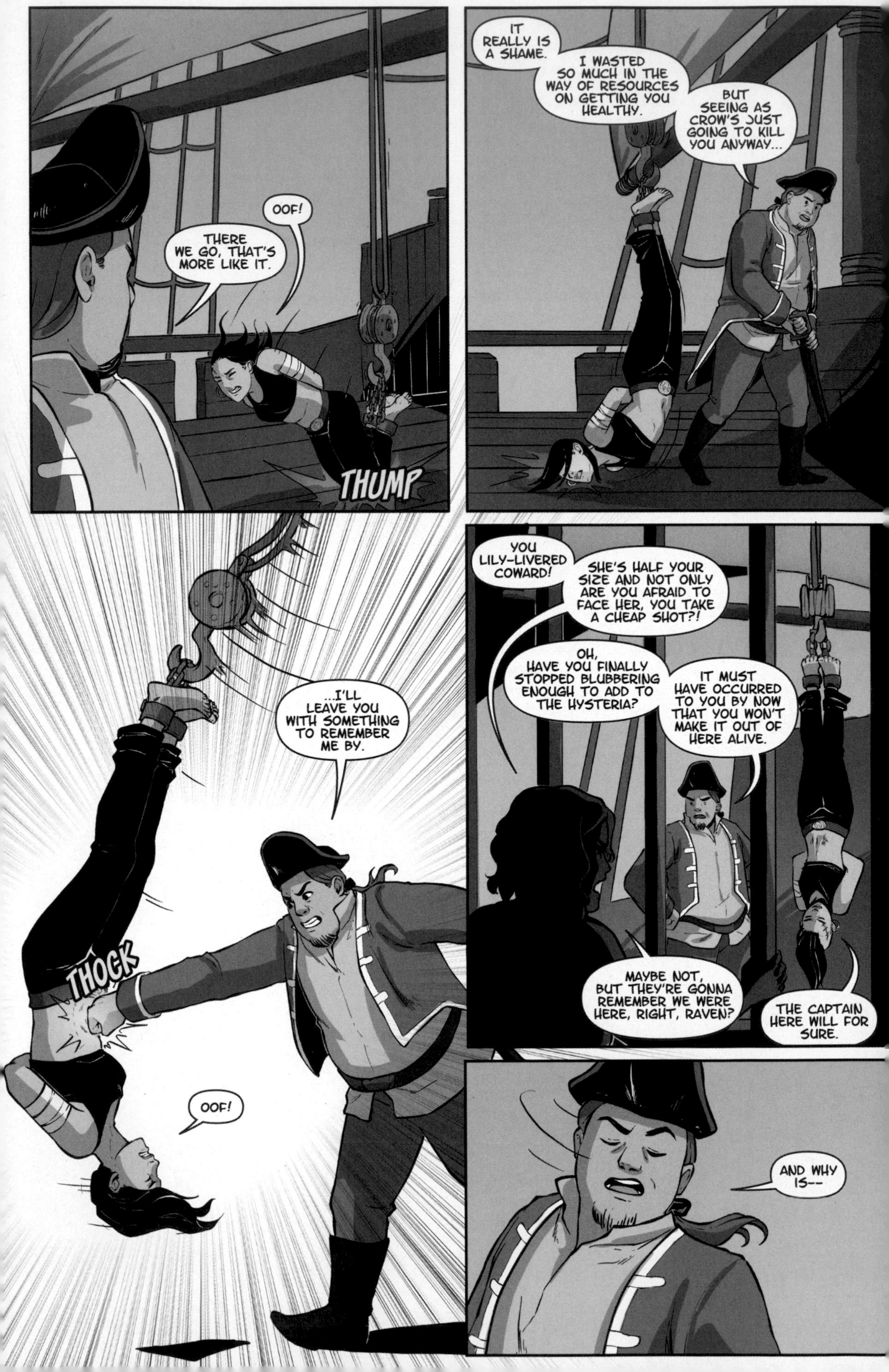

OOF!
THERE WE GO, THAT'S MORE LIKE IT.
THUMP
IT REALLY IS A SHAME.
I WASTED SO MUCH IN THE WAY OF RESOURCES ON GETTING YOU HEALTHY.
BUT SEEING AS CROW'S JUST GOING TO KILL YOU ANYWAY...
...I'LL LEAVE YOU WITH SOMETHING TO REMEMBER ME BY.
THOCK
OOF!
YOU LILY-LIVERED COWARD!
SHE'S HALF YOUR SIZE AND NOT ONLY ARE YOU AFRAID TO FACE HER, YOU TAKE A CHEAP SHOT?!
OH, HAVE YOU FINALLY STOPPED BLUBBERING ENOUGH TO ADD TO THE HYSTERIA?
IT MUST HAVE OCCURRED TO YOU BY NOW THAT YOU WON'T MAKE IT OUT OF HERE ALIVE.
MAYBE NOT, BUT THEY'RE GONNA REMEMBER WE WERE HERE, RIGHT, RAVEN?
THE CAPTAIN HERE WILL FOR SURE.
AND WHY IS--

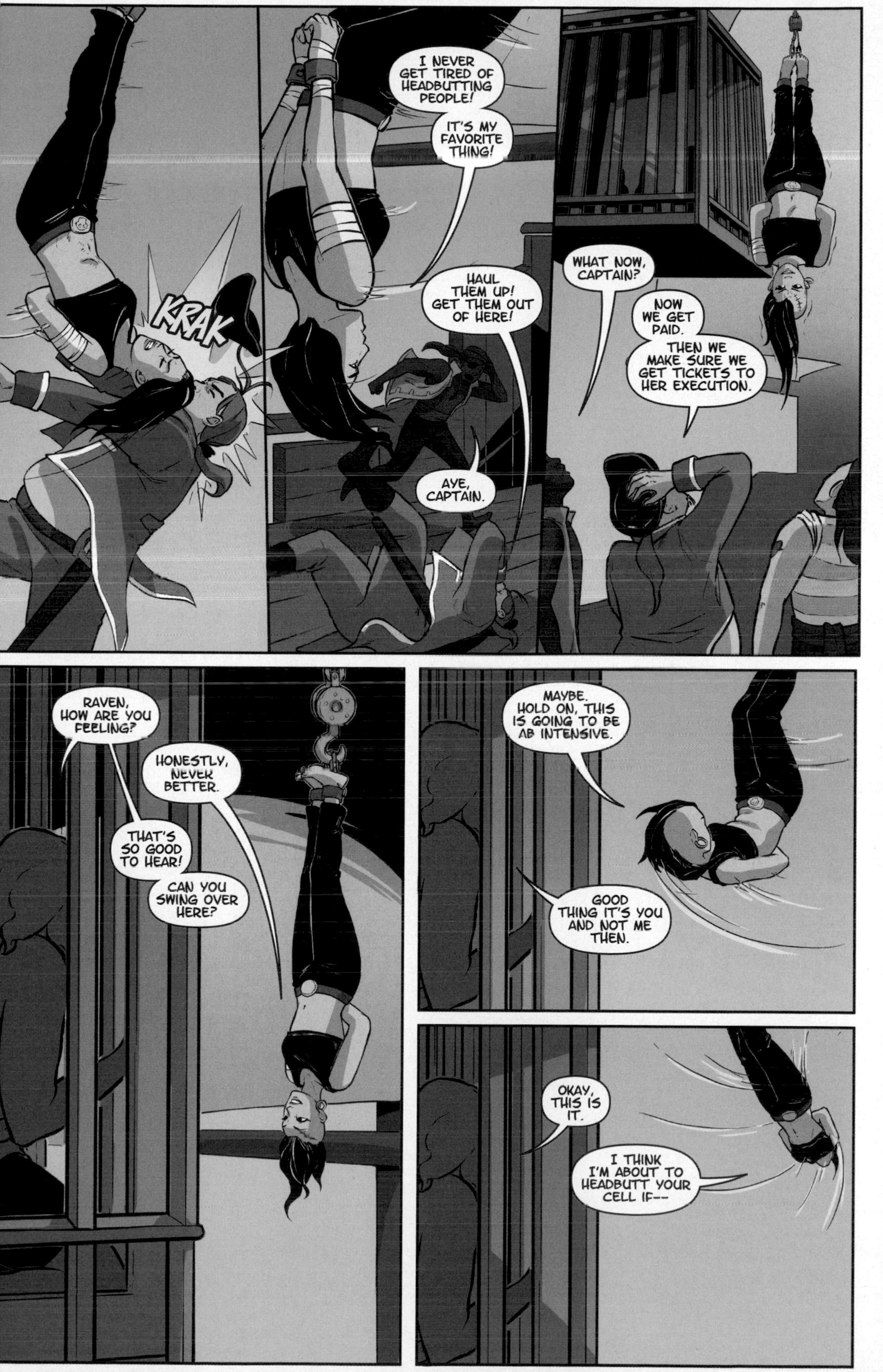
KRAK
I NEVER GET TIRED OF HEADBUTTING PEOPLE!
IT'S MY FAVORITE THING!
HAUL THEM UP! GET THEM OUT OF HERE!
AYE, CAPTAIN.
WHAT NOW, CAPTAIN?
NOW WE GET PAID.
THEN WE MAKE SURE WE GET TICKETS TO HER EXECUTION.
RAVEN, HOW ARE YOU FEELING?
HONESTLY, NEVER BETTER.
THAT'S SO GOOD TO HEAR!
CAN YOU SWING OVER HERE?
MAYBE. HOLD ON, THIS IS GOING TO BE AB INTENSIVE.
GOOD THING IT'S YOU AND NOT ME THEN.
OKAY, THIS IS IT.
I THINK I'M ABOUT TO HEADBUTT YOUR CELL IF--

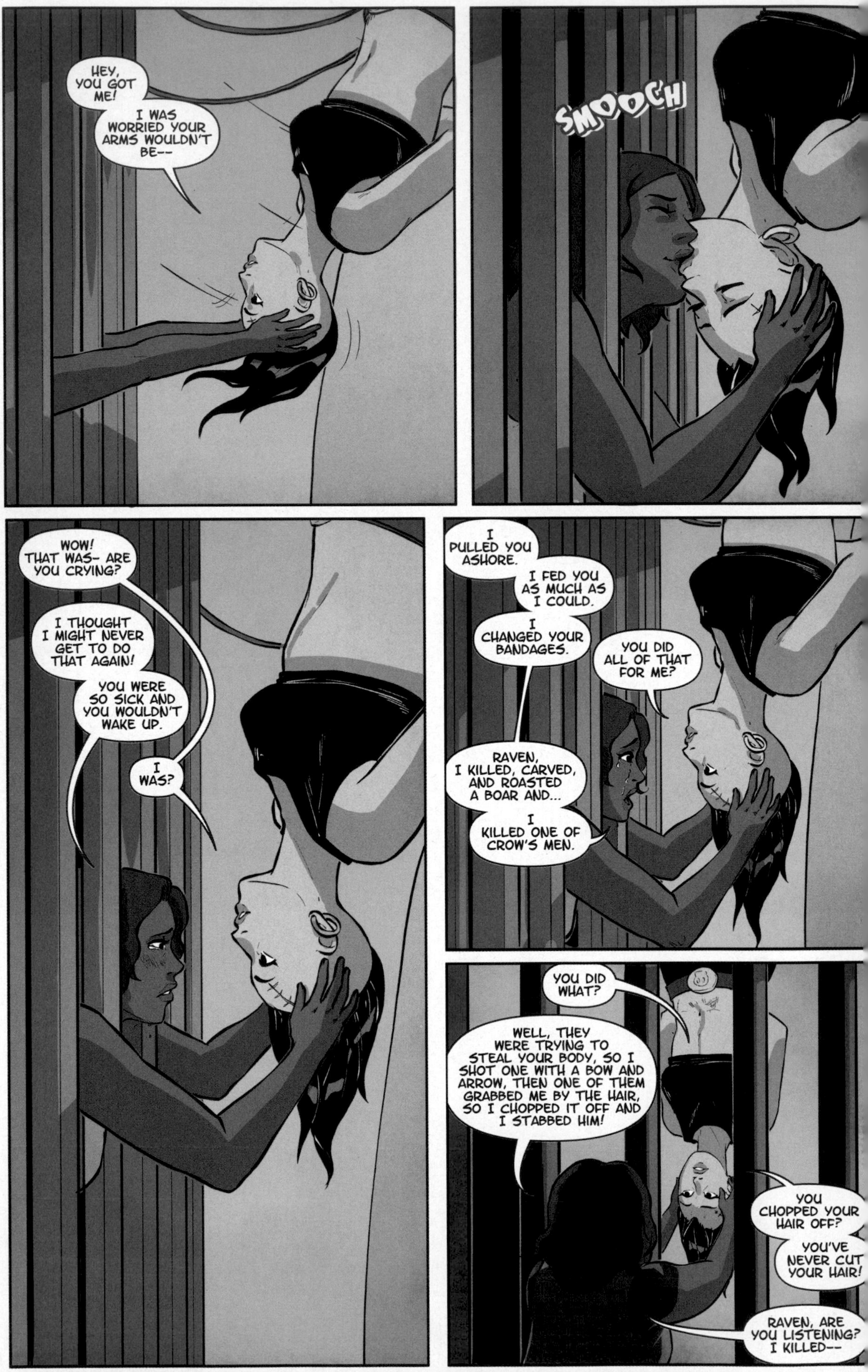
HEY, YOU GOT ME!
I WAS WORRIED YOUR ARMS WOULDN'T BE--
SMOOCH
WOW! THAT WAS- ARE YOU CRYING?
I THOUGHT I MIGHT NEVER GET TO DO THAT AGAIN!
YOU WERE SO SICK AND YOU WOULDN'T WAKE UP.
I WAS?
I PULLED YOU ASHORE.
I FED YOU AS MUCH AS I COULD.
I CHANGED YOUR BANDAGES.
YOU DID ALL OF THAT FOR ME?
RAVEN, I KILLED, CARVED, AND ROASTED A BOAR AND...
I KILLED ONE OF CROW'S MEN.
YOU DID WHAT?
WELL, THEY WERE TRYING TO STEAL YOUR BODY, SO I SHOT ONE WITH A BOW AND ARROW, THEN ONE OF THEM GRABBED ME BY THE HAIR, SO I CHOPPED IT OFF AND I STABBED HIM!
YOU CHOPPED YOUR HAIR OFF?
YOU'VE NEVER CUT YOUR HAIR!
RAVEN, ARE YOU LISTENING? I KILLED--

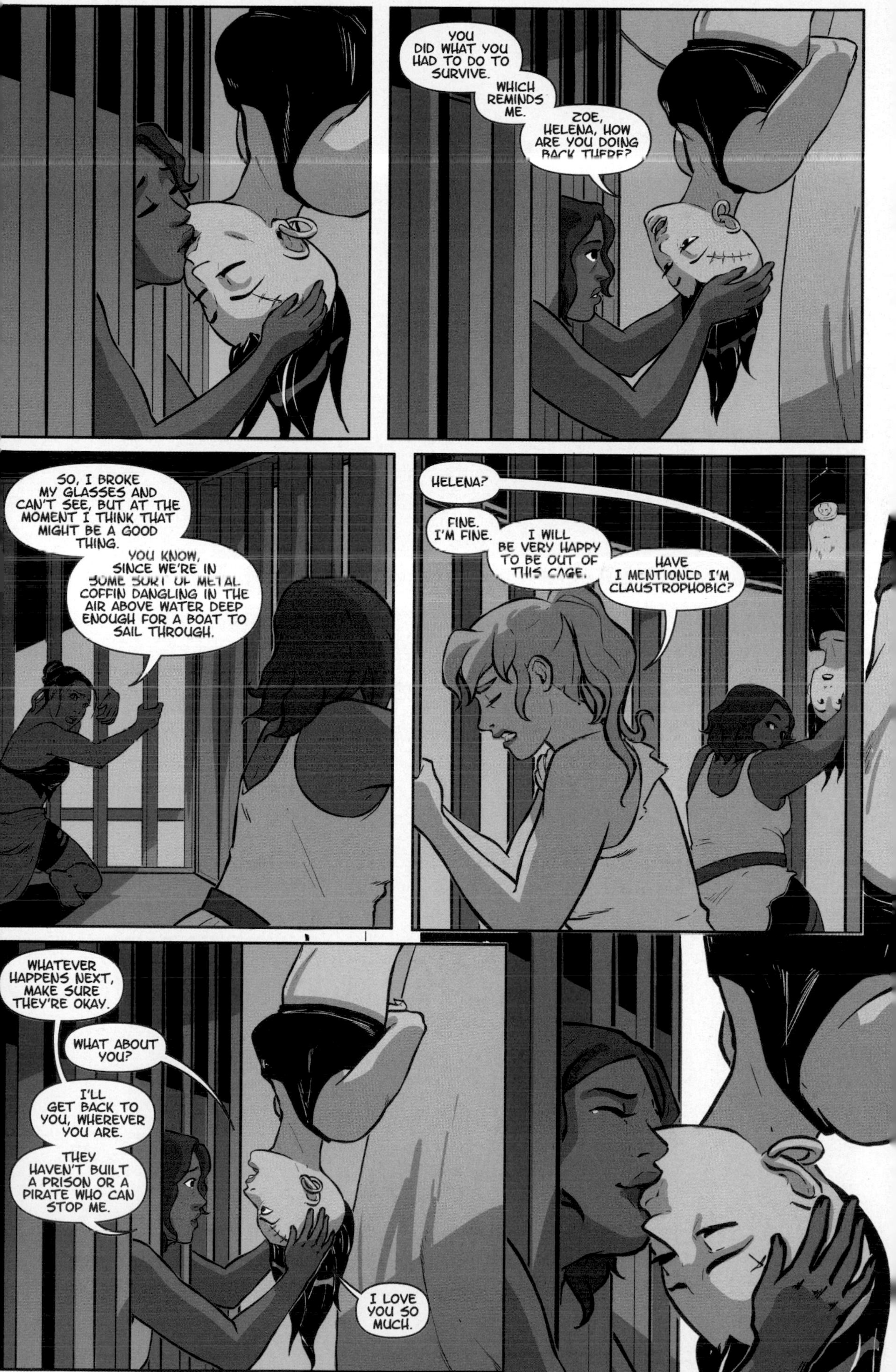
YOU DID WHAT YOU HAD TO DO TO SURVIVE.
WHICH REMINDS ME.
ZOE, HELENA, HOW ARE YOU DOING BACK THERE?
SO, I BROKE MY GLASSES AND CAN'T SEE, BUT AT THE MOMENT I THINK THAT MIGHT BE A GOOD THING.
YOU KNOW, SINCE WE'RE IN SOME SORT OF METAL COFFIN DANGLING IN THE AIR ABOVE WATER DEEP ENOUGH FOR A BOAT TO SAIL THROUGH.
HELENA?
FINE. I'M FINE.
I WILL BE VERY HAPPY TO BE OUT OF THIS CAGE.
HAVE I MENTIONED I'M CLAUSTROPHOBIC?
WHATEVER HAPPENS NEXT, MAKE SURE THEY'RE OKAY.
WHAT ABOUT YOU?
I'LL GET BACK TO YOU, WHEREVER YOU ARE.
THEY HAVEN'T BUILT A PRISON OR A PIRATE WHO CAN STOP ME.
I LOVE YOU SO MUCH.

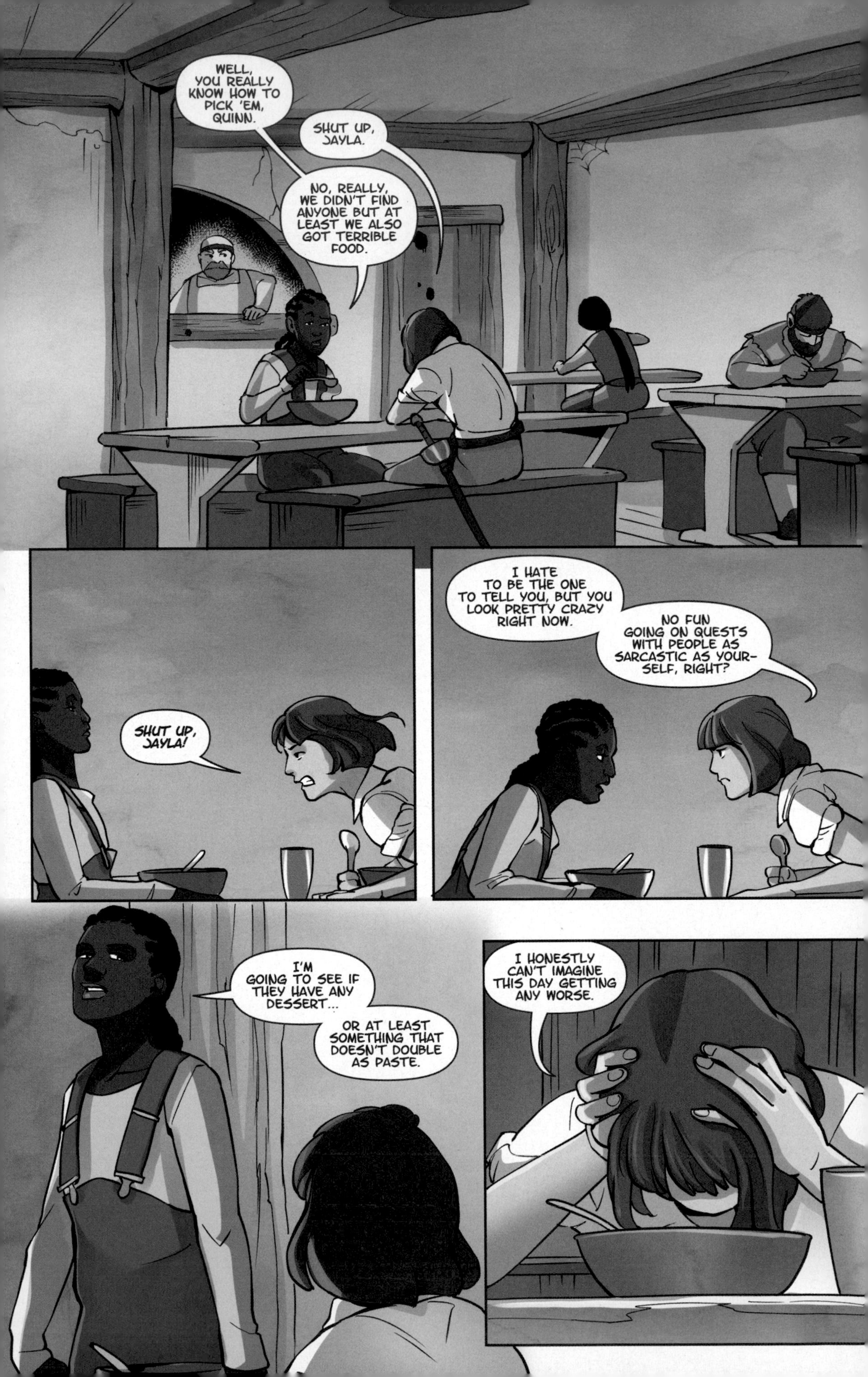
WELL, YOU REALLY KNOW HOW TO PICK 'EM, QUINN.
SHUT UP, JAYLA.
NO, REALLY, WE DIDN'T FIND ANYONE BUT AT LEAST WE ALSO GOT TERRIBLE FOOD.
SHUT UP, JAYLA!
I HATE TO BE THE ONE TO TELL YOU, BUT YOU LOOK PRETTY CRAZY RIGHT NOW.
NO FUN GOING ON QUESTS WITH PEOPLE AS SARCASTIC AS YOUR-SELF, RIGHT?
I'M GOING TO SEE IF THEY HAVE ANY DESSERT...
OR AT LEAST SOMETHING THAT DOESN'T DOUBLE AS PASTE.
I HONESTLY CAN'T IMAGINE THIS DAY GETTING ANY WORSE.

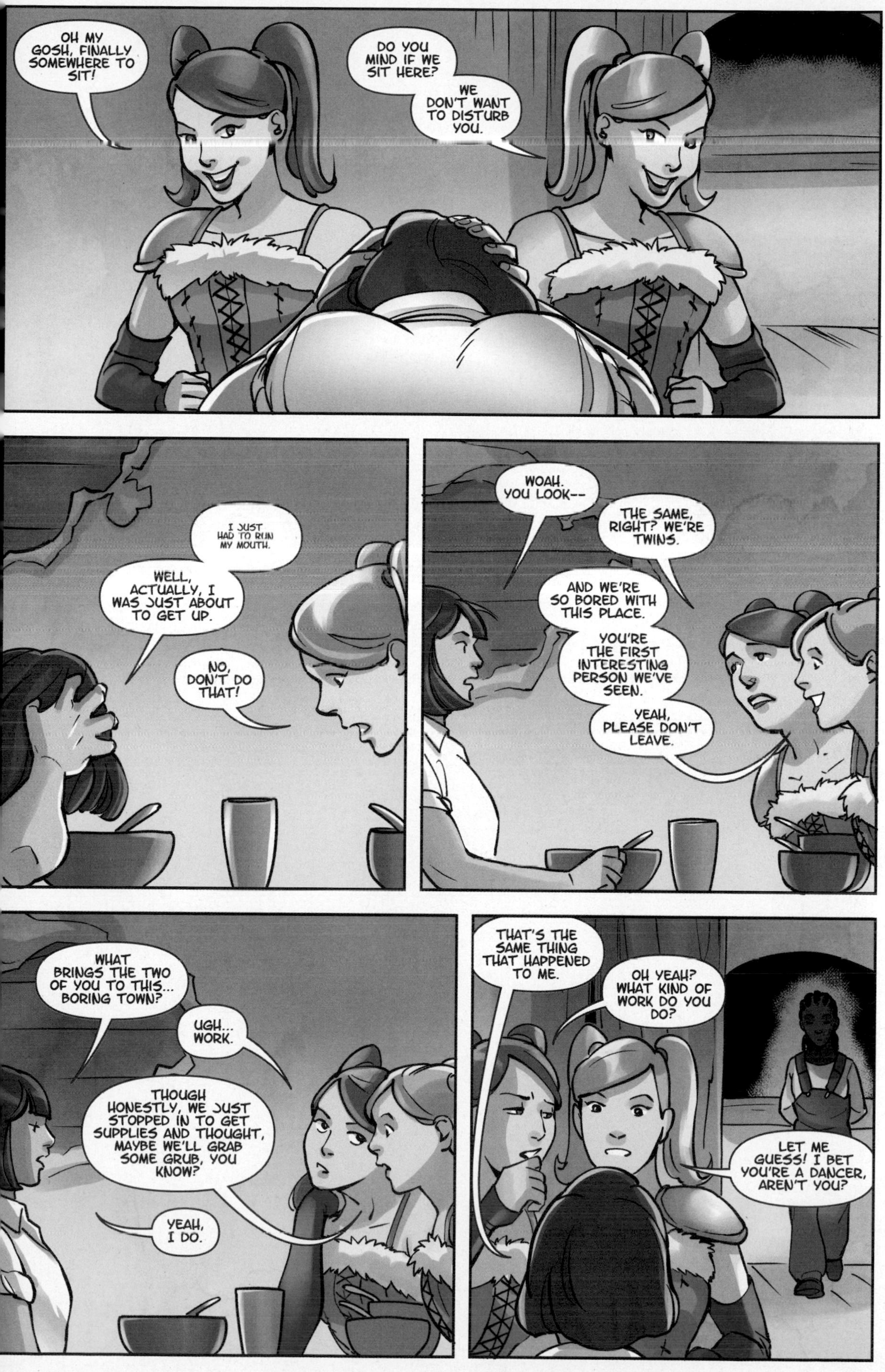
OH MY GOSH, FINALLY SOMEWHERE TO SIT!
DO YOU MIND IF WE SIT HERE?
WE DON'T WANT TO DISTURB YOU.
I JUST HAD TO RUN MY MOUTH.
WELL, ACTUALLY, I WAS JUST ABOUT TO GET UP.
NO, DON'T DO THAT!
WOAH. YOU LOOK--
THE SAME, RIGHT? WE'RE TWINS.
AND WE'RE SO BORED WITH THIS PLACE.
YOU'RE THE FIRST INTERESTING PERSON WE'VE SEEN.
YEAH, PLEASE DON'T LEAVE.
WHAT BRINGS THE TWO OF YOU TO THIS... BORING TOWN?
UGH... WORK.
THOUGH HONESTLY, WE JUST STOPPED IN TO GET SUPPLIES AND THOUGHT, MAYBE WE'LL GRAB SOME GRUB, YOU KNOW?
YEAH, I DO.
THAT'S THE SAME THING THAT HAPPENED TO ME.
OH YEAH? WHAT KIND OF WORK DO YOU DO?
LET ME GUESS! I BET YOU'RE A DANCER, AREN'T YOU?

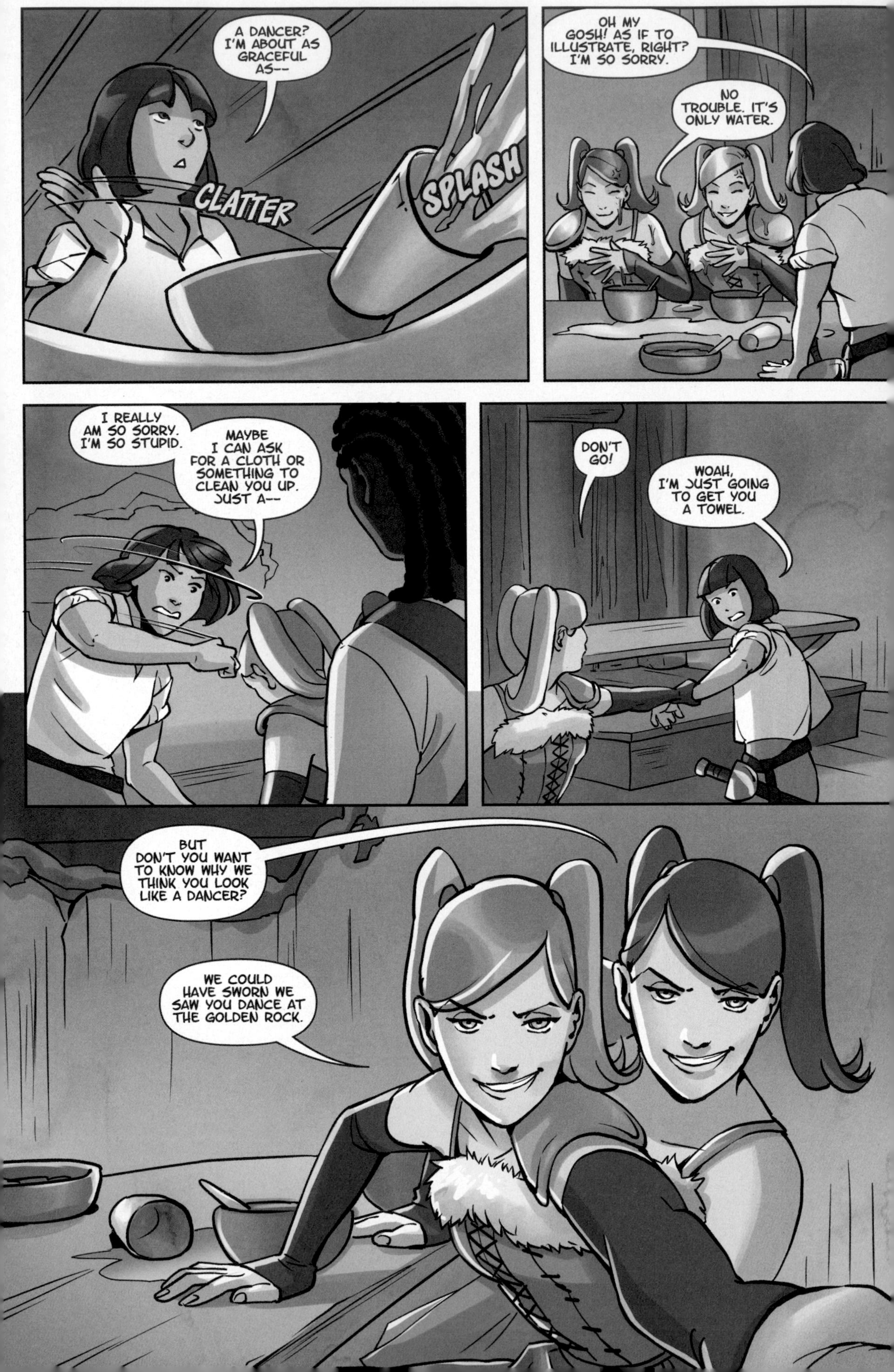
A DANCER? I'M ABOUT AS GRACEFUL AS--
CLATTER
SPLASH
OH MY GOSH! AS IF TO ILLUSTRATE, RIGHT? I'M SO SORRY.
NO TROUBLE. IT'S ONLY WATER.
I REALLY AM SO SORRY. I'M SO STUPID.
MAYBE I CAN ASK FOR A CLOTH OR SOMETHING TO CLEAN YOU UP. JUST A--
DON'T GO!
WOAH, I'M JUST GOING TO GET YOU A TOWEL.
BUT DON'T YOU WANT TO KNOW WHY WE THINK YOU LOOK LIKE A DANCER?
WE COULD HAVE SWORN WE SAW YOU DANCE AT THE GOLDEN ROCK.

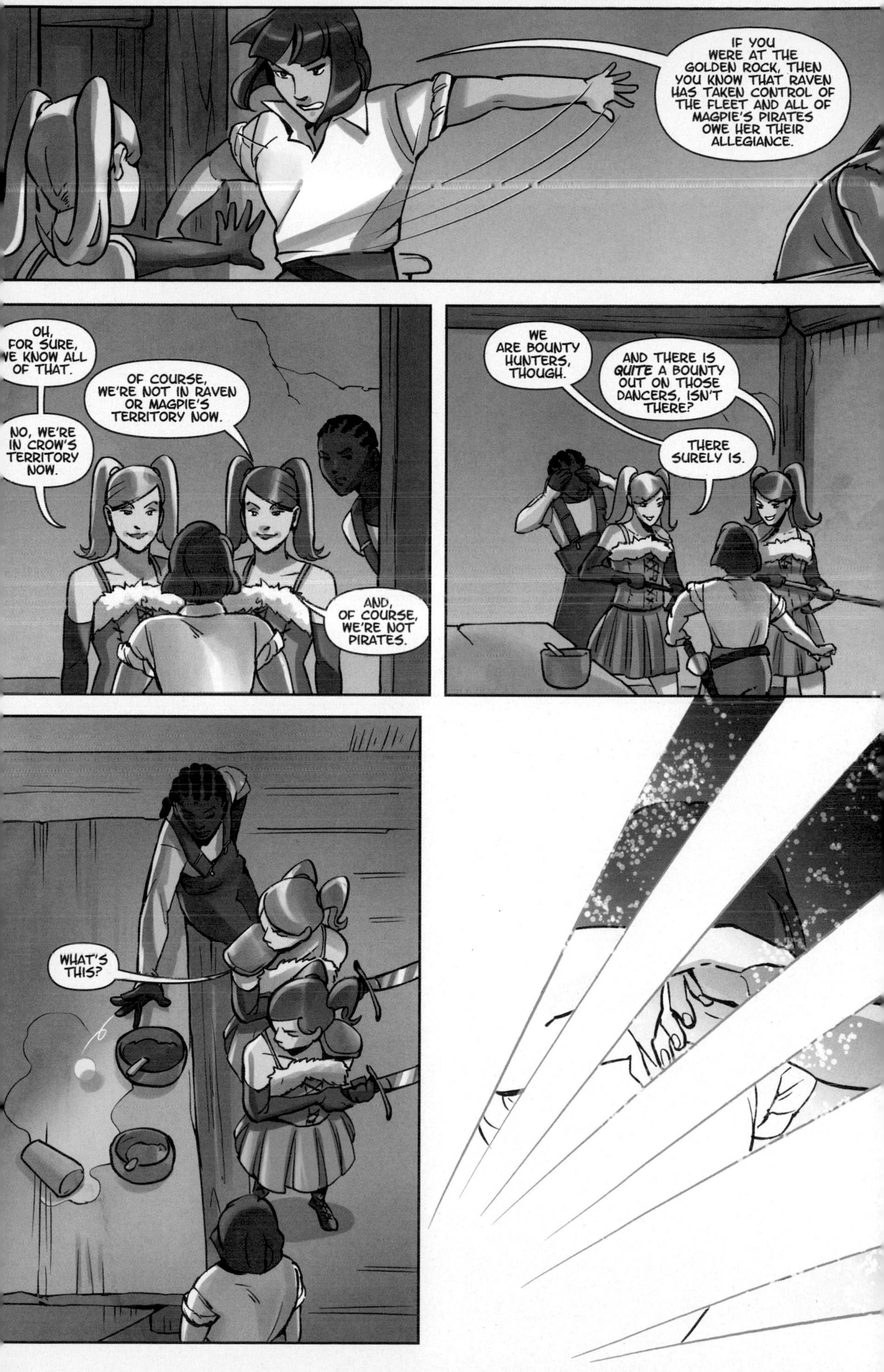
IF YOU WERE AT THE GOLDEN ROCK, THEN YOU KNOW THAT RAVEN HAS TAKEN CONTROL OF THE FLEET AND ALL OF MAGPIE'S PIRATES OWE HER THEIR ALLEGIANCE.
OH, FOR SURE, WE KNOW ALL OF THAT.
NO, WE'RE IN CROW'S TERRITORY NOW.
OF COURSE, WE'RE NOT IN RAVEN OR MAGPIE'S TERRITORY NOW.
AND, OF COURSE, WE'RE NOT PIRATES.
WE ARE BOUNTY HUNTERS, THOUGH.
AND THERE IS QUITE A BOUNTY OUT ON THOSE DANCERS, ISN'T THERE?
THERE SURELY IS.
WHAT'S THIS?

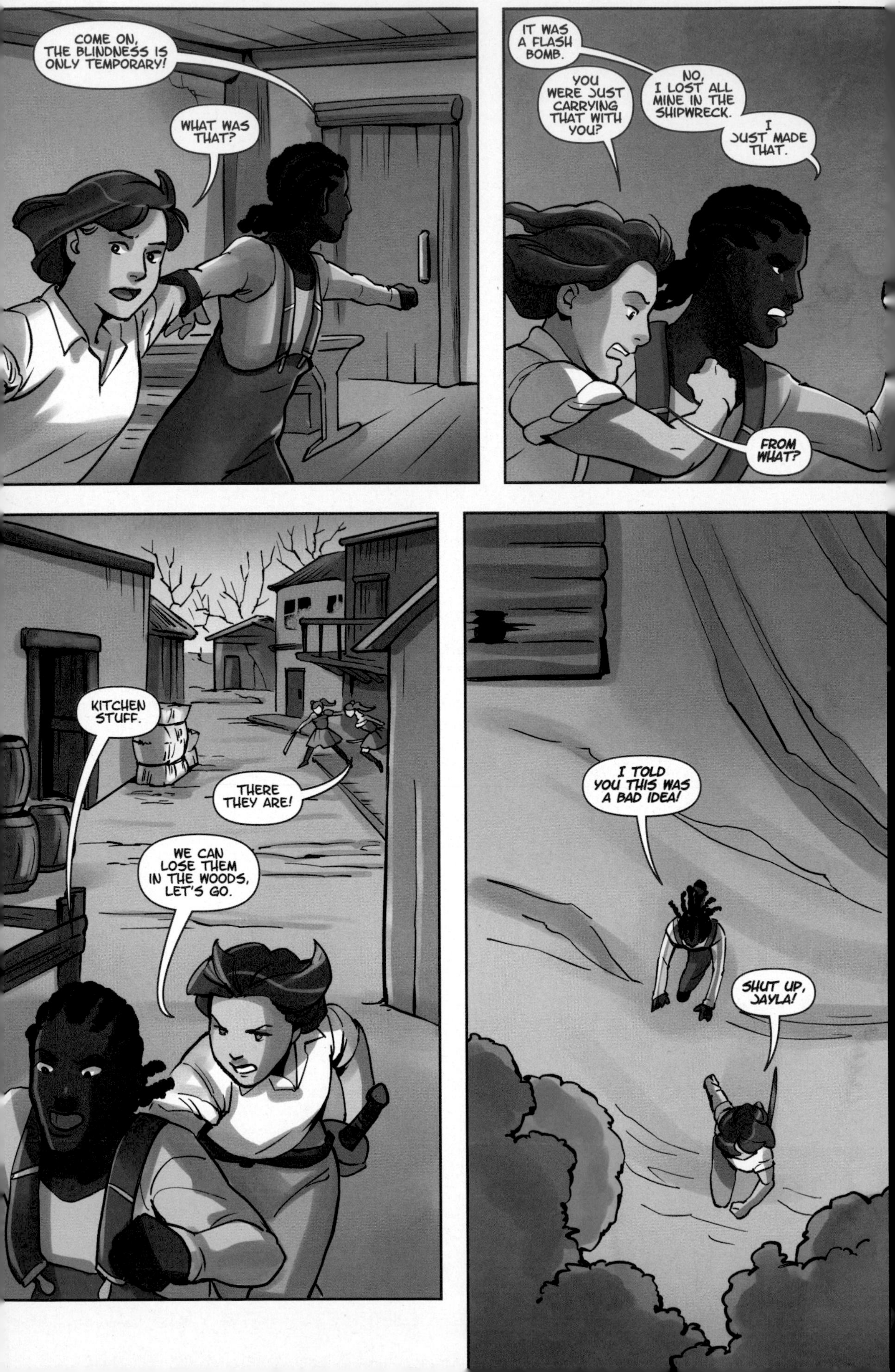
COME ON, THE BLINDNESS IS ONLY TEMPORARY!
WHAT WAS THAT?
IT WAS A FLASH BOMB.
YOU WERE JUST CARRYING THAT WITH YOU?
NO, I LOST ALL MINE IN THE SHIPWRECK.
I JUST MADE THAT.
FROM WHAT?
KITCHEN STUFF.
THERE THEY ARE!
WE CAN LOSE THEM IN THE WOODS, LET'S GO.
I TOLD YOU THIS WAS A BAD IDEA!
SHUT UP, JAYLA!

Princeless

Raven

The Pirate Princess

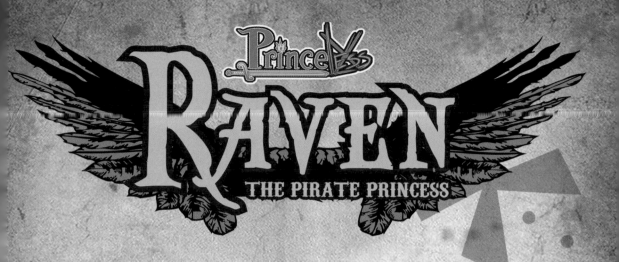

Year Three: Monsters of the Deep

Chapter Ten: In the Belly of the Beast

Written By: Jeremy Whitley

Pencils By:
(Pages 1-9, 20-21, 24) Xenia Pamfil
(Pages 10-17, 19, 22-23) Telênia Albuquerque

Inks By:
Pocket Owl

Colors By:
(Pages 1-9, 20-21, 24) Lexillo
(Pages 10-17, 19, 22-23) Valentina Pinto

Lettered By: Alex Scherkenbach

Cover By: Telenia Albuquerque

Bryan Seaton: Publisher - Vito Delsante: Editor In Chief
Jason Martin: Publisher-Danger Zone
Chad Cicconi: Deck Swabber

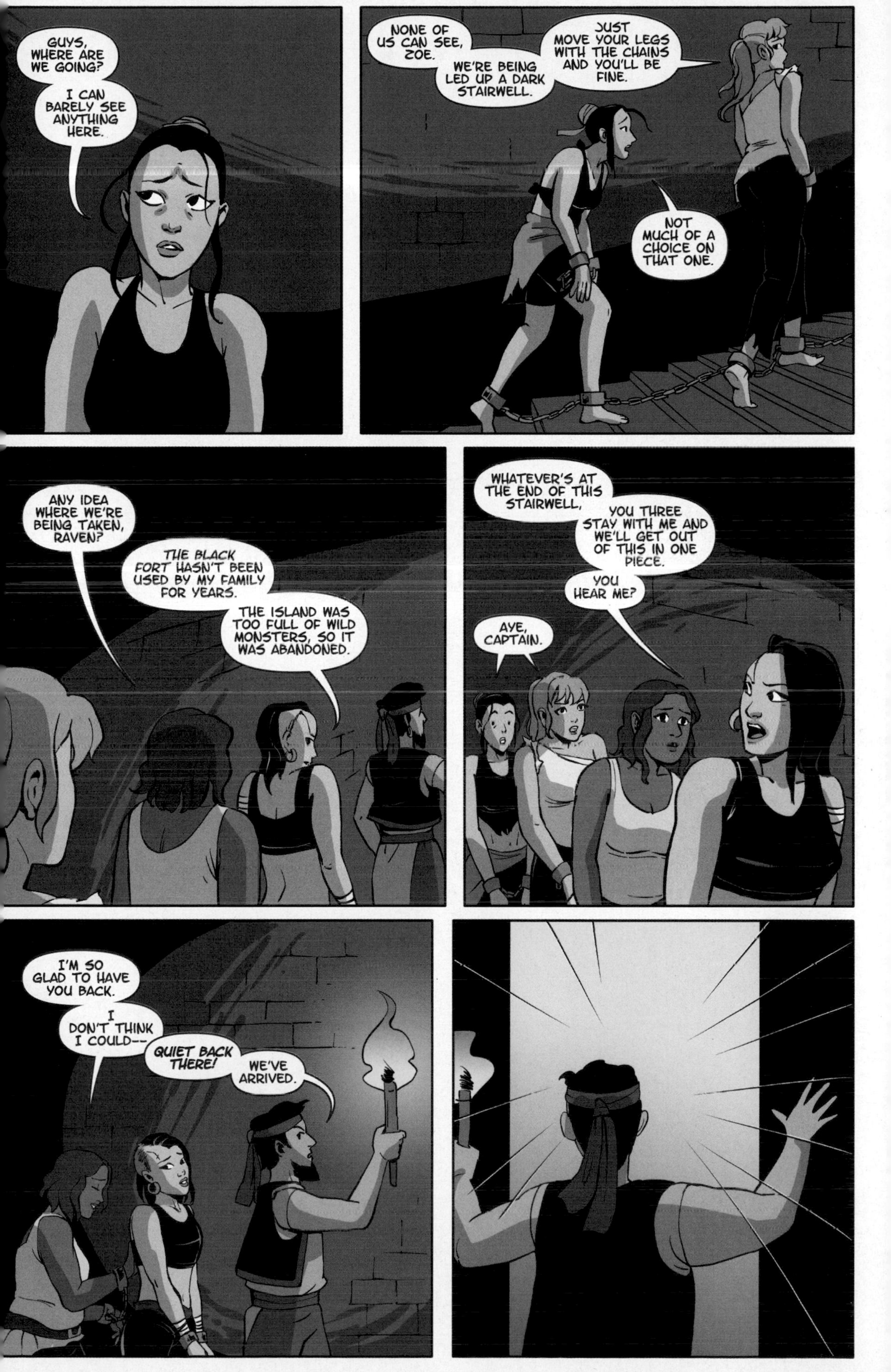
GUYS, WHERE ARE WE GOING?
I CAN BARELY SEE ANYTHING HERE.
NONE OF US CAN SEE, ZOE.
WE'RE BEING LED UP A DARK STAIRWELL.
JUST MOVE YOUR LEGS WITH THE CHAINS AND YOU'LL BE FINE.
NOT MUCH OF A CHOICE ON THAT ONE.
ANY IDEA WHERE WE'RE BEING TAKEN, RAVEN?
THE BLACK FORT HASN'T BEEN USED BY MY FAMILY FOR YEARS.
THE ISLAND WAS TOO FULL OF WILD MONSTERS, SO IT WAS ABANDONED.
WHATEVER'S AT THE END OF THIS STAIRWELL,
YOU THREE STAY WITH ME AND WE'LL GET OUT OF THIS IN ONE PIECE.
YOU HEAR ME?
AYE, CAPTAIN.
I'M SO GLAD TO HAVE YOU BACK.
I DON'T THINK I COULD--
QUIET BACK THERE!
WE'VE ARRIVED.

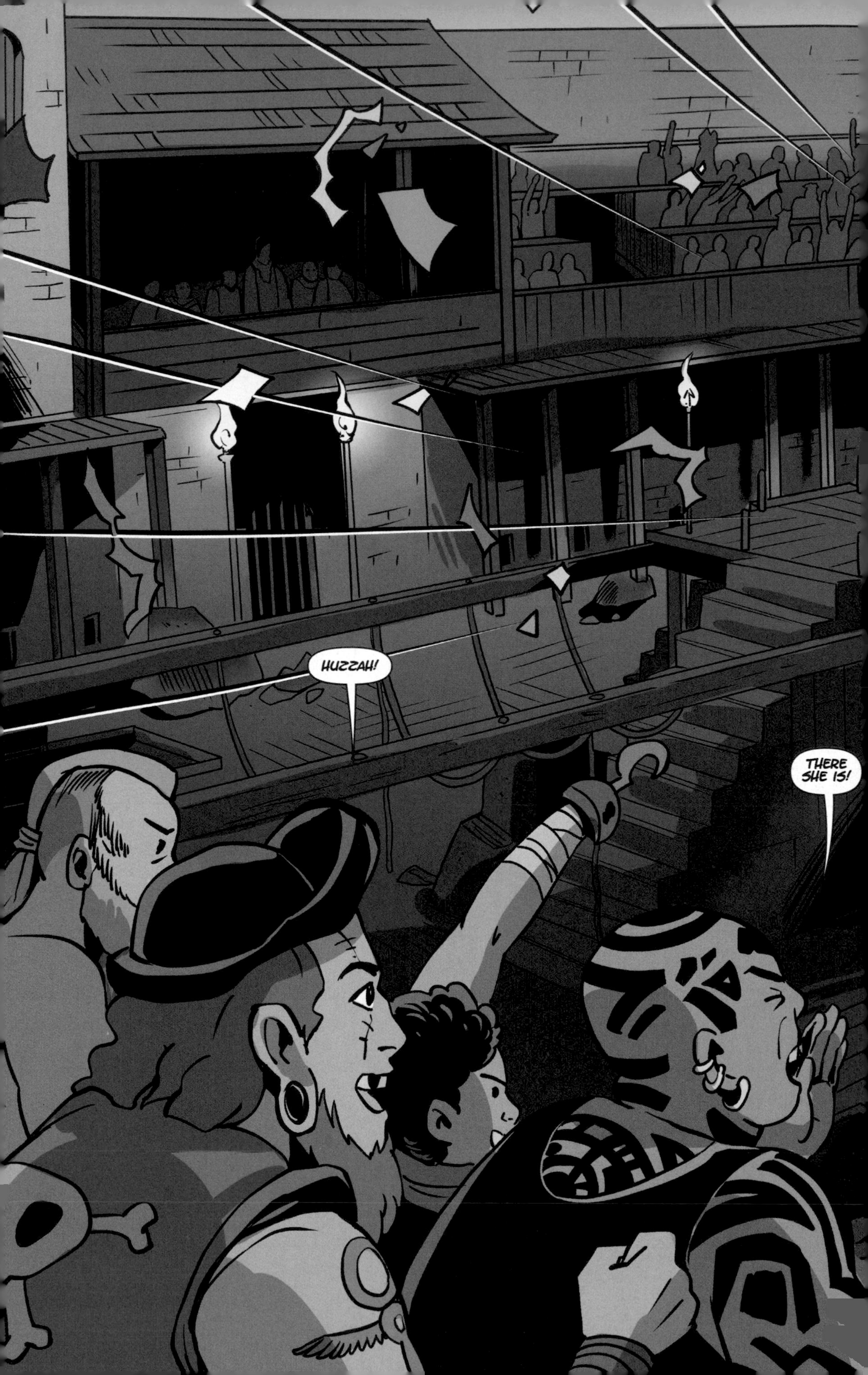
HUZZAH!
THERE SHE IS!

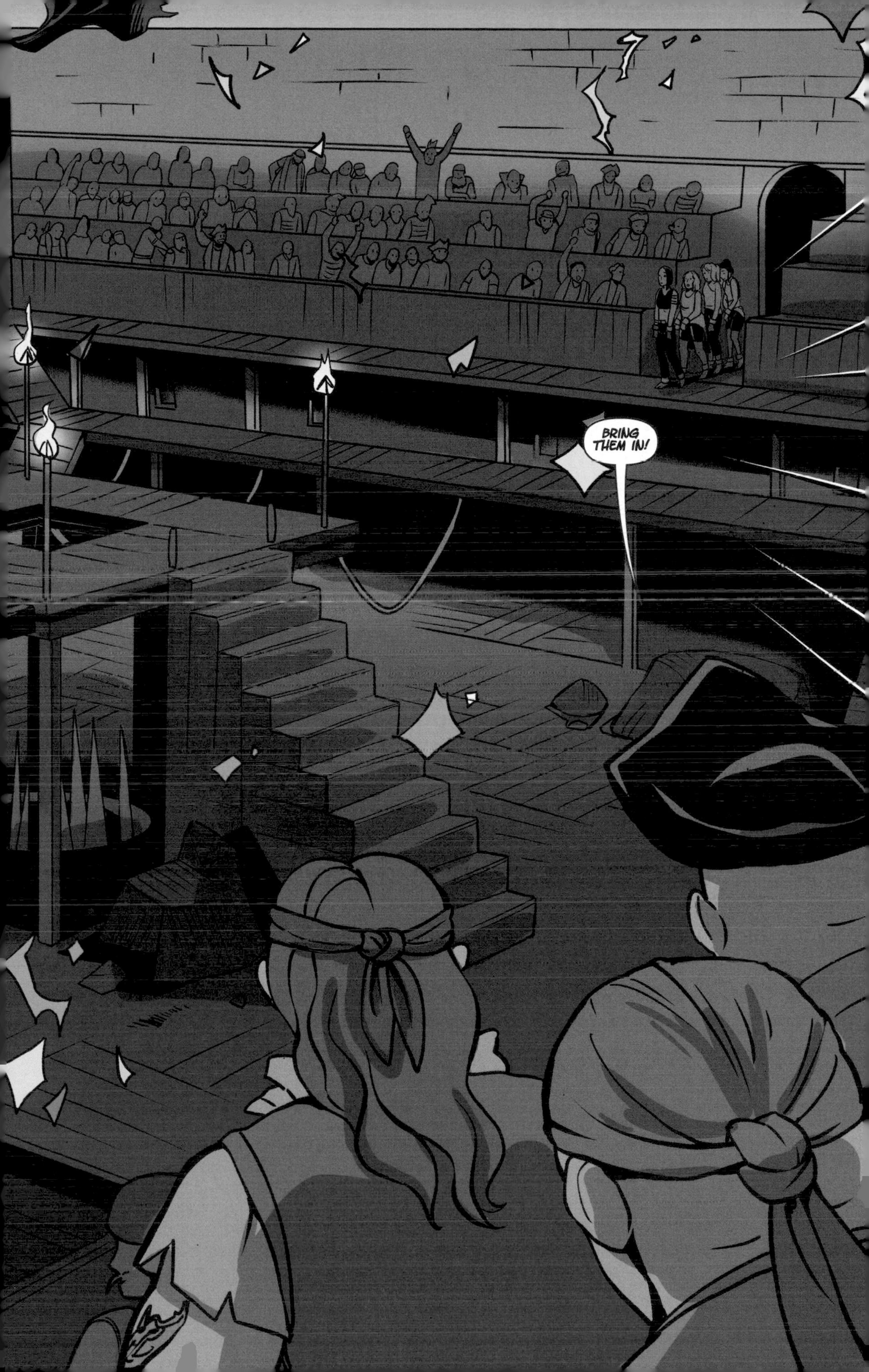
BRING THEM IN!

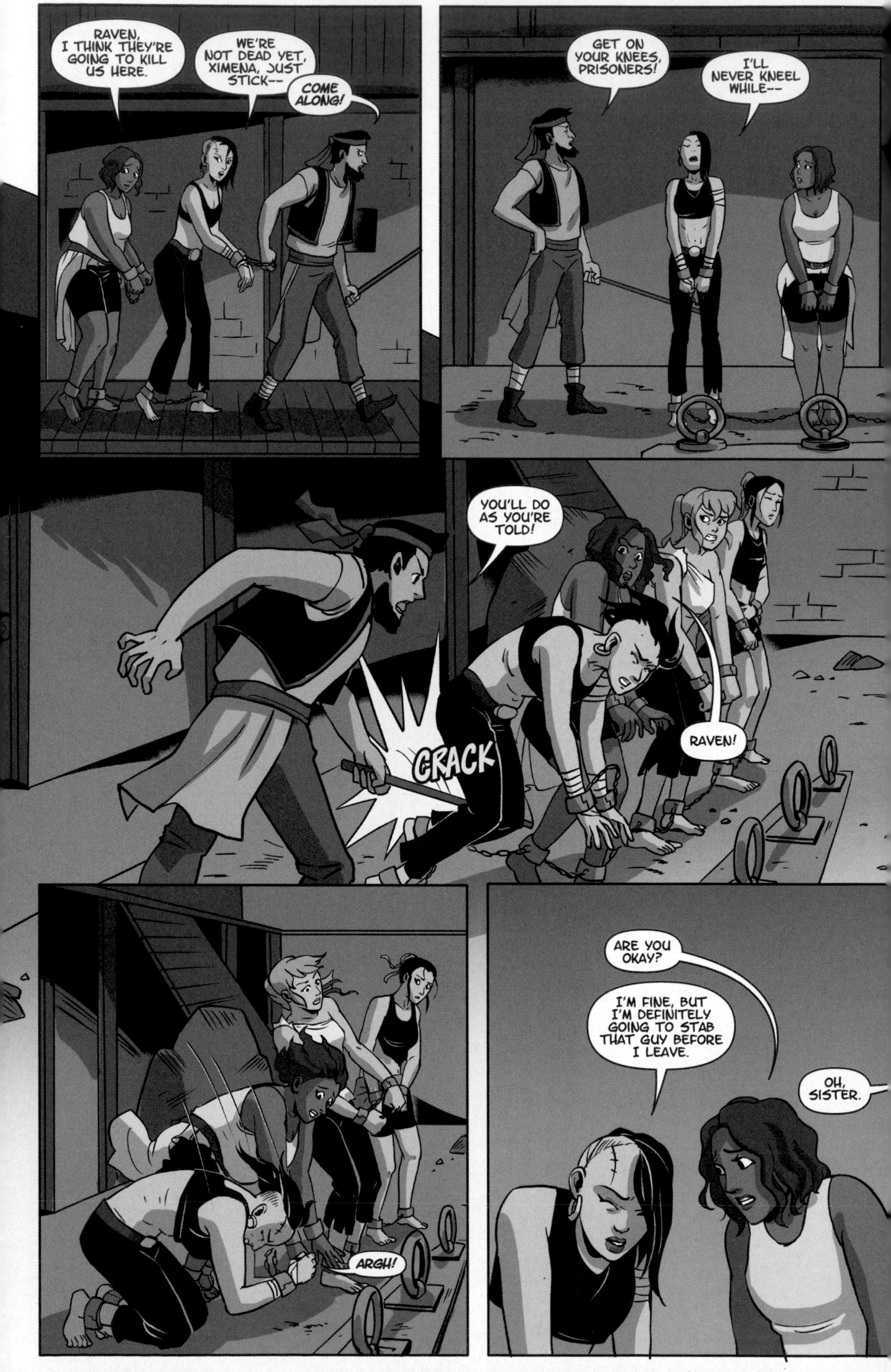
RAVEN, I THINK THEY'RE GOING TO KILL US HERE.
WE'RE NOT DEAD YET, XIMENA, JUST STICK--
COME ALONG!
GET ON YOUR KNEES, PRISONERS!
I'LL NEVER KNEEL WHILE--
YOU'LL DO AS YOU'RE TOLD!
CRACK
RAVEN!
ARGH!
ARE YOU OKAY?
I'M FINE, BUT I'M DEFINITELY GOING TO STAB THAT GUY BEFORE I LEAVE.
OH, SISTER.

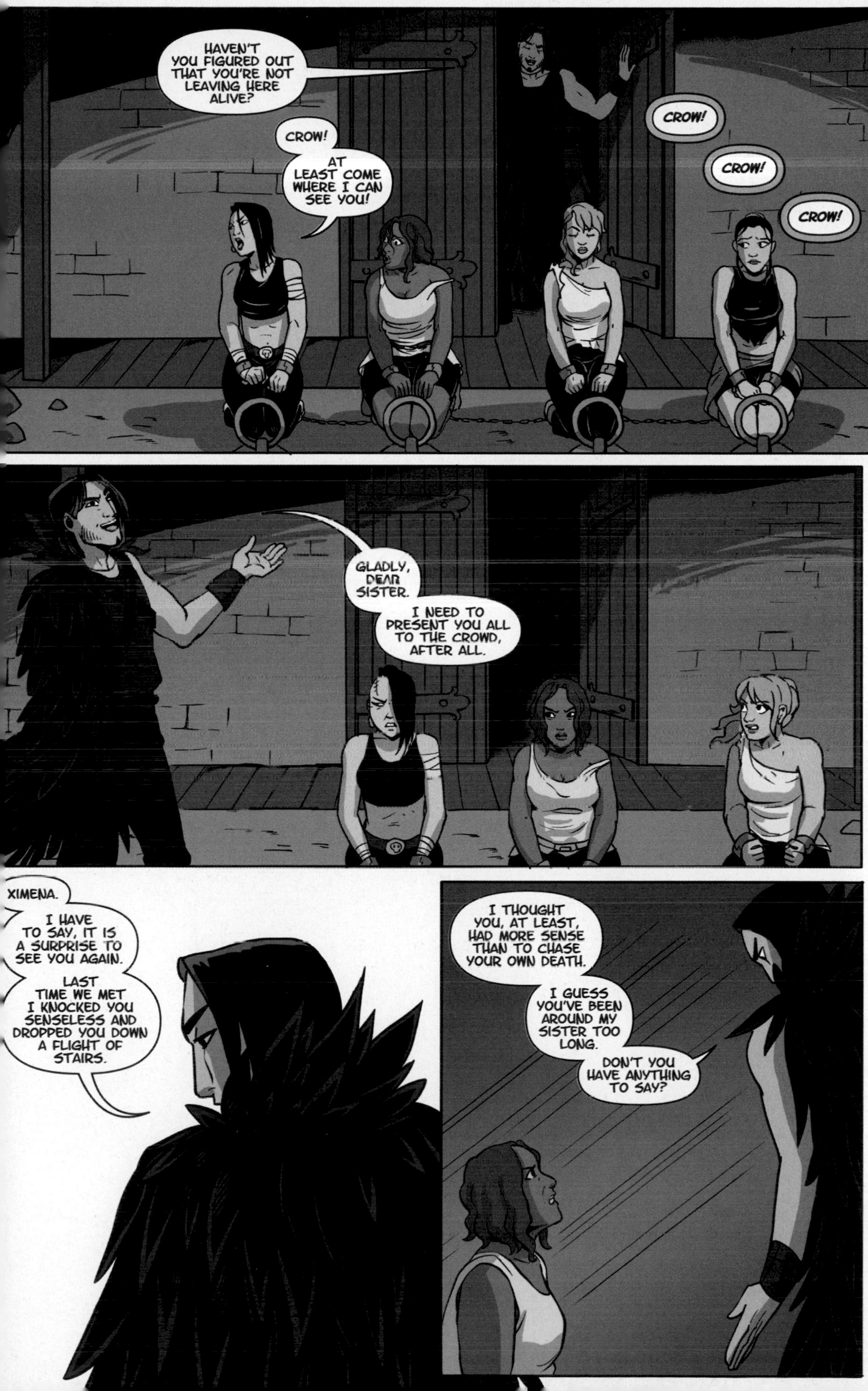
HAVEN'T YOU FIGURED OUT THAT YOU'RE NOT LEAVING HERE ALIVE?
CROW!
AT LEAST COME WHERE I CAN SEE YOU!
CROW!
CROW!
CROW!
GLADLY, DEAR SISTER.
I NEED TO PRESENT YOU ALL TO THE CROWD, AFTER ALL.
XIMENA.
I HAVE TO SAY, IT IS A SURPRISE TO SEE YOU AGAIN.
LAST TIME WE MET I KNOCKED YOU SENSELESS AND DROPPED YOU DOWN A FLIGHT OF STAIRS.
I THOUGHT YOU, AT LEAST, HAD MORE SENSE THAN TO CHASE YOUR OWN DEATH.
I GUESS YOU'VE BEEN AROUND MY SISTER TOO LONG.
DON'T YOU HAVE ANYTHING TO SAY?

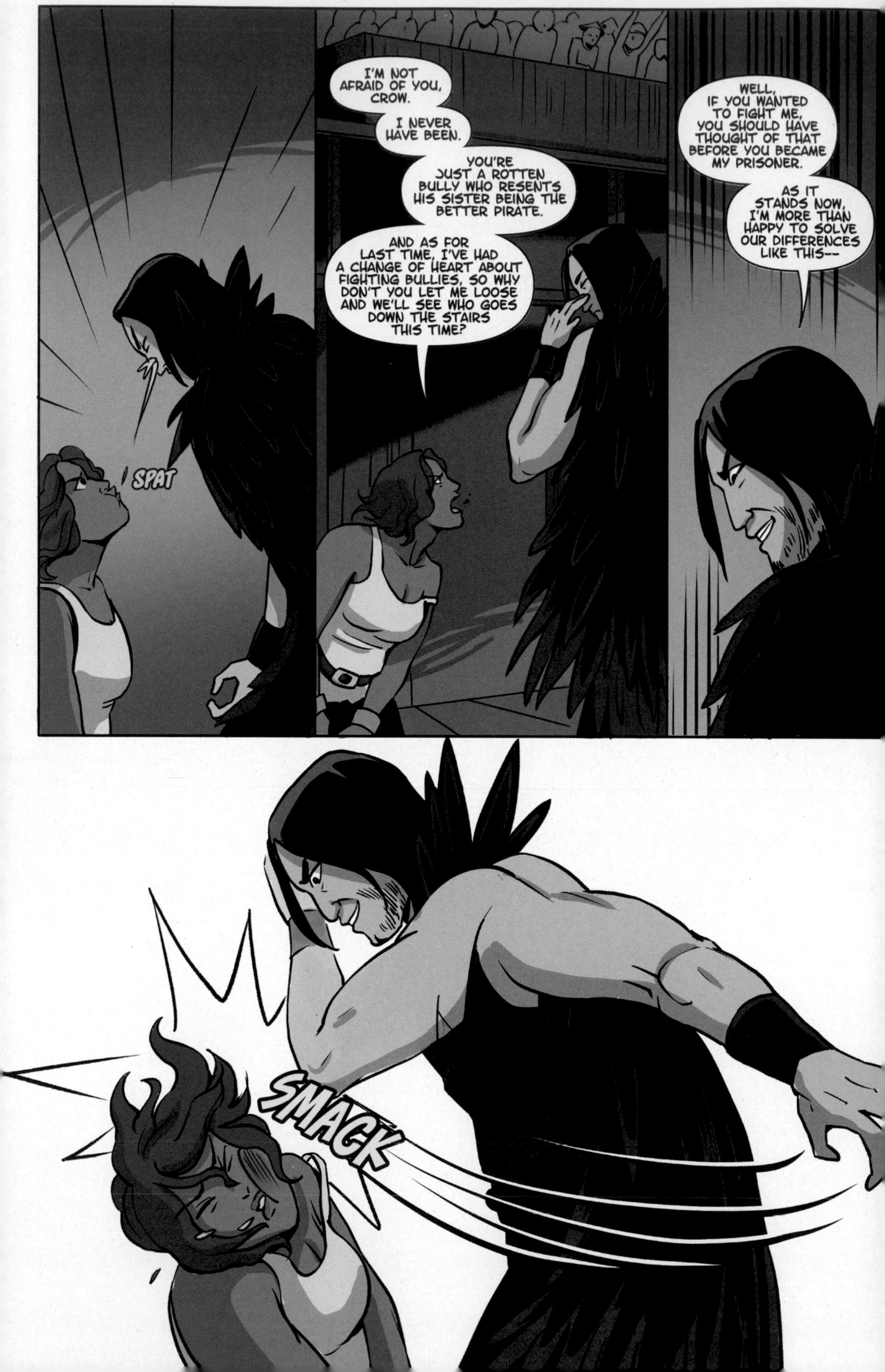
SPAT
I'M NOT AFRAID OF YOU, CROW.
I NEVER HAVE BEEN.
YOU'RE JUST A ROTTEN BULLY WHO RESENTS HIS SISTER BEING THE BETTER PIRATE.
AND AS FOR LAST TIME, I'VE HAD A CHANGE OF HEART ABOUT FIGHTING BULLIES, SO WHY DON'T YOU LET ME LOOSE AND WE'LL SEE WHO GOES DOWN THE STAIRS THIS TIME?
WELL, IF YOU WANTED TO FIGHT ME, YOU SHOULD HAVE THOUGHT OF THAT BEFORE YOU BECAME MY PRISONER.
AS IT STANDS NOW, I'M MORE THAN HAPPY TO SOLVE OUR DIFFERENCES LIKE THIS--
SMACK

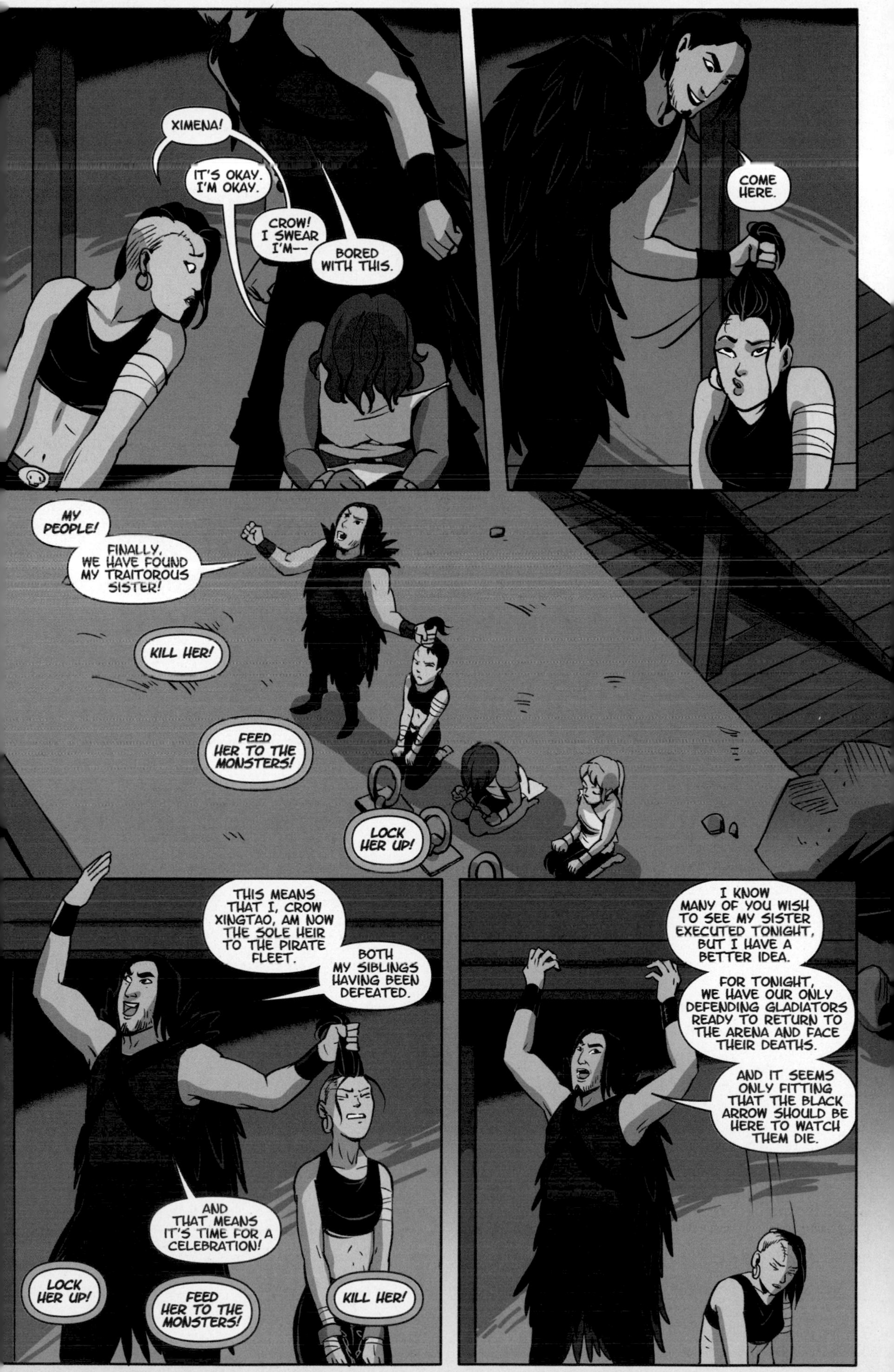
XIMENA!
IT'S OKAY. I'M OKAY.
CROW! I SWEAR I'M--
BORED WITH THIS.
COME HERE.
MY PEOPLE!
FINALLY, WE HAVE FOUND MY TRAITOROUS SISTER!
KILL HER!
FEED HER TO THE MONSTERS!
LOCK HER UP!
THIS MEANS THAT I, CROW XINGTAO, AM NOW THE SOLE HEIR TO THE PIRATE FLEET.
BOTH MY SIBLINGS HAVING BEEN DEFEATED.
AND THAT MEANS IT'S TIME FOR A CELEBRATION!
LOCK HER UP!
FEED HER TO THE MONSTERS!
KILL HER!
I KNOW MANY OF YOU WISH TO SEE MY SISTER EXECUTED TONIGHT, BUT I HAVE A BETTER IDEA.
FOR TONIGHT, WE HAVE OUR ONLY DEFENDING GLADIATORS READY TO RETURN TO THE ARENA AND FACE THEIR DEATHS.
AND IT SEEMS ONLY FITTING THAT THE BLACK ARROW SHOULD BE HERE TO WATCH THEM DIE.

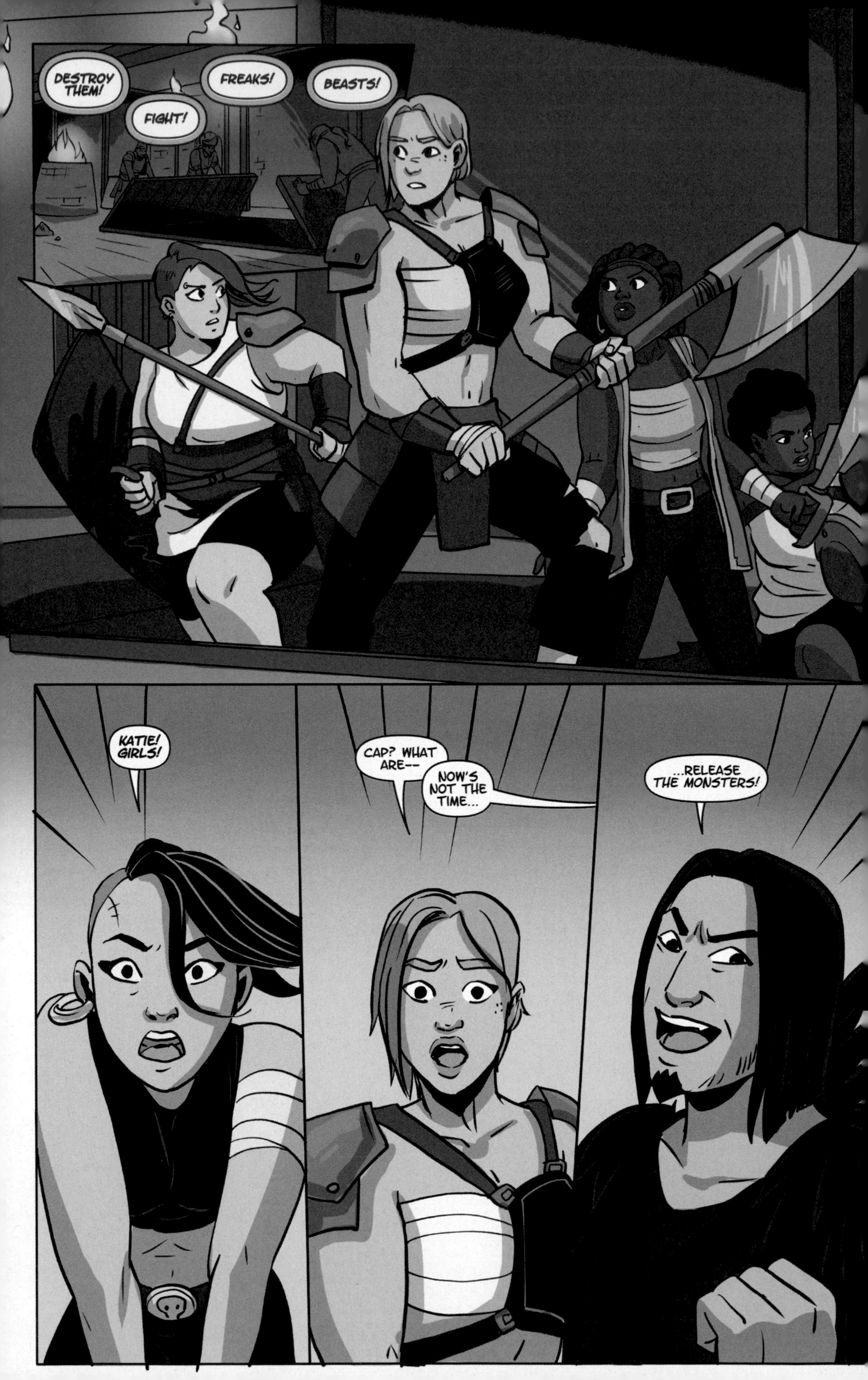
DESTROY THEM!
FIGHT!
FREAKS!
BEASTS!
KATIE! GIRLS!
CAP? WHAT ARE--
NOW'S NOT THE TIME...
...RELEASE THE MONSTERS!

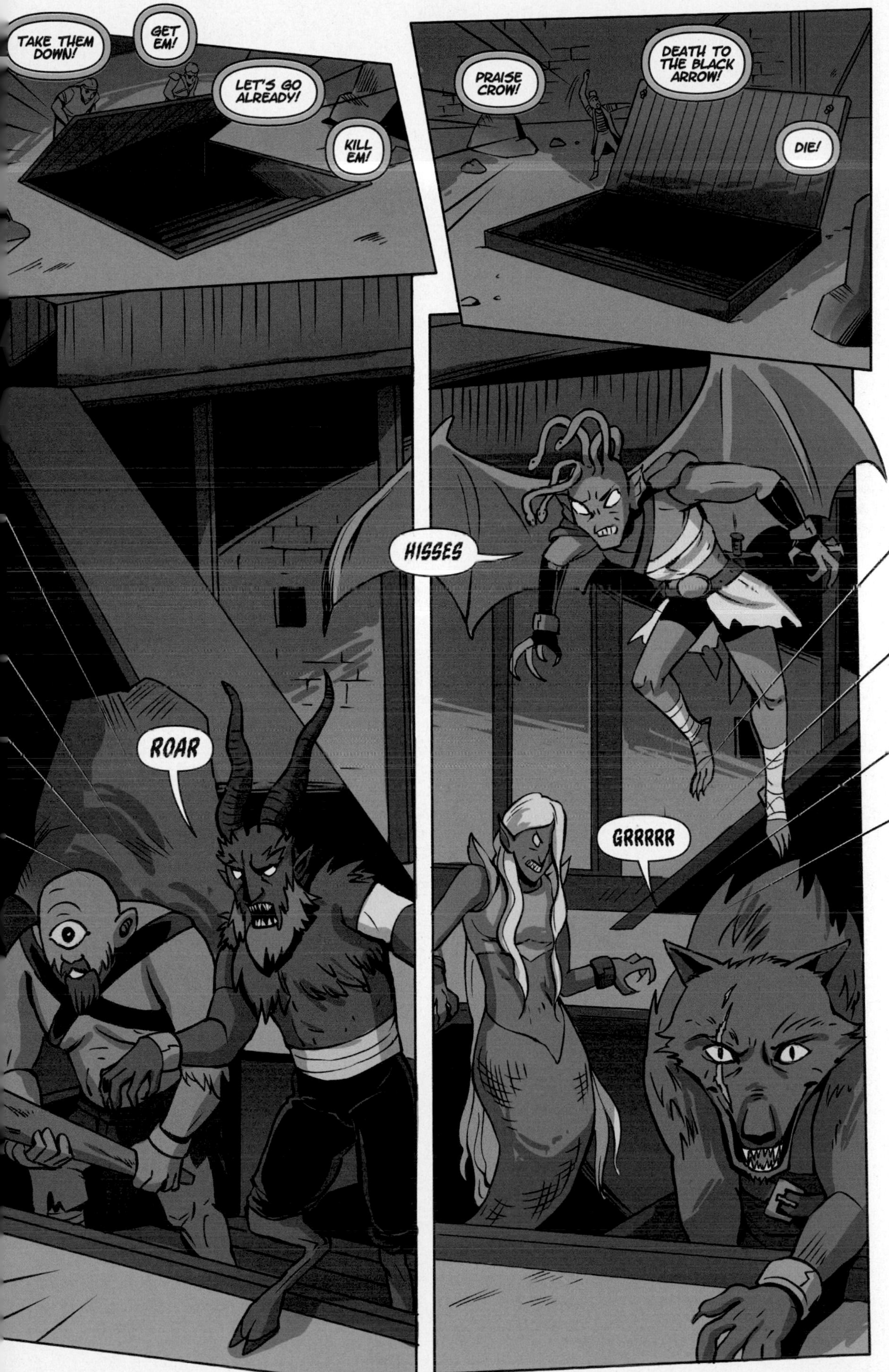
TAKE THEM DOWN!
GET EM!
LET'S GO ALREADY!
KILL EM!
PRAISE CROW!
DEATH TO THE BLACK ARROW!
DIE!
ROAR
HISSES
GRRRRR

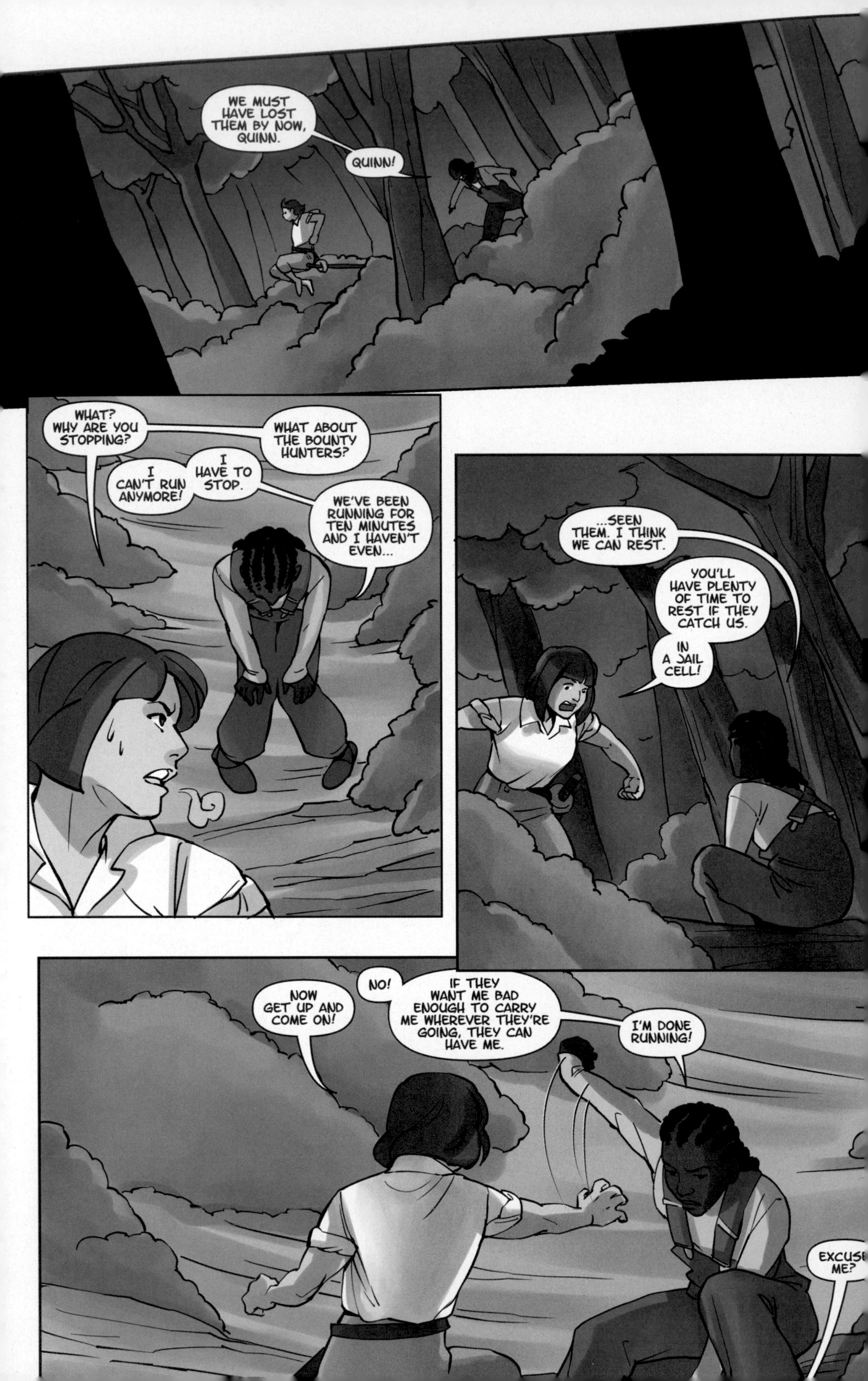
WE MUST HAVE LOST THEM BY NOW, QUINN.
QUINN!
WHAT? WHY ARE YOU STOPPING?
WHAT ABOUT THE BOUNTY HUNTERS?
I CAN'T RUN ANYMORE!
I HAVE TO STOP.
WE'VE BEEN RUNNING FOR TEN MINUTES AND I HAVEN'T EVEN...
...SEEN THEM. I THINK WE CAN REST.
YOU'LL HAVE PLENTY OF TIME TO REST IF THEY CATCH US.
IN A JAIL CELL!
NOW GET UP AND COME ON!
NO!
IF THEY WANT ME BAD ENOUGH TO CARRY ME WHEREVER THEY'RE GOING, THEY CAN HAVE ME.
I'M DONE RUNNING!
EXCUSE ME?

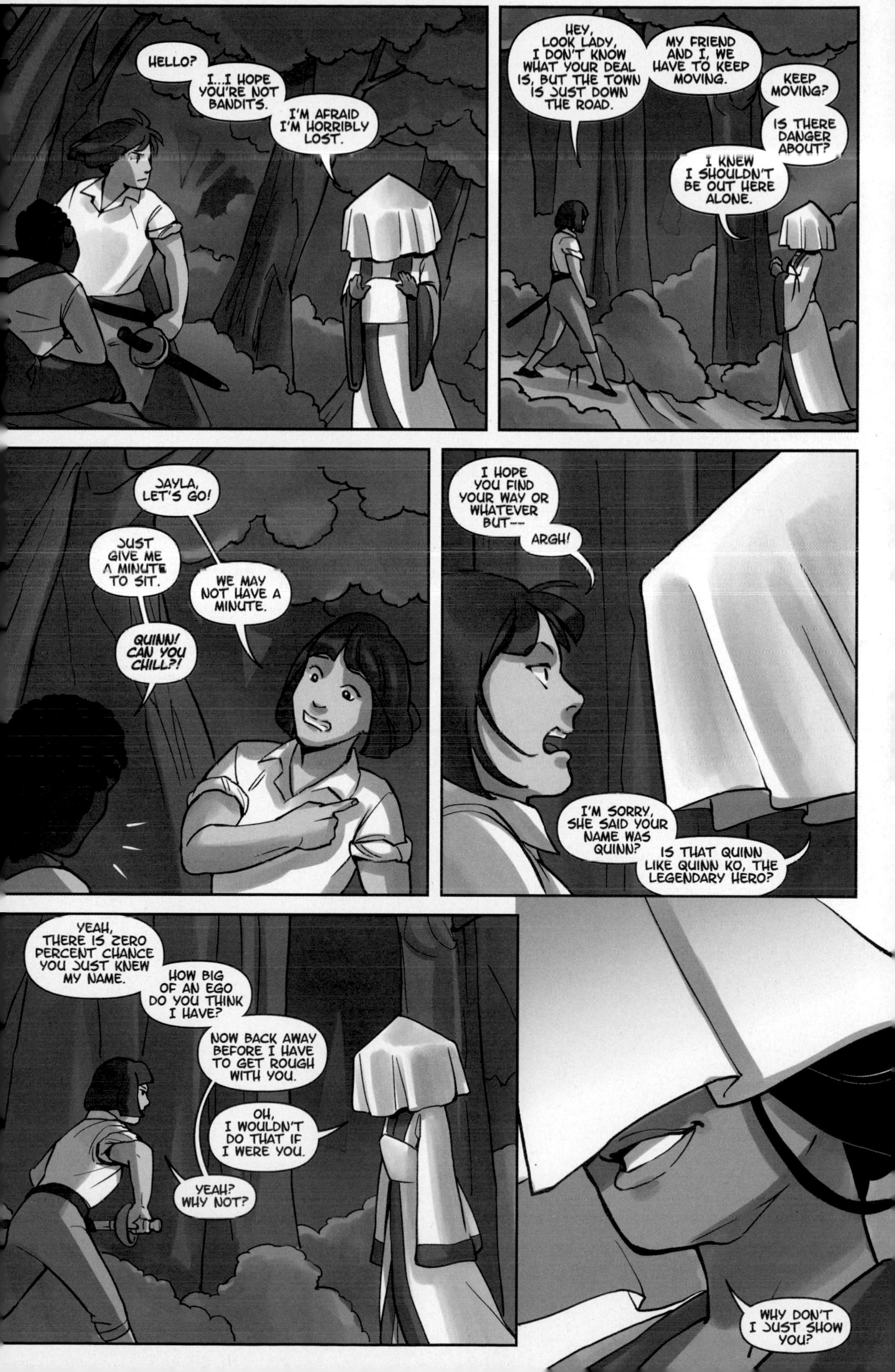
HELLO?
I...I HOPE YOU'RE NOT BANDITS.
I'M AFRAID I'M HORRIBLY LOST.
HEY, LOOK LADY, I DON'T KNOW WHAT YOUR DEAL IS, BUT THE TOWN IS JUST DOWN THE ROAD.
MY FRIEND AND I, WE HAVE TO KEEP MOVING.
KEEP MOVING?
IS THERE DANGER ABOUT?
I KNEW I SHOULDN'T BE OUT HERE ALONE.
JAYLA, LET'S GO!
JUST GIVE ME A MINUTE TO SIT.
WE MAY NOT HAVE A MINUTE.
QUINN! CAN YOU CHILL?!
I HOPE YOU FIND YOUR WAY OR WHATEVER BUT--
ARGH!
I'M SORRY, SHE SAID YOUR NAME WAS QUINN?
IS THAT QUINN LIKE QUINN KO, THE LEGENDARY HERO?
YEAH, THERE IS ZERO PERCENT CHANCE YOU JUST KNEW MY NAME.
HOW BIG OF AN EGO DO YOU THINK I HAVE?
NOW BACK AWAY BEFORE I HAVE TO GET ROUGH WITH YOU.
OH, I WOULDN'T DO THAT IF I WERE YOU.
YEAH? WHY NOT?
WHY DON'T I JUST SHOW YOU?

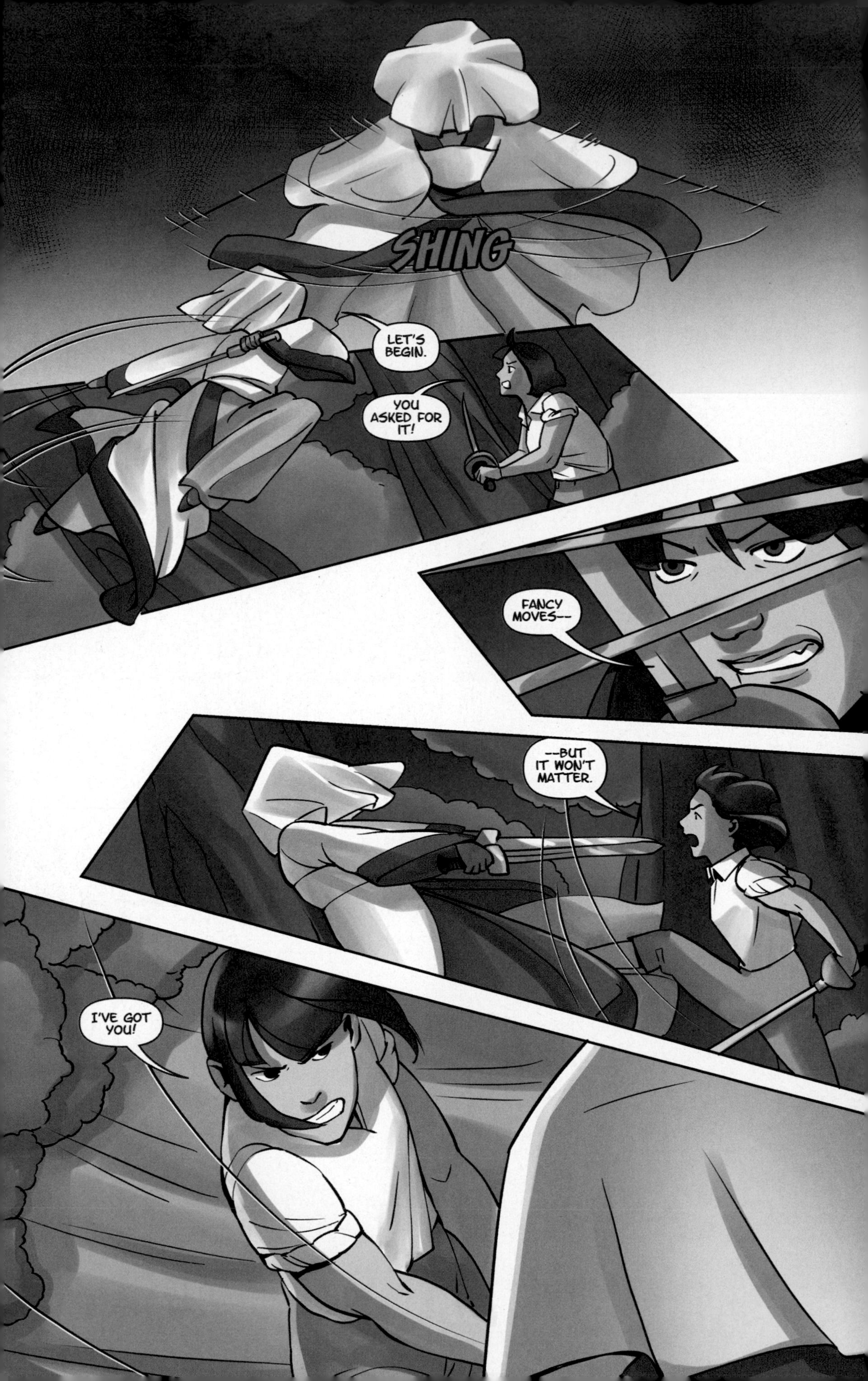
SHING
LET'S BEGIN.
YOU ASKED FOR IT!
FANCY MOVES--
--BUT IT WON'T MATTER.
I'VE GOT YOU!

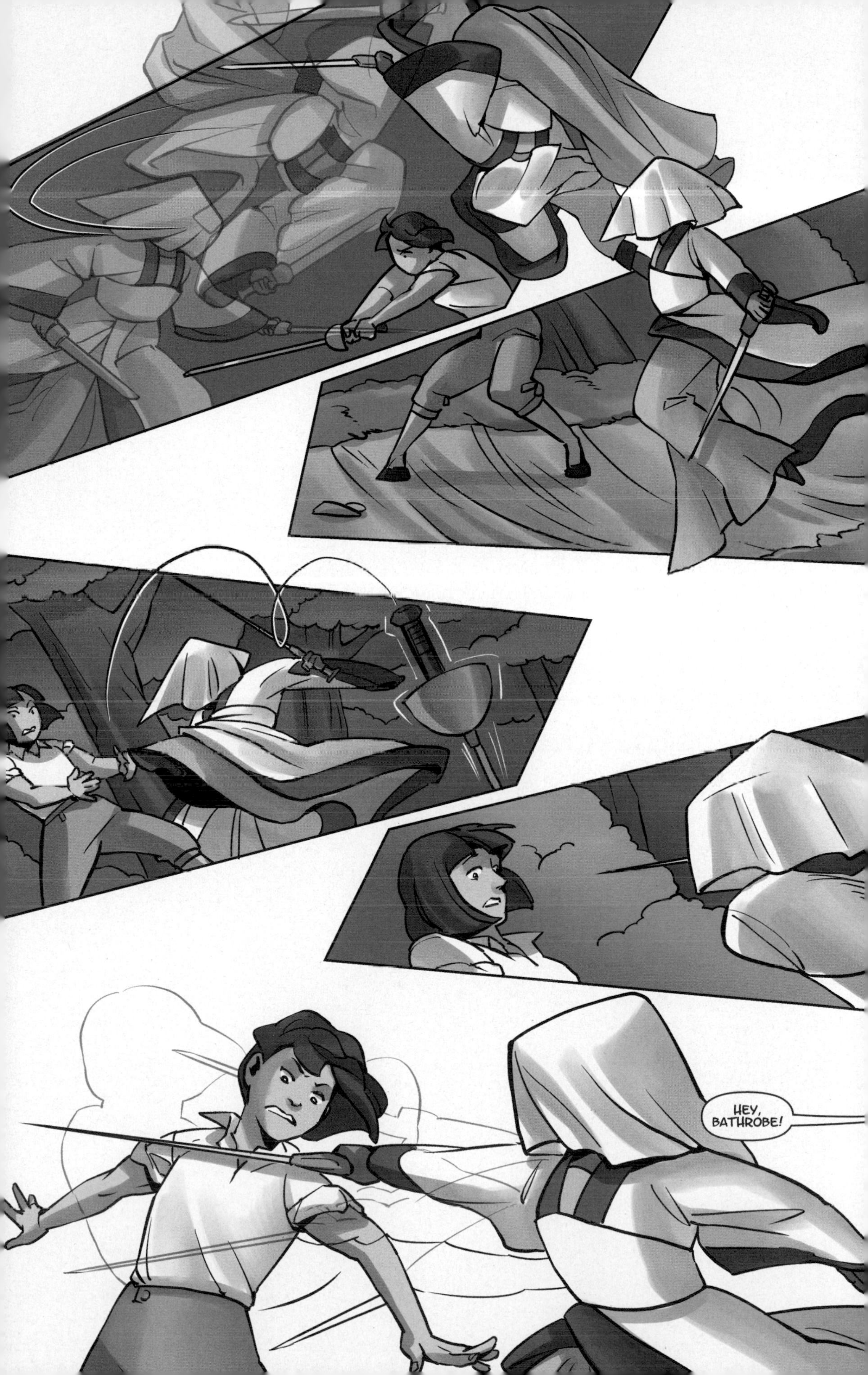
HEY, BATHROBE!

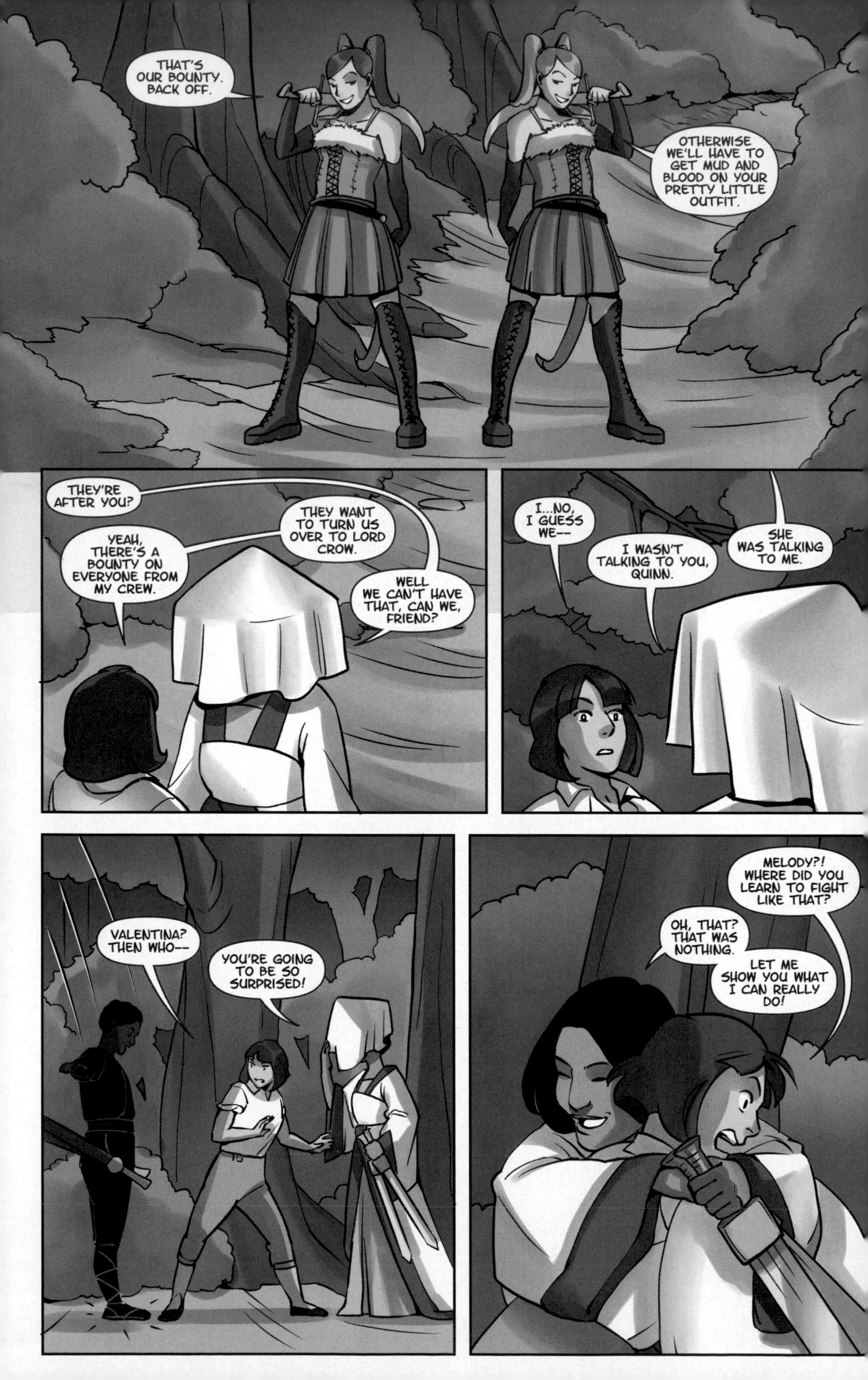
THAT'S OUR BOUNTY. BACK OFF.
OTHERWISE WE'LL HAVE TO GET MUD AND BLOOD ON YOUR PRETTY LITTLE OUTFIT.
THEY'RE AFTER YOU?
YEAH, THERE'S A BOUNTY ON EVERYONE FROM MY CREW.
THEY WANT TO TURN US OVER TO LORD CROW.
WELL WE CAN'T HAVE THAT, CAN WE, FRIEND?
I...NO, I GUESS WE--
I WASN'T TALKING TO YOU, QUINN.
SHE WAS TALKING TO ME.
VALENTINA? THEN WHO--
YOU'RE GOING TO BE SO SURPRISED!
MELODY?! WHERE DID YOU LEARN TO FIGHT LIKE THAT?
OH, THAT? THAT WAS NOTHING.
LET ME SHOW YOU WHAT I CAN REALLY DO!

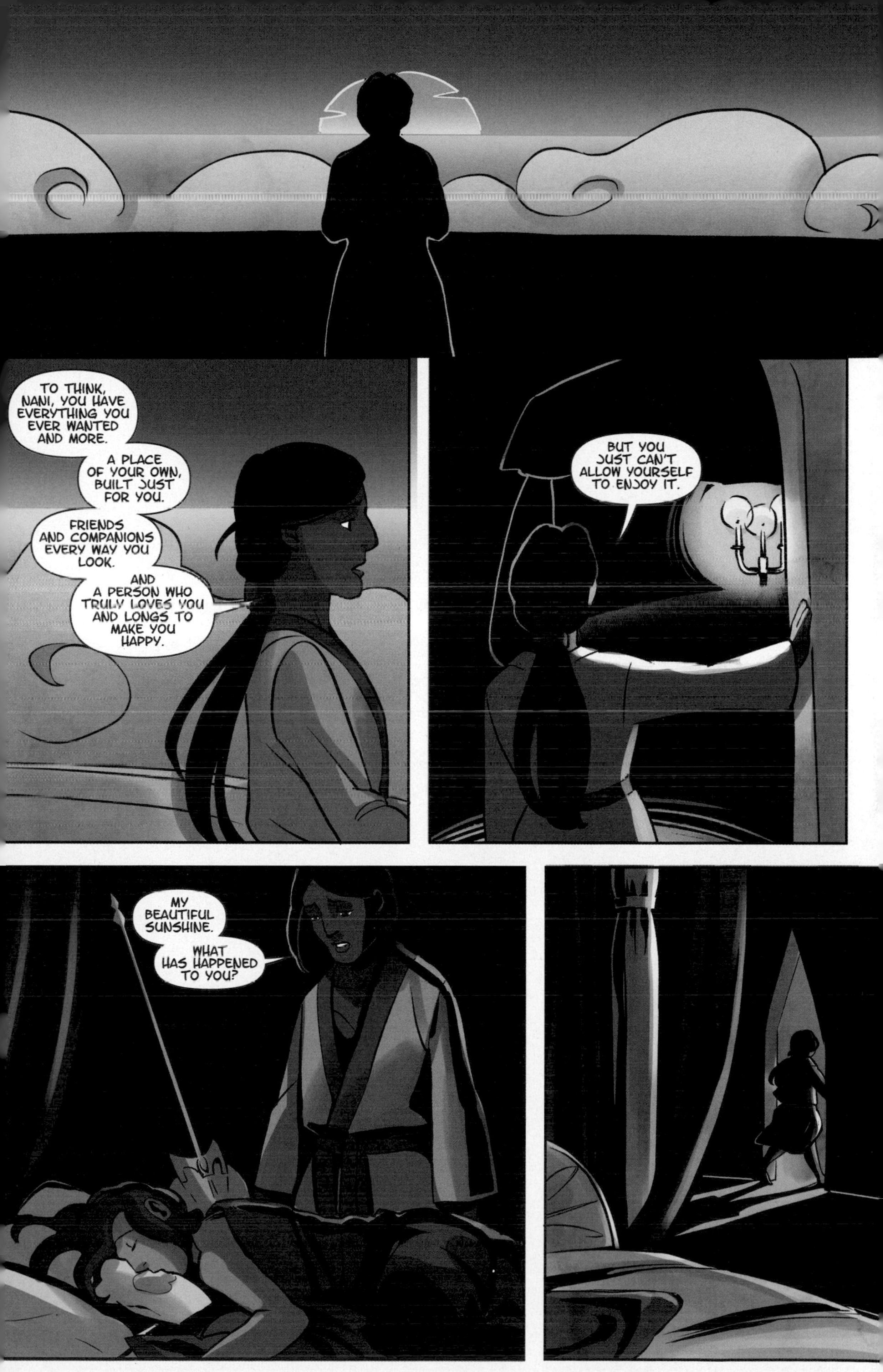
TO THINK, NANI, YOU HAVE EVERYTHING YOU EVER WANTED AND MORE.
A PLACE OF YOUR OWN, BUILT JUST FOR YOU.
FRIENDS AND COMPANIONS EVERY WAY YOU LOOK.
AND A PERSON WHO TRULY LOVES YOU AND LONGS TO MAKE YOU HAPPY.
BUT YOU JUST CAN'T ALLOW YOURSELF TO ENJOY IT.
MY BEAUTIFUL SUNSHINE.
WHAT HAS HAPPENED TO YOU?

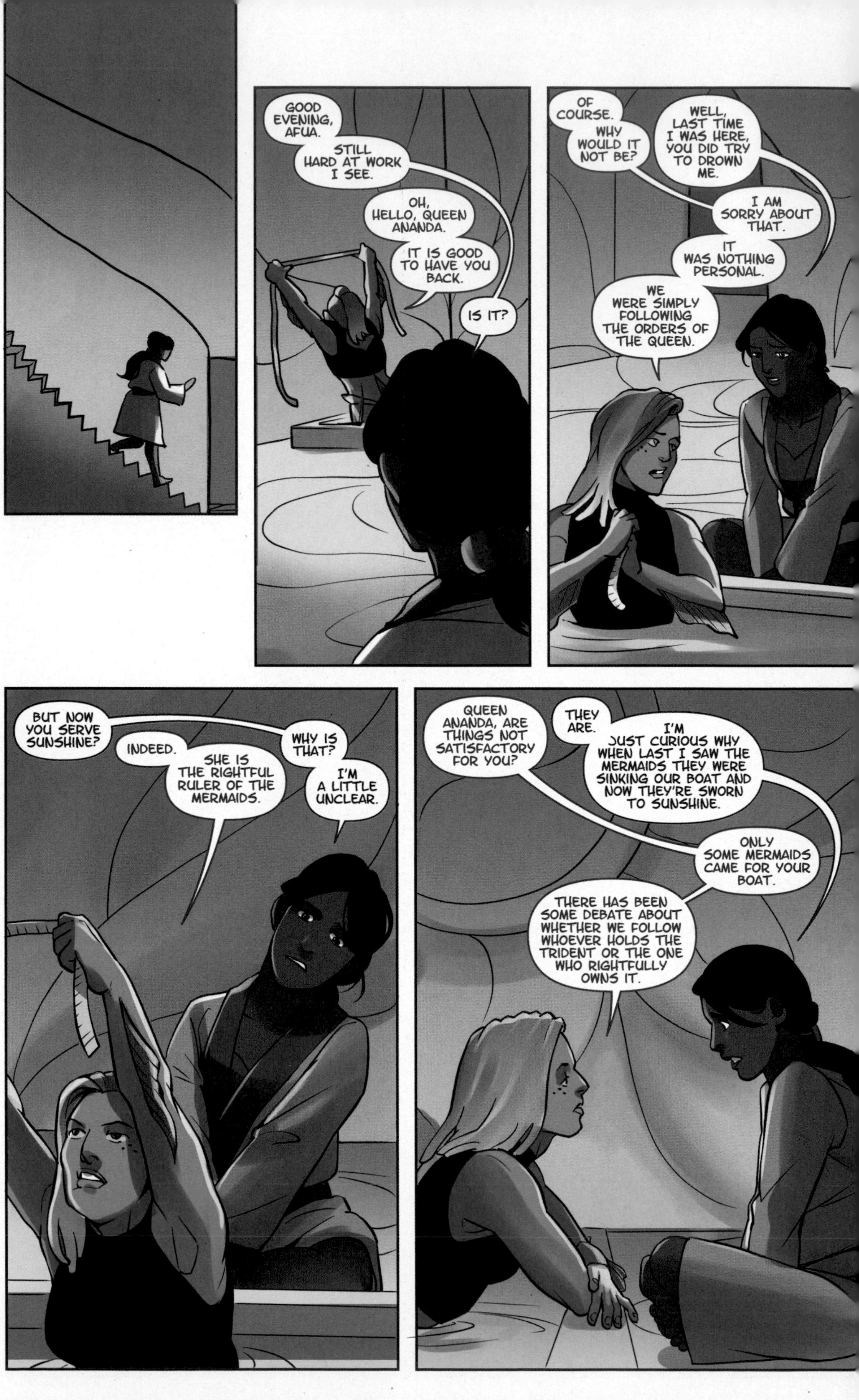
GOOD EVENING, AFUA.
STILL HARD AT WORK I SEE.
OH, HELLO, QUEEN ANANDA.
IT IS GOOD TO HAVE YOU BACK.
IS IT?
OF COURSE.
WHY WOULD IT NOT BE?
WELL, LAST TIME I WAS HERE, YOU DID TRY TO DROWN ME.
I AM SORRY ABOUT THAT.
IT WAS NOTHING PERSONAL.
WE WERE SIMPLY FOLLOWING THE ORDERS OF THE QUEEN.
BUT NOW YOU SERVE SUNSHINE?
INDEED.
SHE IS THE RIGHTFUL RULER OF THE MERMAIDS.
WHY IS THAT?
I'M A LITTLE UNCLEAR.
QUEEN ANANDA, ARE THINGS NOT SATISFACTORY FOR YOU?
THEY ARE.
I'M JUST CURIOUS WHY WHEN LAST I SAW THE MERMAIDS THEY WERE SINKING OUR BOAT AND NOW THEY'RE SWORN TO SUNSHINE.
ONLY SOME MERMAIDS CAME FOR YOUR BOAT.
THERE HAS BEEN SOME DEBATE ABOUT WHETHER WE FOLLOW WHOEVER HOLDS THE TRIDENT OR THE ONE WHO RIGHTFULLY OWNS IT.

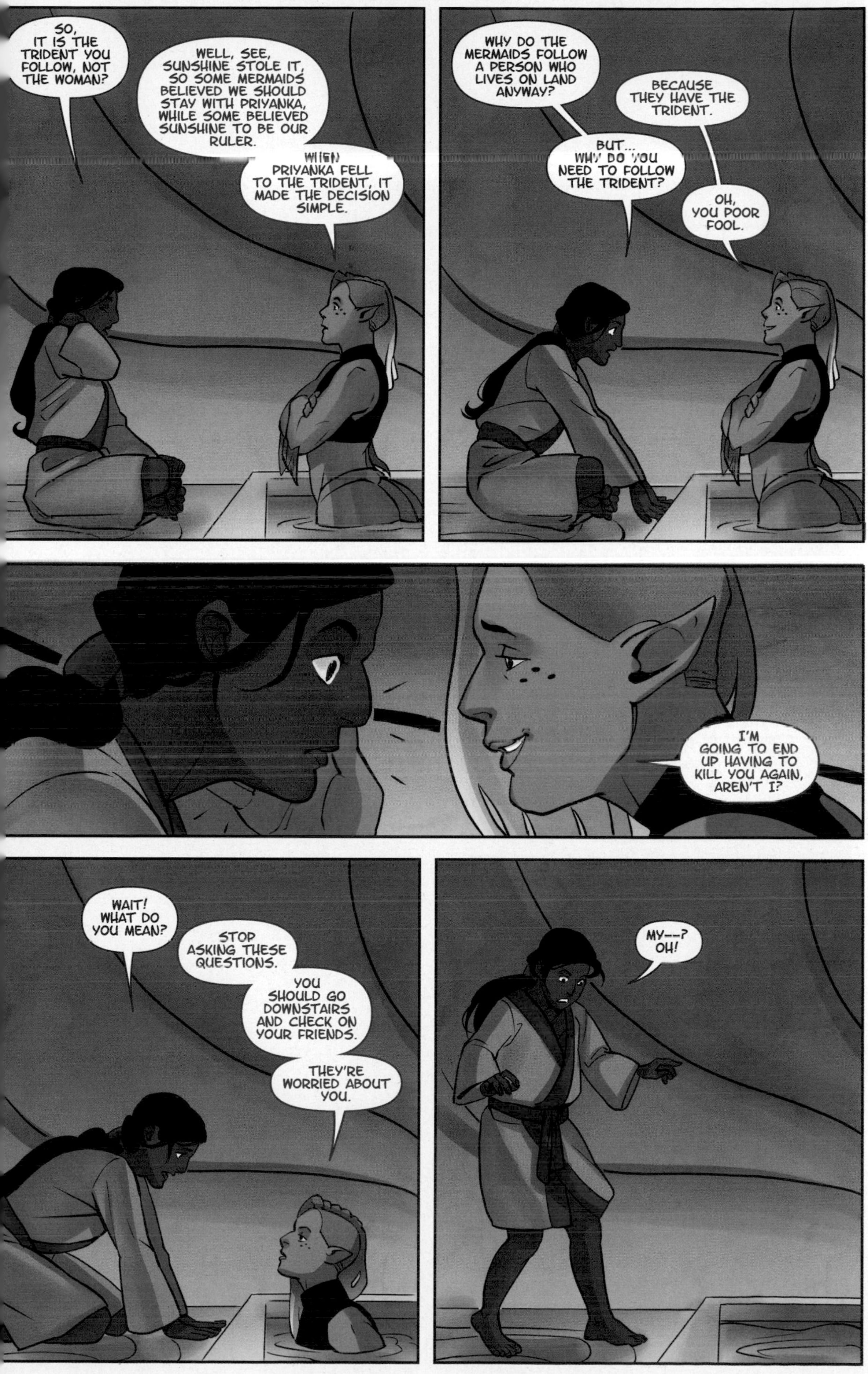
SO, IT IS THE TRIDENT YOU FOLLOW, NOT THE WOMAN?
WELL, SEE, SUNSHINE STOLE IT, SO SOME MERMAIDS BELIEVED WE SHOULD STAY WITH PRIYANKA, WHILE SOME BELIEVED SUNSHINE TO BE OUR RULER.
WHEN PRIYANKA FELL TO THE TRIDENT, IT MADE THE DECISION SIMPLE.
WHY DO THE MERMAIDS FOLLOW A PERSON WHO LIVES ON LAND ANYWAY?
BECAUSE THEY HAVE THE TRIDENT.
BUT... WHY DO YOU NEED TO FOLLOW THE TRIDENT?
OH, YOU POOR FOOL.
I'M GOING TO END UP HAVING TO KILL YOU AGAIN, AREN'T I?
WAIT! WHAT DO YOU MEAN?
STOP ASKING THESE QUESTIONS.
YOU SHOULD GO DOWNSTAIRS AND CHECK ON YOUR FRIENDS.
THEY'RE WORRIED ABOUT YOU.
MY--? OH!

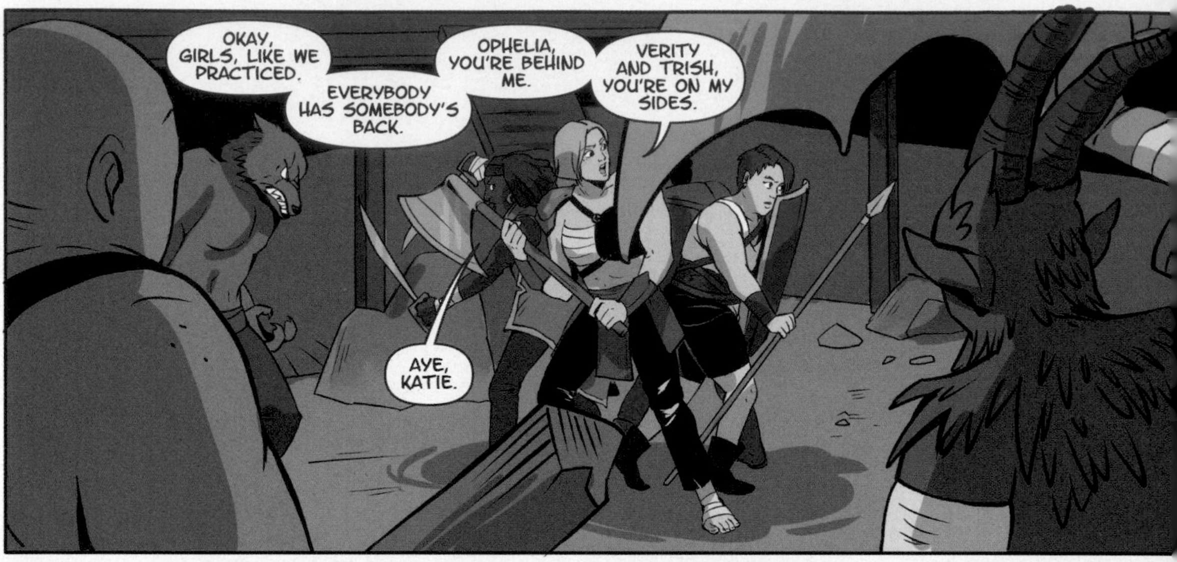
OKAY, GIRLS, LIKE WE PRACTICED.
EVERYBODY HAS SOMEBODY'S BACK.
OPHELIA, YOU'RE BEHIND ME.
VERITY AND TRISH, YOU'RE ON MY SIDES.
AYE, KATIE.

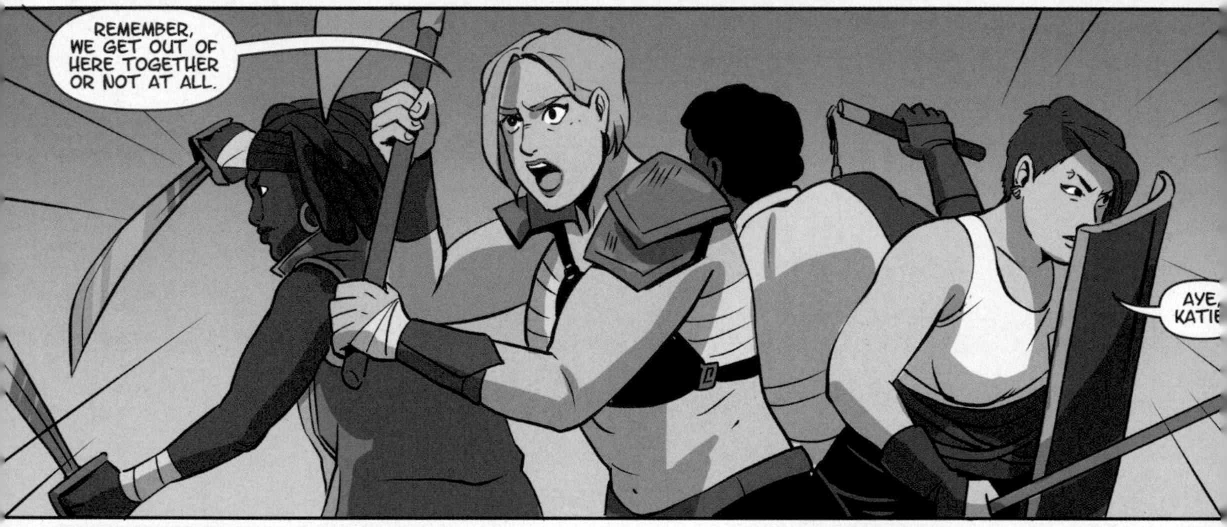
REMEMBER, WE GET OUT OF HERE TOGETHER OR NOT AT ALL.
AYE, KATIE

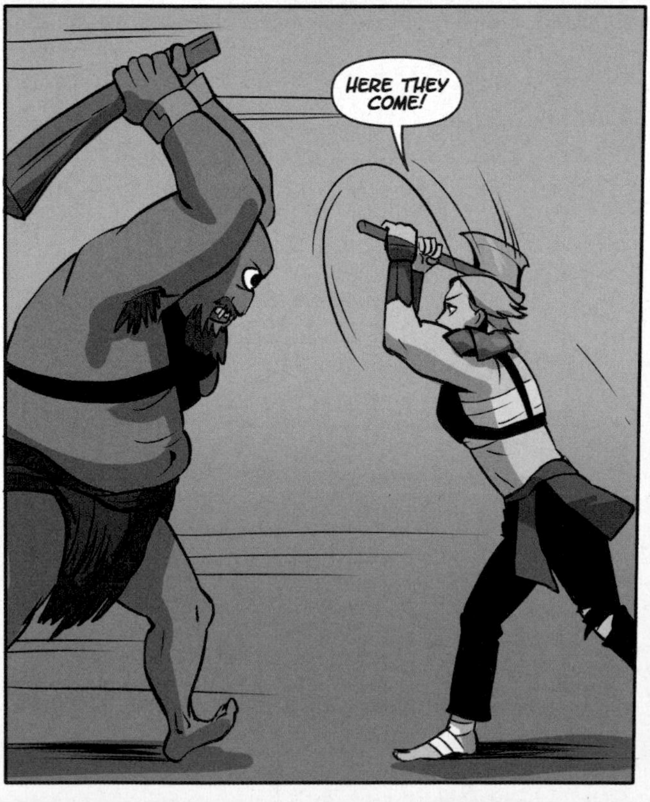
HERE THEY COME!

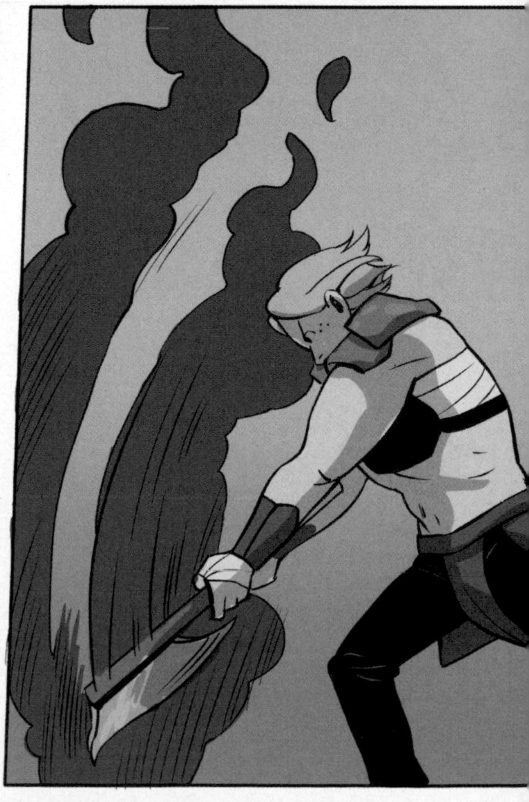

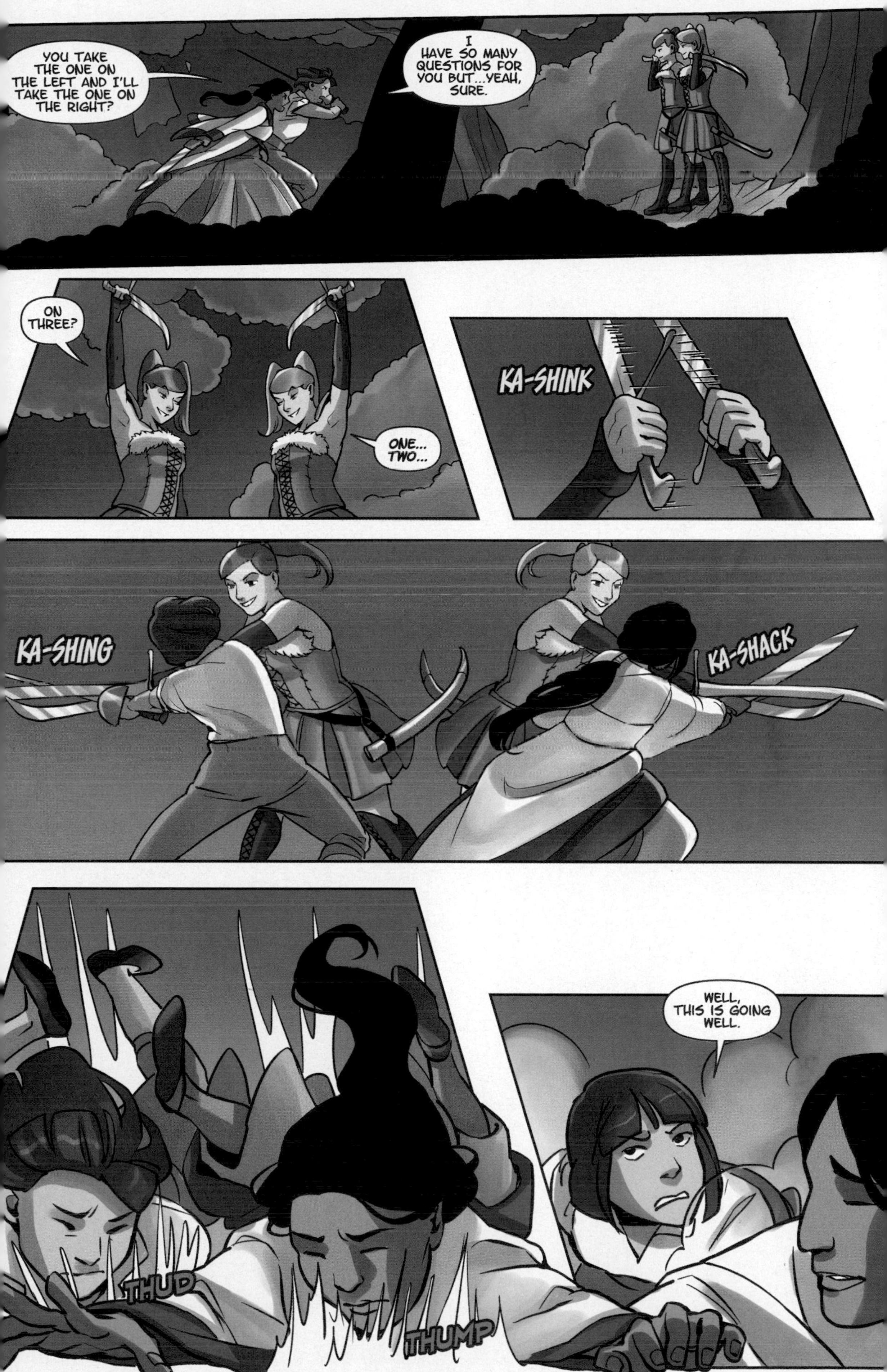
YOU TAKE THE ONE ON THE LEFT AND I'LL TAKE THE ONE ON THE RIGHT?
I HAVE SO MANY QUESTIONS FOR YOU BUT...YEAH, SURE.
ON THREE?
ONE... TWO...
KA-SHINK
KA-SHING
KA-SHACK
THUD
THUMP
WELL, THIS IS GOING WELL.

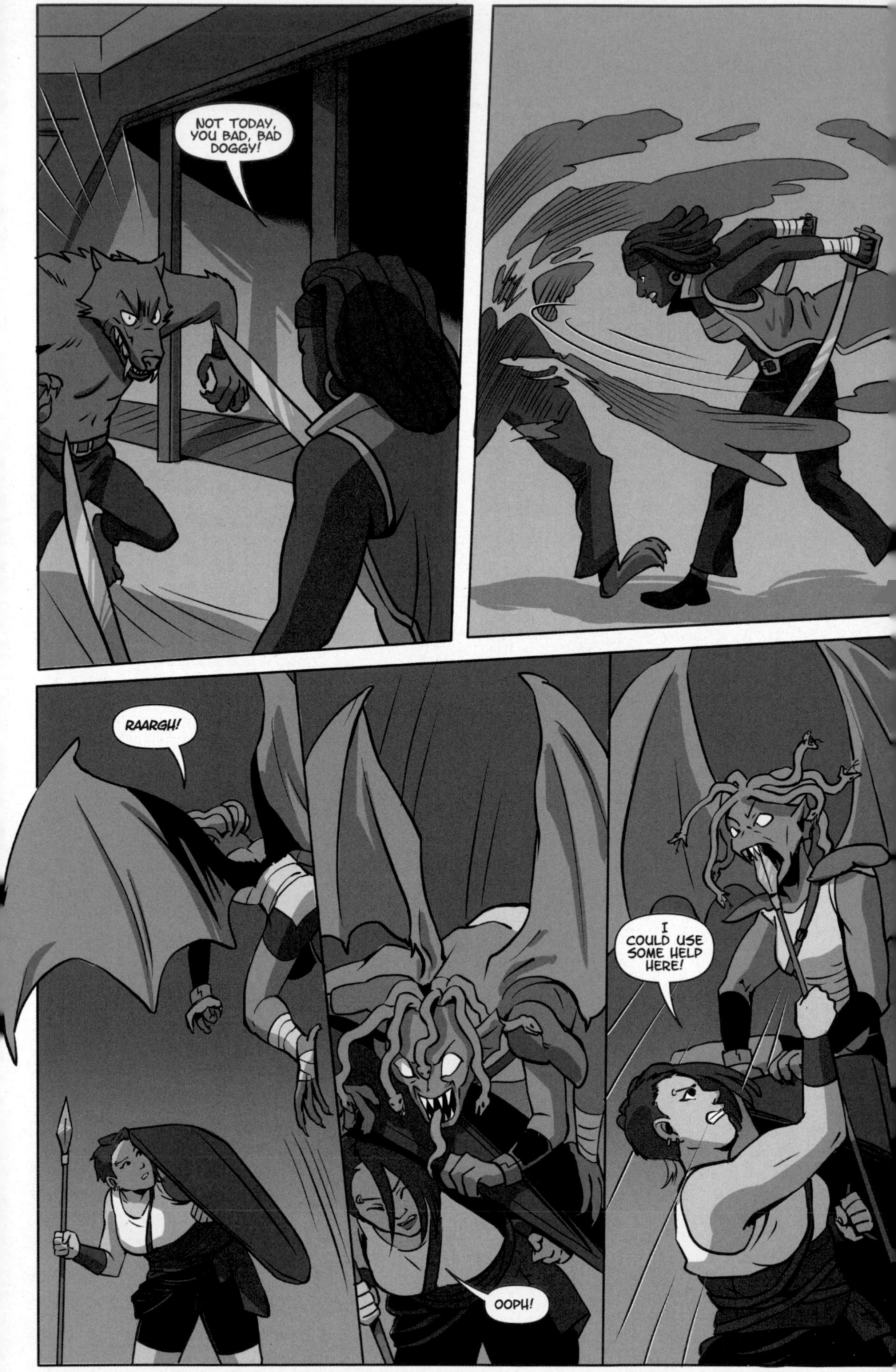
NOT TODAY, YOU BAD, BAD DOGGY!
RAARGH!
OOPH!
I COULD USE SOME HELP HERE!

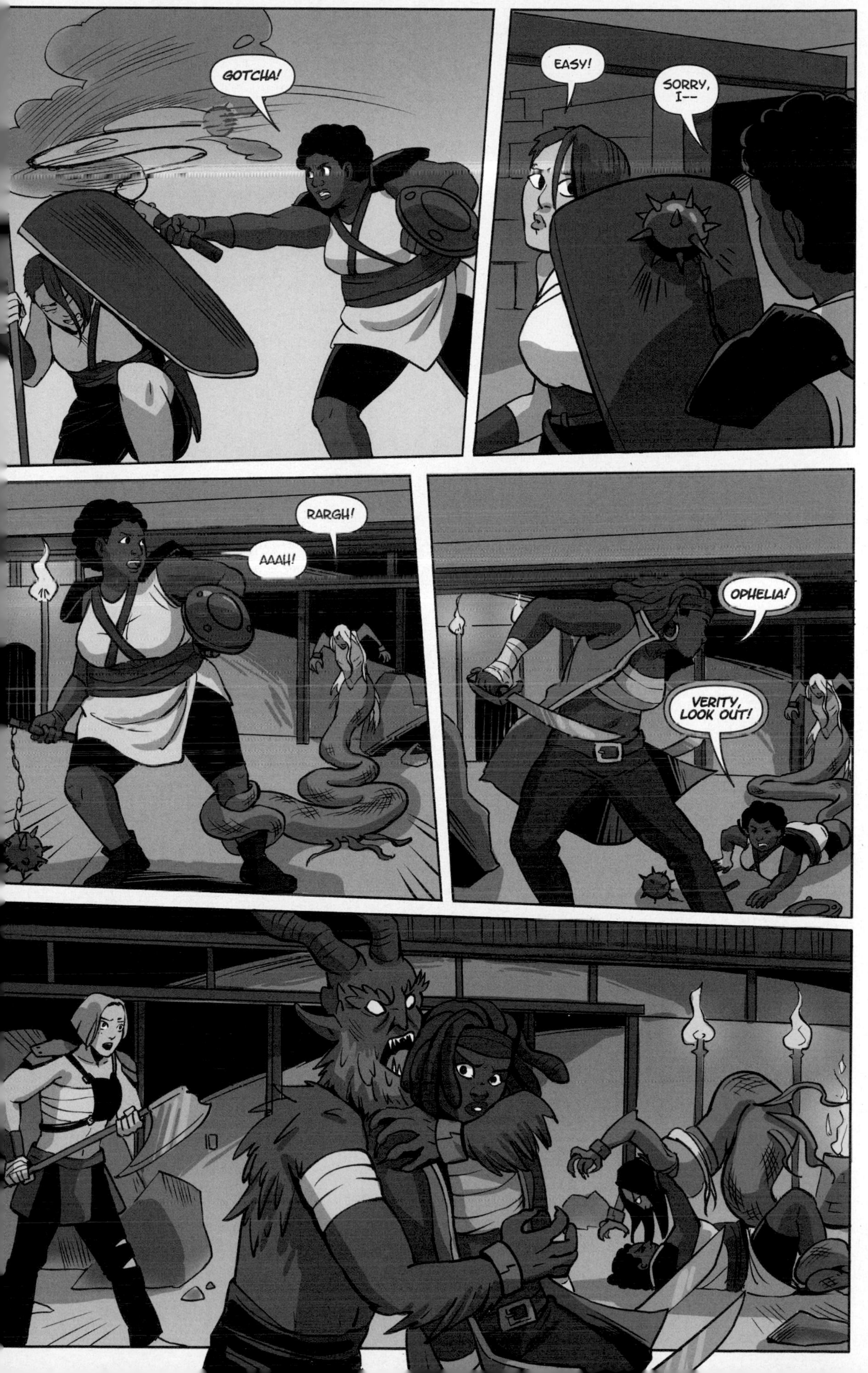
GOTCHA!
EASY!
SORRY, I--
RARGH!
AAAH!
OPHELIA!
VERITY, LOOK OUT!

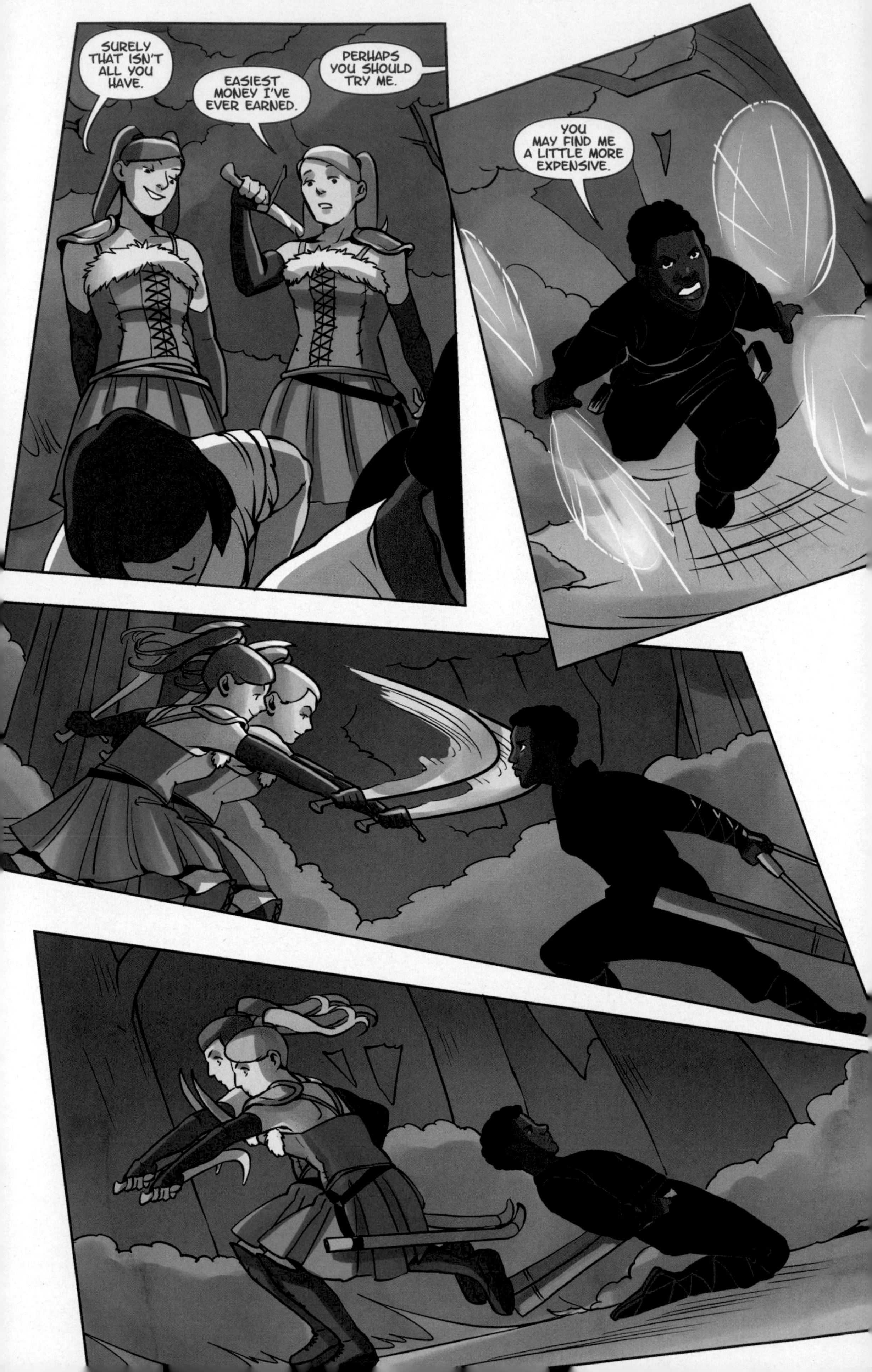
SURELY THAT ISN'T ALL YOU HAVE.
EASIEST MONEY I'VE EVER EARNED.
PERHAPS YOU SHOULD TRY ME.
YOU MAY FIND ME A LITTLE MORE EXPENSIVE.

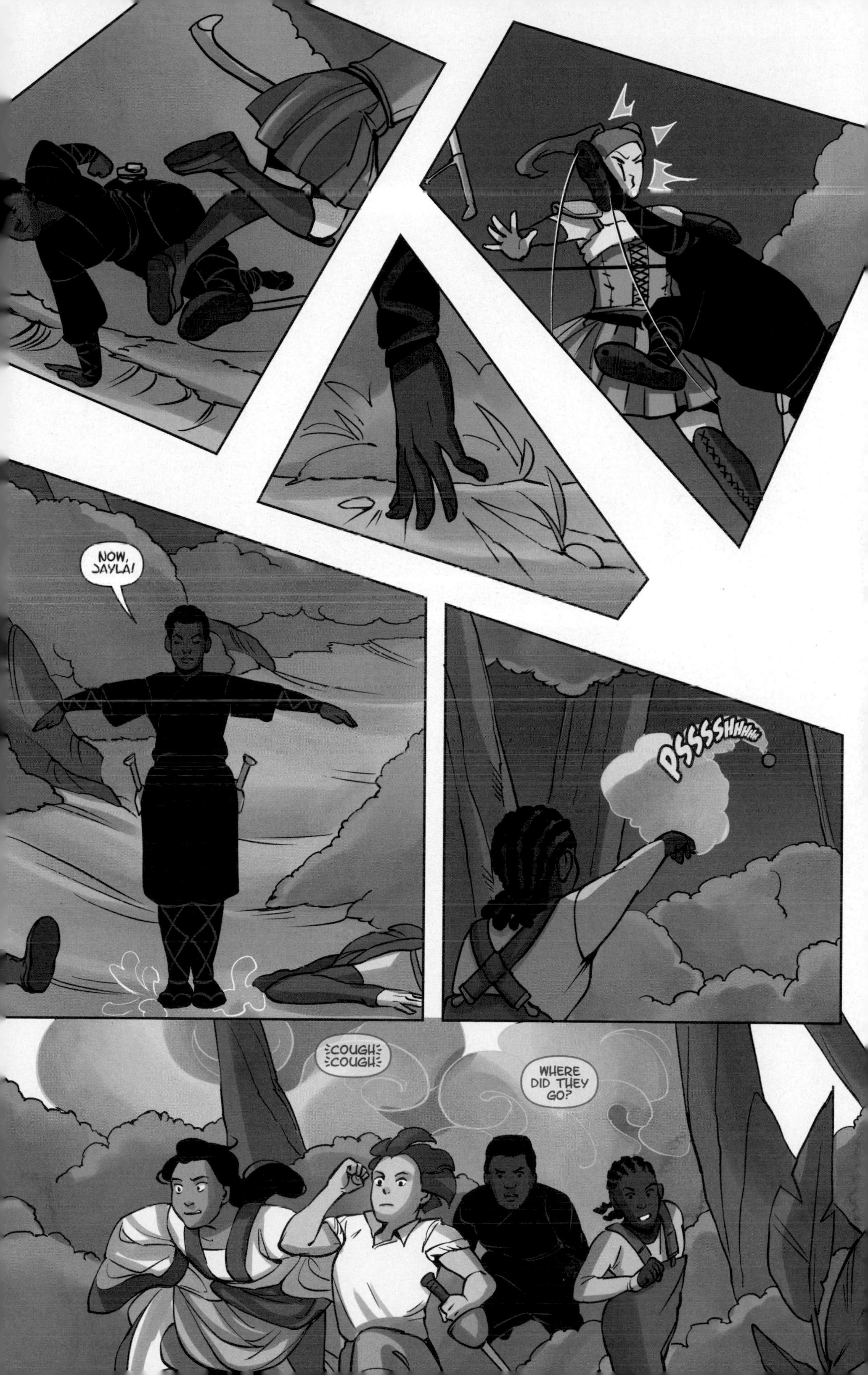

NOW, JAYLA!
PSSSSHHHH
COUGH COUGH
WHERE DID THEY GO?

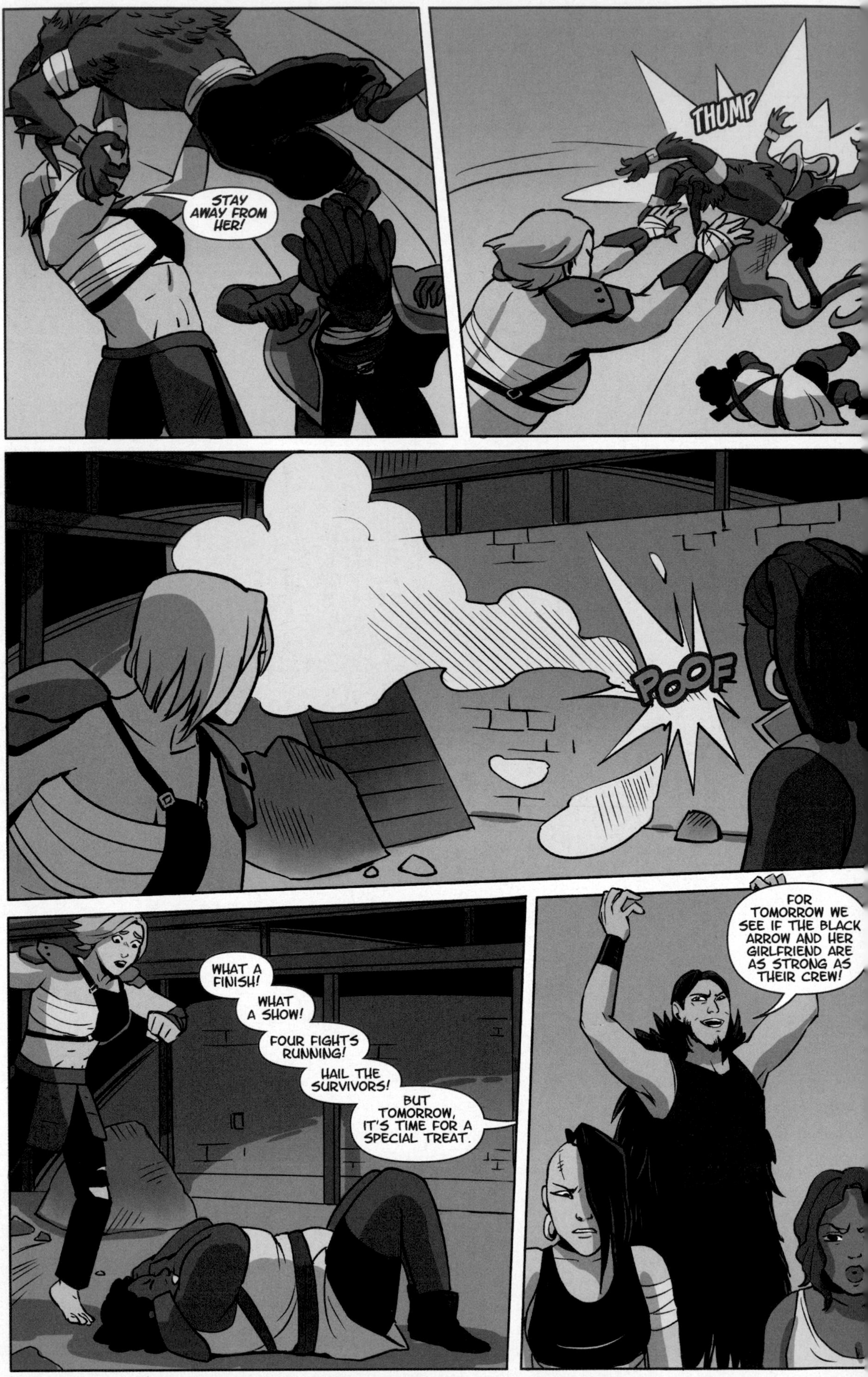
STAY AWAY FROM HER!
THUMP
POOF
WHAT A FINISH!
WHAT A SHOW!
FOUR FIGHTS RUNNING!
HAIL THE SURVIVORS!
BUT TOMORROW, IT'S TIME FOR A SPECIAL TREAT.
FOR TOMORROW WE SEE IF THE BLACK ARROW AND HER GIRLFRIEND ARE AS STRONG AS THEIR CREW!

Year Three: Monsters of the Deep

Chapter Eleven: Prisoners

Written By: Jeremy Whitley

Pencils By:
(Pages 1-5, 8-14, 19-24) Telênia Albuquerque
(Pages 6-7, 15-18) Xenia Pamfil

Inks By:
Pocket Owl

Colors By:
(Pages 1-5, 8-14, 19-24) Valentina Pinto
(Pages 6-7, 15-18) Lexillo

Lettered By: Alex Scherkenbach

Cover By: Telenia Albuquerque

Bryan Seaton: Publisher - Vito Delsante: Editor In Chief
Jason Martin: Publisher-Danger Zone
Chad Cicconi: Deck Swabber

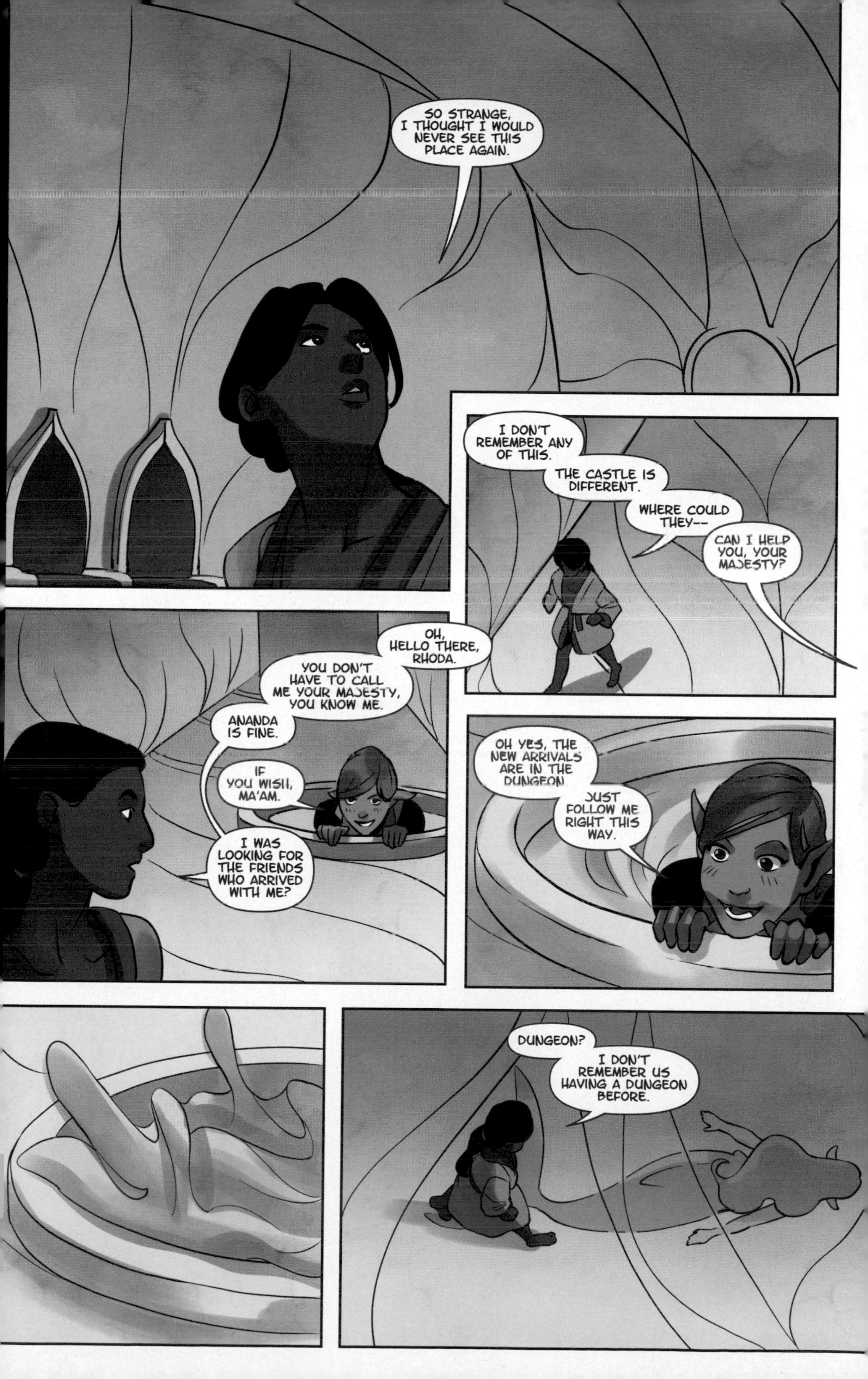
SO STRANGE, I THOUGHT I WOULD NEVER SEE THIS PLACE AGAIN.
I DON'T REMEMBER ANY OF THIS.
THE CASTLE IS DIFFERENT.
WHERE COULD THEY--
CAN I HELP YOU, YOUR MAJESTY?
OH, HELLO THERE, RHODA.
YOU DON'T HAVE TO CALL ME YOUR MAJESTY, YOU KNOW ME.
ANANDA IS FINE.
IF YOU WISH, MA'AM.
I WAS LOOKING FOR THE FRIENDS WHO ARRIVED WITH ME?
OH YES, THE NEW ARRIVALS ARE IN THE DUNGEON.
JUST FOLLOW ME RIGHT THIS WAY.
DUNGEON?
I DON'T REMEMBER US HAVING A DUNGEON BEFORE.

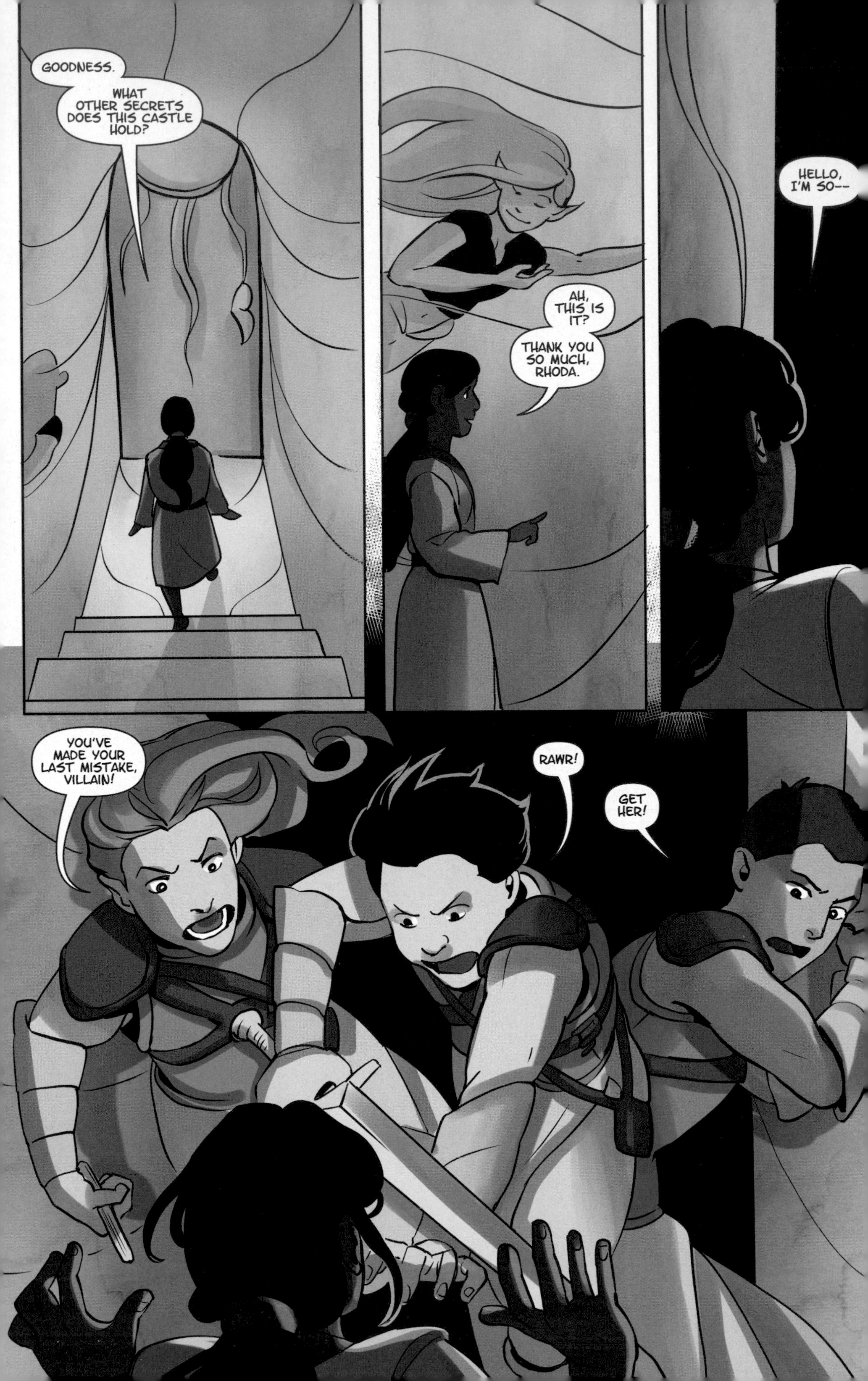
GOODNESS.
WHAT OTHER SECRETS DOES THIS CASTLE HOLD?
AH, THIS IS IT?
THANK YOU SO MUCH, RHODA.
HELLO, I'M SO--
YOU'VE MADE YOUR LAST MISTAKE, VILLAIN!
RAWR!
GET HER!

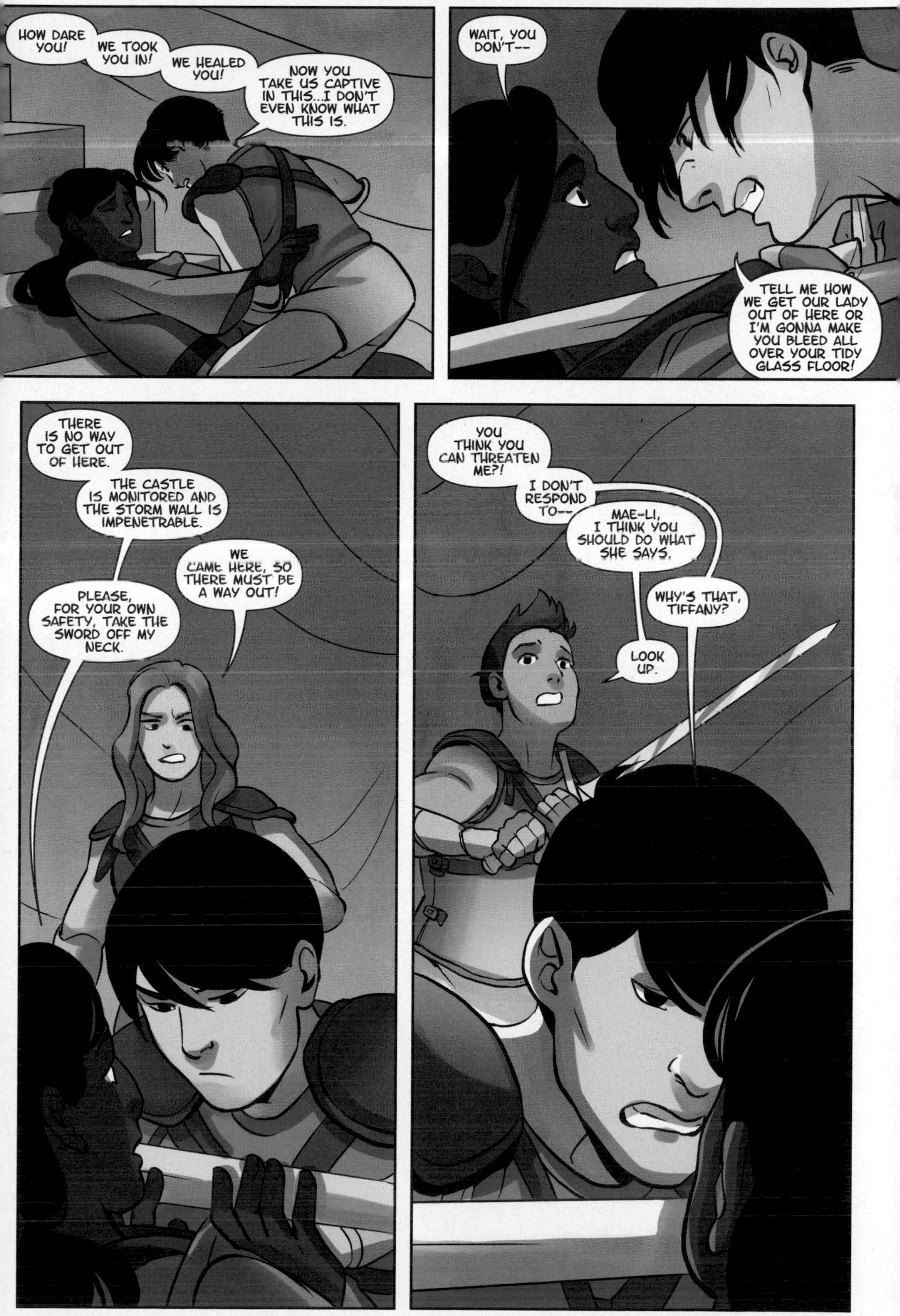

HOW DARE YOU!
WE TOOK YOU IN!
WE HEALED YOU!
NOW YOU TAKE US CAPTIVE IN THIS...I DON'T EVEN KNOW WHAT THIS IS.
WAIT, YOU DON'T--
TELL ME HOW WE GET OUR LADY OUT OF HERE OR I'M GONNA MAKE YOU BLEED ALL OVER YOUR TIDY GLASS FLOOR!
THERE IS NO WAY TO GET OUT OF HERE.
THE CASTLE IS MONITORED AND THE STORM WALL IS IMPENETRABLE.
WE CAME HERE, SO THERE MUST BE A WAY OUT!
PLEASE, FOR YOUR OWN SAFETY, TAKE THE SWORD OFF MY NECK.
YOU THINK YOU CAN THREATEN ME?!
I DON'T RESPOND TO--
MAE-LI, I THINK YOU SHOULD DO WHAT SHE SAYS.
WHY'S THAT, TIFFANY?
LOOK UP.

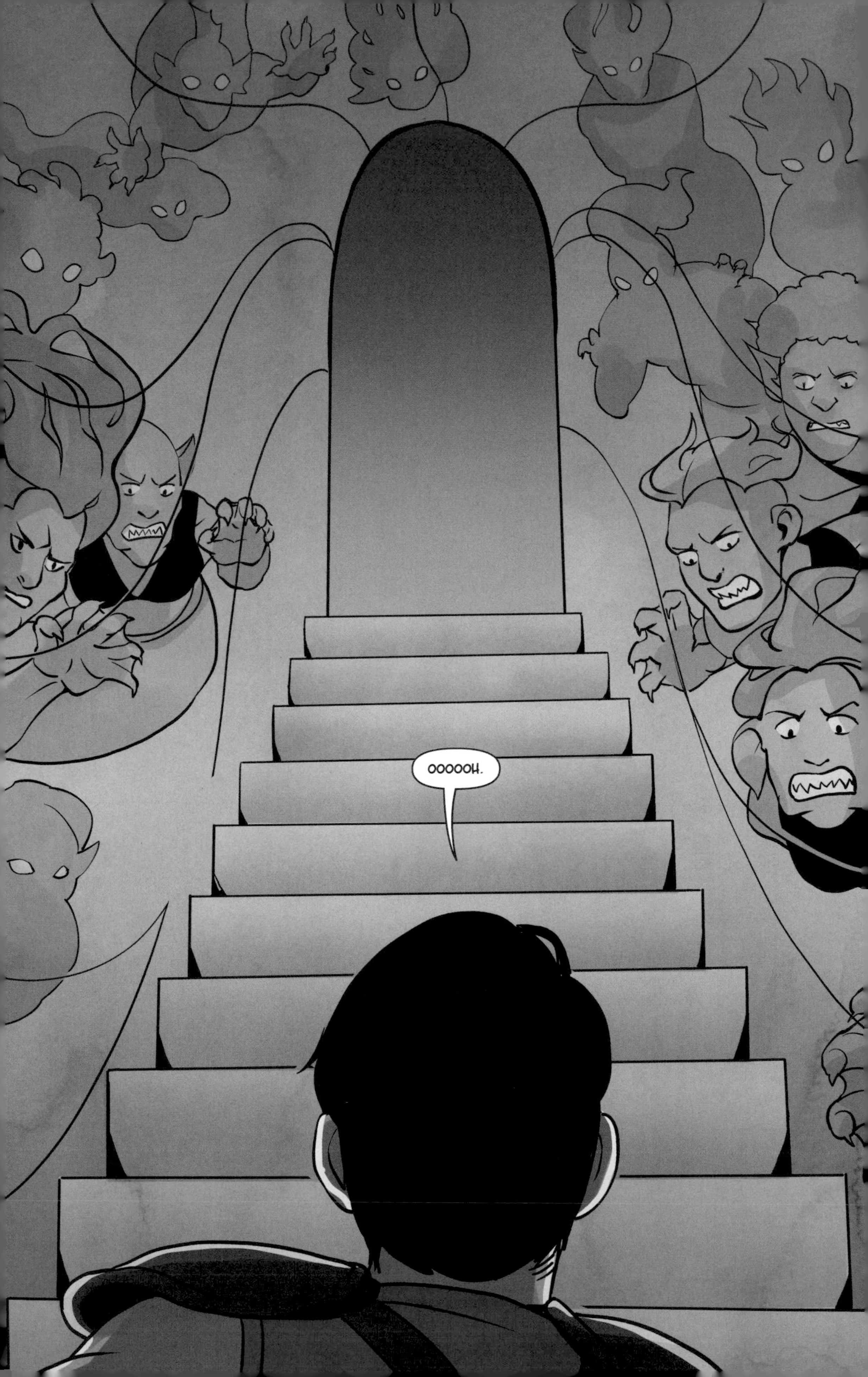
OOOOOH.

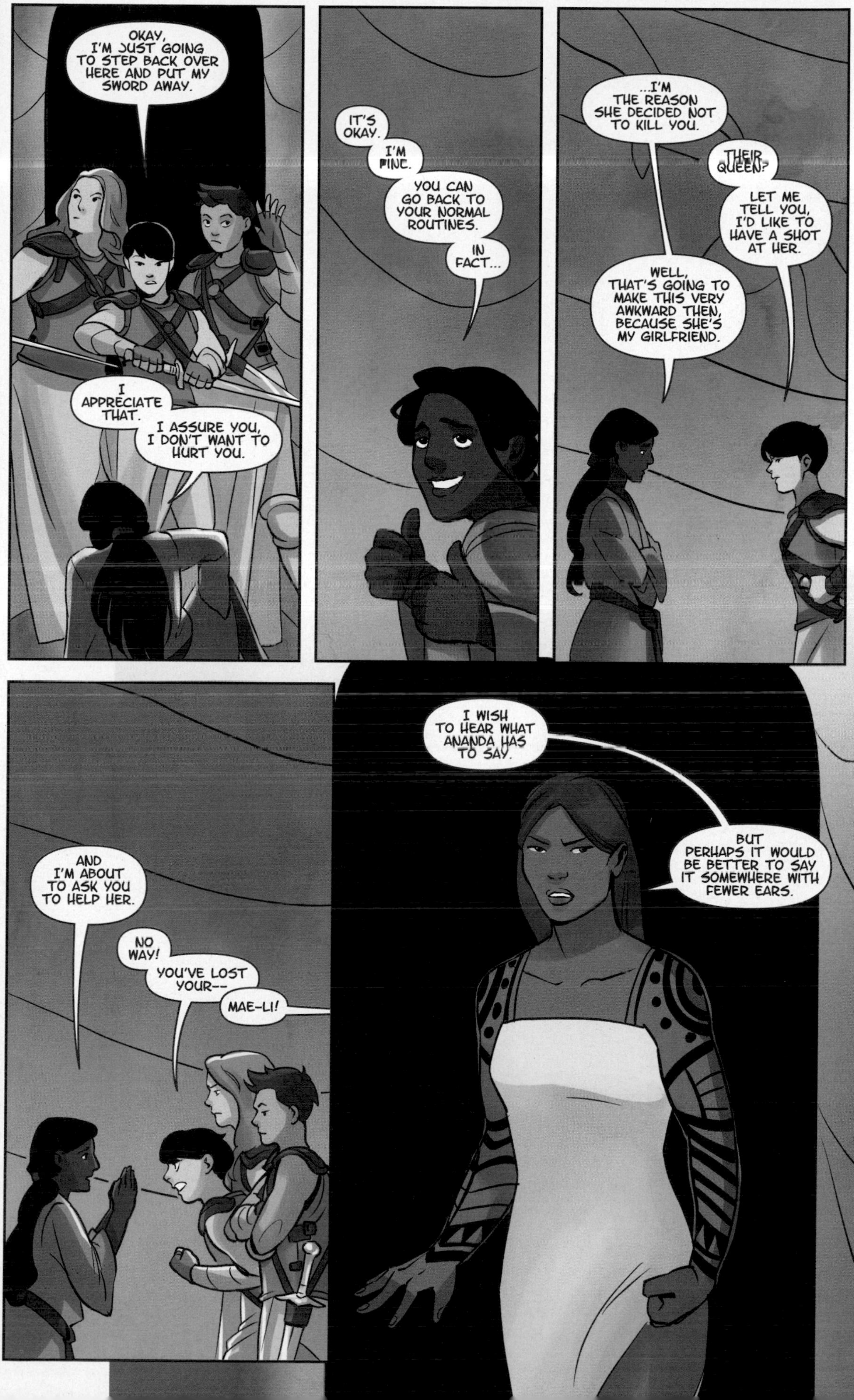
OKAY, I'M JUST GOING TO STEP BACK OVER HERE AND PUT MY SWORD AWAY.
I APPRECIATE THAT.
I ASSURE YOU, I DON'T WANT TO HURT YOU.
IT'S OKAY.
I'M FINE.
YOU CAN GO BACK TO YOUR NORMAL ROUTINES.
IN FACT...
...I'M THE REASON SHE DECIDED NOT TO KILL YOU.
THEIR QUEEN?
LET ME TELL YOU, I'D LIKE TO HAVE A SHOT AT HER.
WELL, THAT'S GOING TO MAKE THIS VERY AWKWARD THEN, BECAUSE SHE'S MY GIRLFRIEND.
AND I'M ABOUT TO ASK YOU TO HELP HER.
NO WAY!
YOU'VE LOST YOUR--
MAE-LI!
I WISH TO HEAR WHAT ANANDA HAS TO SAY.
BUT PERHAPS IT WOULD BE BETTER TO SAY IT SOMEWHERE WITH FEWER EARS.

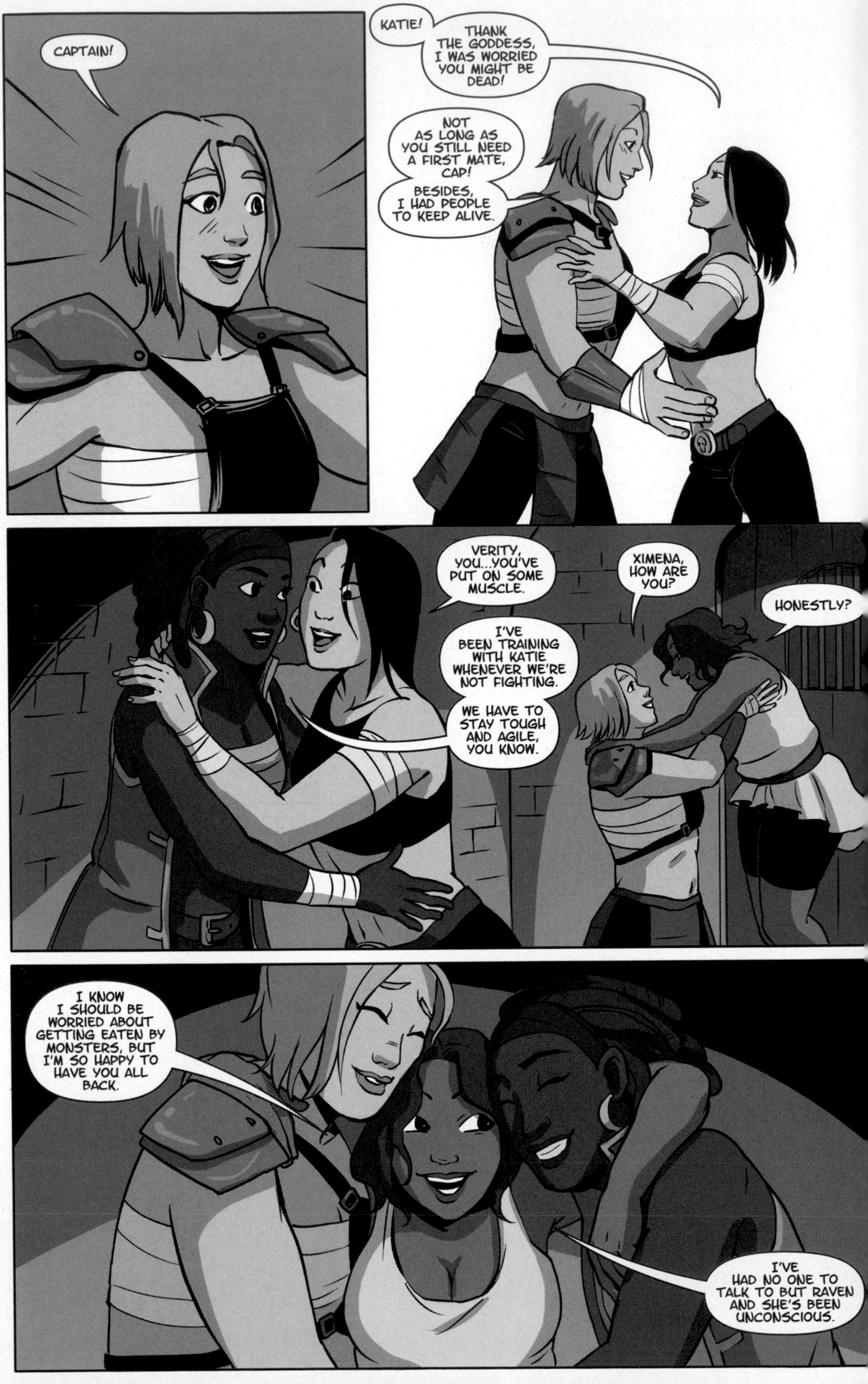
CAPTAIN!
KATIE!
THANK THE GODDESS, I WAS WORRIED YOU MIGHT BE DEAD!
NOT AS LONG AS YOU STILL NEED A FIRST MATE, CAP!
BESIDES, I HAD PEOPLE TO KEEP ALIVE.
VERITY, YOU...YOU'VE PUT ON SOME MUSCLE.
I'VE BEEN TRAINING WITH KATIE WHENEVER WE'RE NOT FIGHTING.
WE HAVE TO STAY TOUGH AND AGILE, YOU KNOW.
XIMENA, HOW ARE YOU?
HONESTLY?
I KNOW I SHOULD BE WORRIED ABOUT GETTING EATEN BY MONSTERS, BUT I'M SO HAPPY TO HAVE YOU ALL BACK.
I'VE HAD NO ONE TO TALK TO BUT RAVEN AND SHE'S BEEN UNCONSCIOUS.

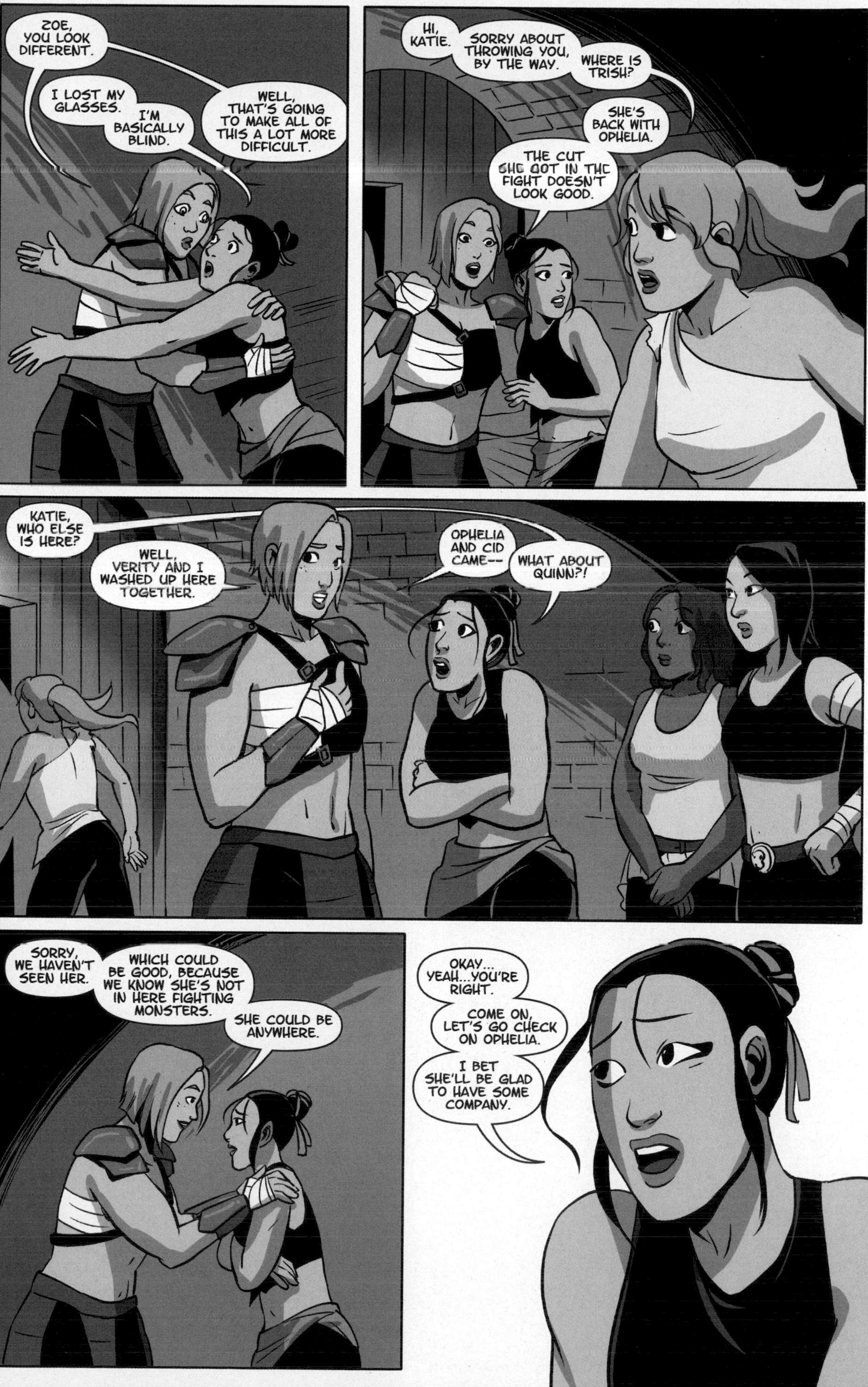
ZOE, YOU LOOK DIFFERENT.
I LOST MY GLASSES.
I'M BASICALLY BLIND.
WELL, THAT'S GOING TO MAKE ALL OF THIS A LOT MORE DIFFICULT.
HI, KATIE.
SORRY ABOUT THROWING YOU, BY THE WAY.
WHERE IS TRISH?
SHE'S BACK WITH OPHELIA.
THE CUT SHE GOT IN THE FIGHT DOESN'T LOOK GOOD.
KATIE, WHO ELSE IS HERE?
WELL, VERITY AND I WASHED UP HERE TOGETHER.
OPHELIA AND CID CAME--
WHAT ABOUT QUINN?!
SORRY, WE HAVEN'T SEEN HER.
WHICH COULD BE GOOD, BECAUSE WE KNOW SHE'S NOT IN HERE FIGHTING MONSTERS.
SHE COULD BE ANYWHERE.
OKAY... YEAH...YOU'RE RIGHT.
COME ON, LET'S GO CHECK ON OPHELIA.
I BET SHE'LL BE GLAD TO HAVE SOME COMPANY.

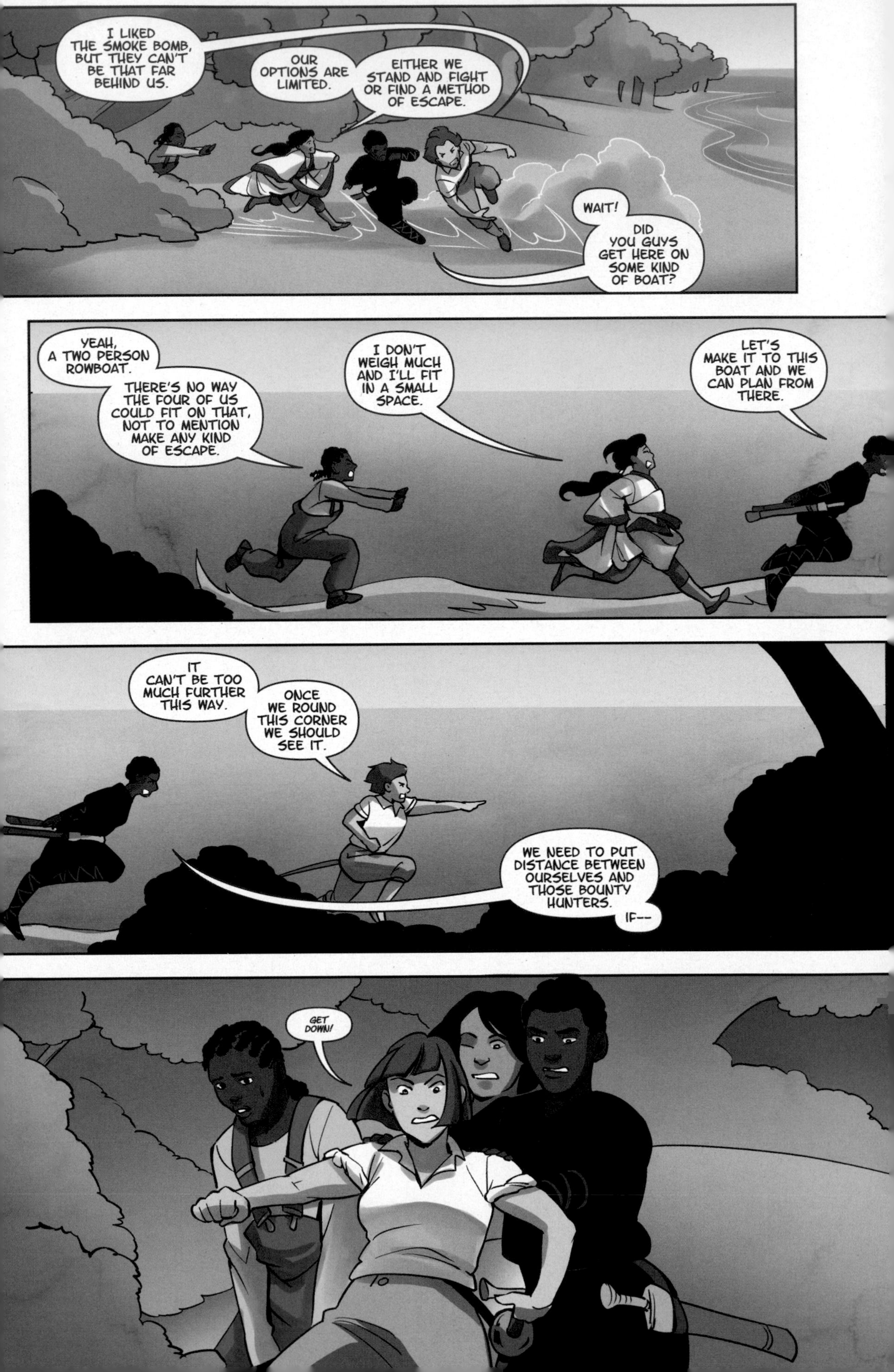
I LIKED THE SMOKE BOMB, BUT THEY CAN'T BE THAT FAR BEHIND US.
OUR OPTIONS ARE LIMITED.
EITHER WE STAND AND FIGHT OR FIND A METHOD OF ESCAPE.
WAIT!
DID YOU GUYS GET HERE ON SOME KIND OF BOAT?
YEAH, A TWO PERSON ROWBOAT.
THERE'S NO WAY THE FOUR OF US COULD FIT ON THAT, NOT TO MENTION MAKE ANY KIND OF ESCAPE.
I DON'T WEIGH MUCH AND I'LL FIT IN A SMALL SPACE.
LET'S MAKE IT TO THIS BOAT AND WE CAN PLAN FROM THERE.
IT CAN'T BE TOO MUCH FURTHER THIS WAY.
ONCE WE ROUND THIS CORNER WE SHOULD SEE IT.
WE NEED TO PUT DISTANCE BETWEEN OURSELVES AND THOSE BOUNTY HUNTERS.
IF--
GET DOWN!

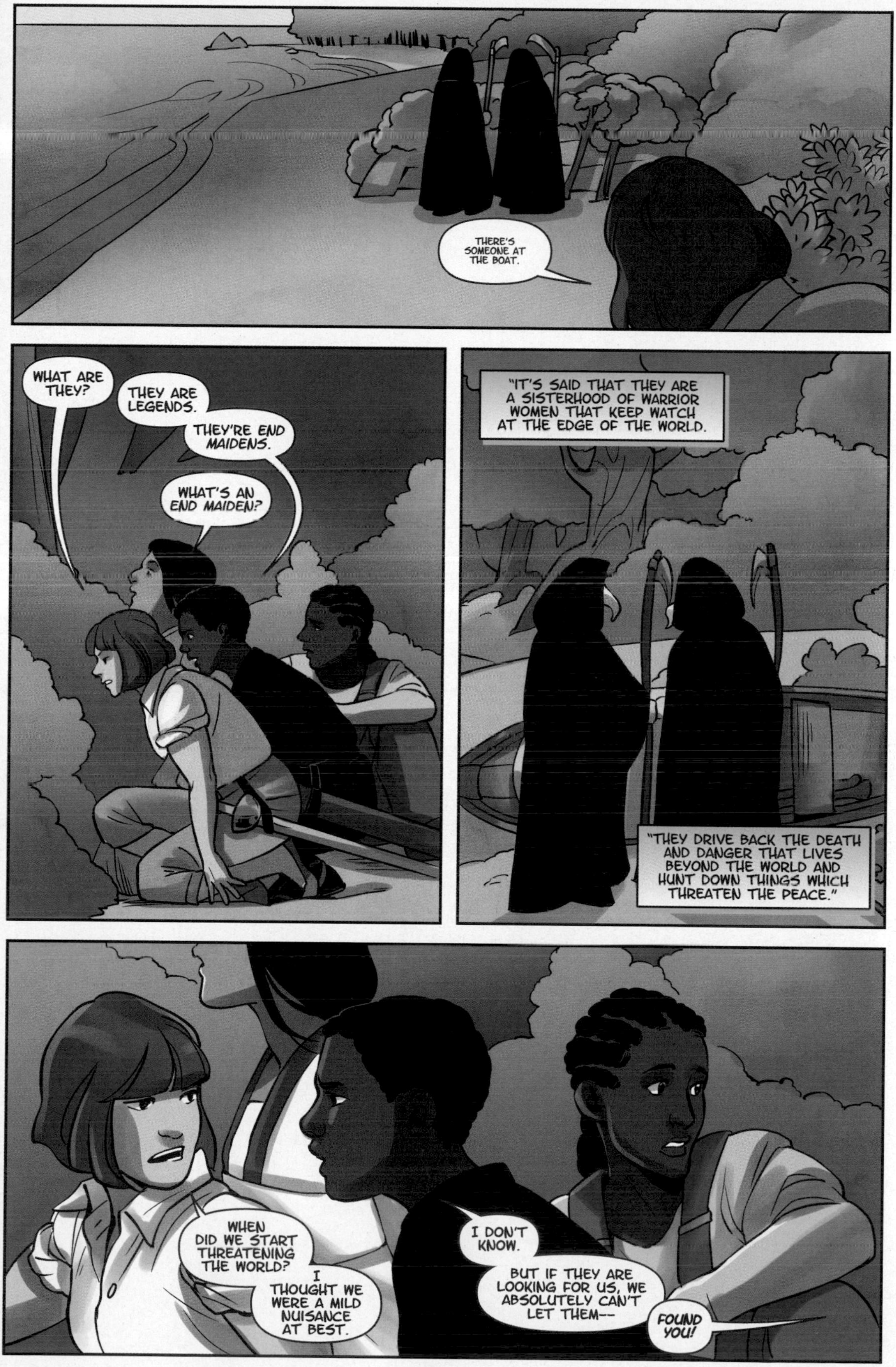
THERE'S SOMEONE AT THE BOAT.
WHAT ARE THEY?
THEY ARE LEGENDS.
THEY'RE END MAIDENS.
WHAT'S AN END MAIDEN?
"IT'S SAID THAT THEY ARE A SISTERHOOD OF WARRIOR WOMEN THAT KEEP WATCH AT THE EDGE OF THE WORLD.
"THEY DRIVE BACK THE DEATH AND DANGER THAT LIVES BEYOND THE WORLD AND HUNT DOWN THINGS WHICH THREATEN THE PEACE."
WHEN DID WE START THREATENING THE WORLD?
I THOUGHT WE WERE A MILD NUISANCE AT BEST.
I DON'T KNOW.
BUT IF THEY ARE LOOKING FOR US, WE ABSOLUTELY CAN'T LET THEM--
FOUND YOU!

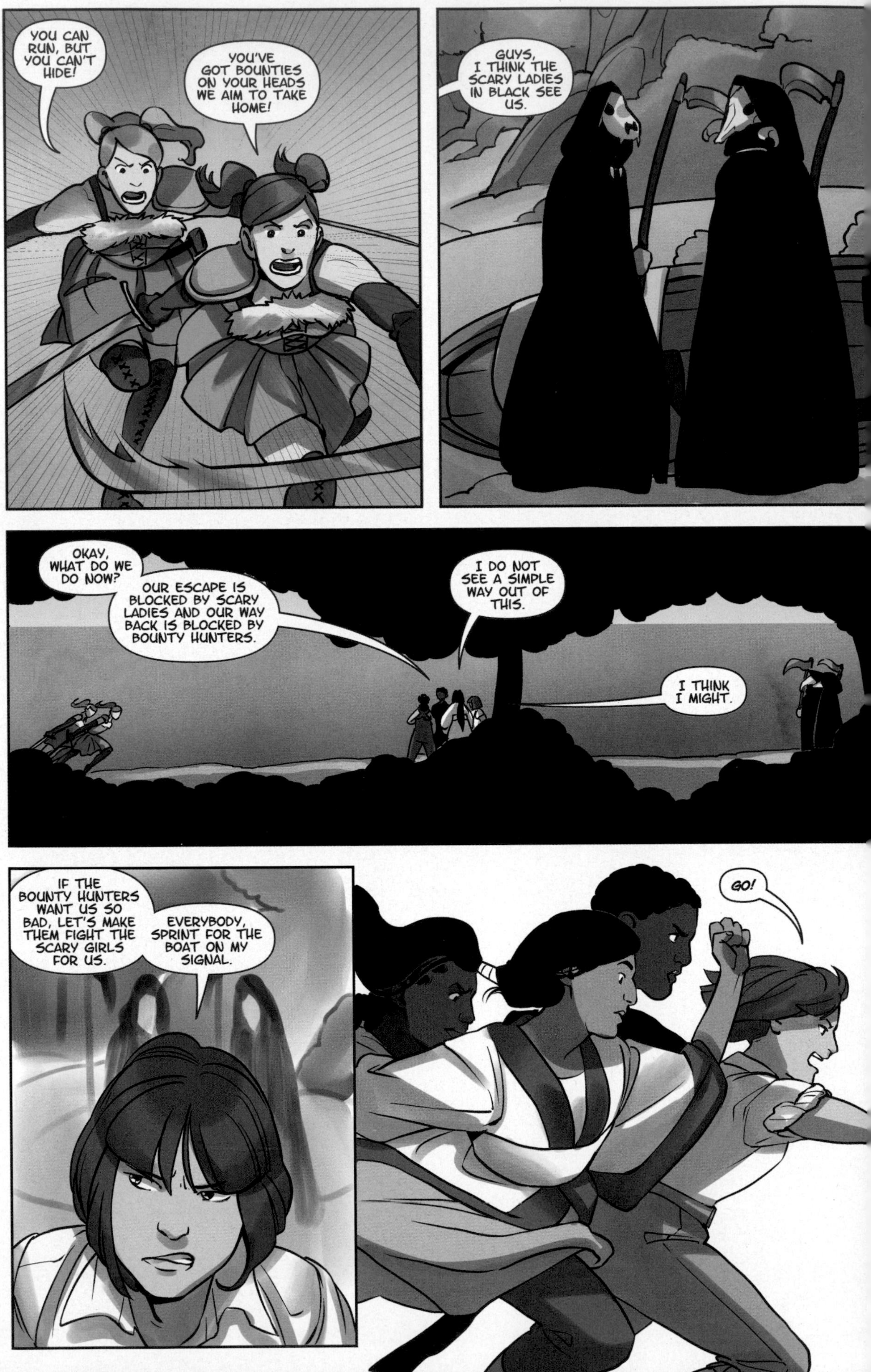
YOU CAN RUN, BUT YOU CAN'T HIDE!
YOU'VE GOT BOUNTIES ON YOUR HEADS WE AIM TO TAKE HOME!
GUYS, I THINK THE SCARY LADIES IN BLACK SEE US.
OKAY, WHAT DO WE DO NOW?
OUR ESCAPE IS BLOCKED BY SCARY LADIES AND OUR WAY BACK IS BLOCKED BY BOUNTY HUNTERS.
I DO NOT SEE A SIMPLE WAY OUT OF THIS.
I THINK I MIGHT.
IF THE BOUNTY HUNTERS WANT US SO BAD, LET'S MAKE THEM FIGHT THE SCARY GIRLS FOR US.
EVERYBODY, SPRINT FOR THE BOAT ON MY SIGNAL.
GO!

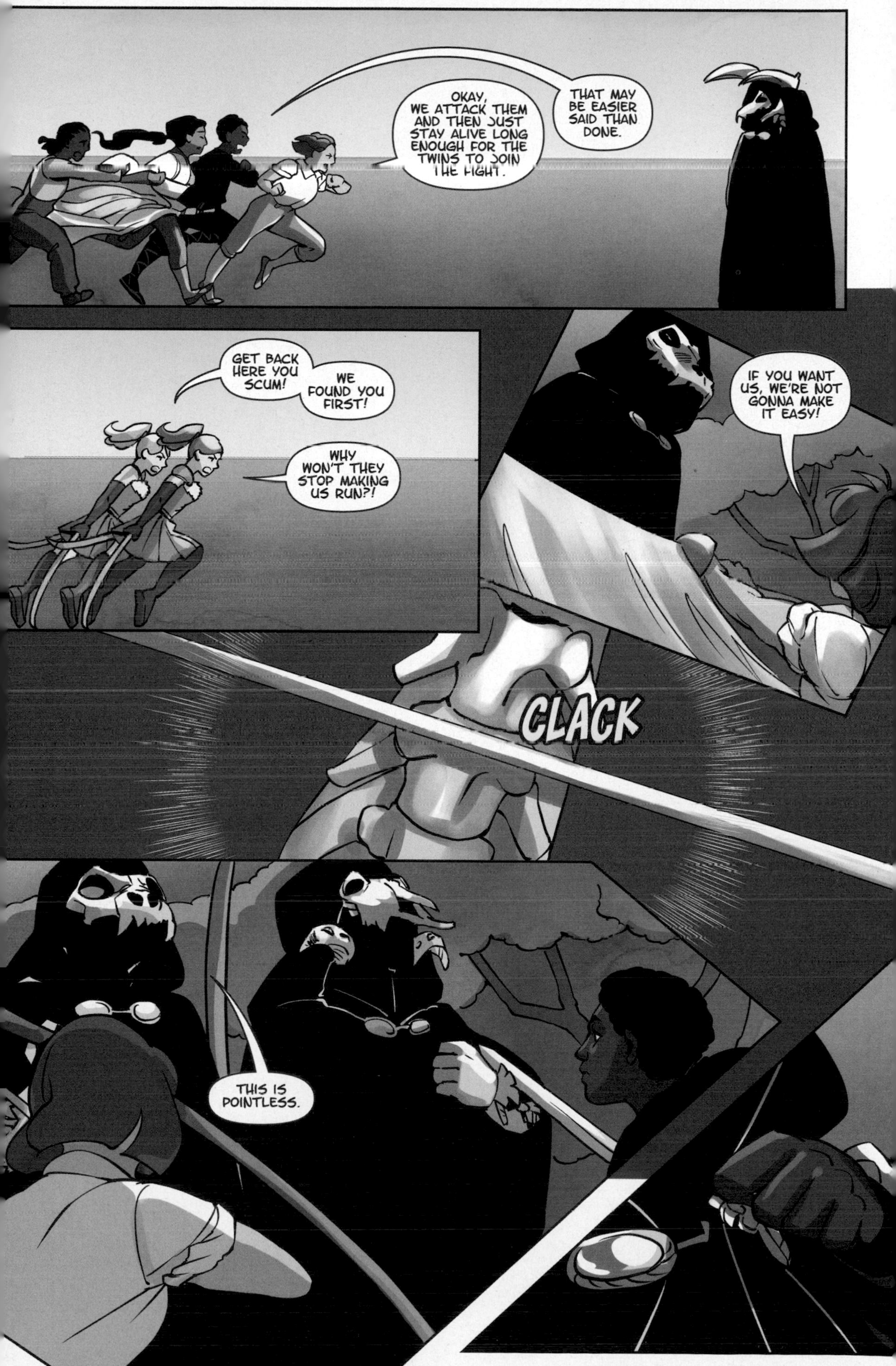
OKAY, WE ATTACK THEM AND THEN JUST STAY ALIVE LONG ENOUGH FOR THE TWINS TO JOIN THE FIGHT.
THAT MAY BE EASIER SAID THAN DONE.
GET BACK HERE YOU SCUM!
WE FOUND YOU FIRST!
WHY WON'T THEY STOP MAKING US RUN?!
IF YOU WANT US, WE'RE NOT GONNA MAKE IT EASY!
CLACK
THIS IS POINTLESS.

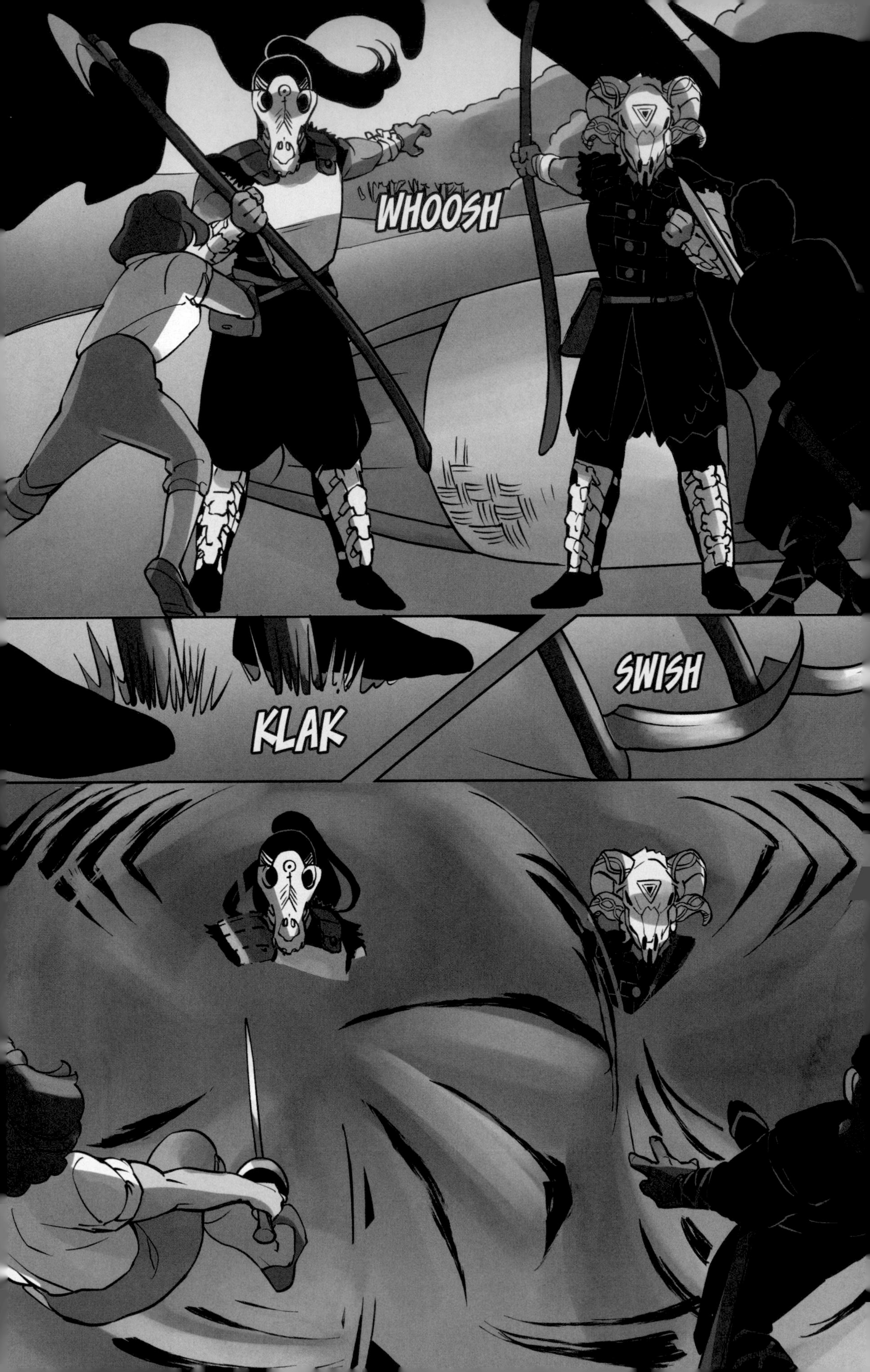
WHOOSH
KLAK
SWISH

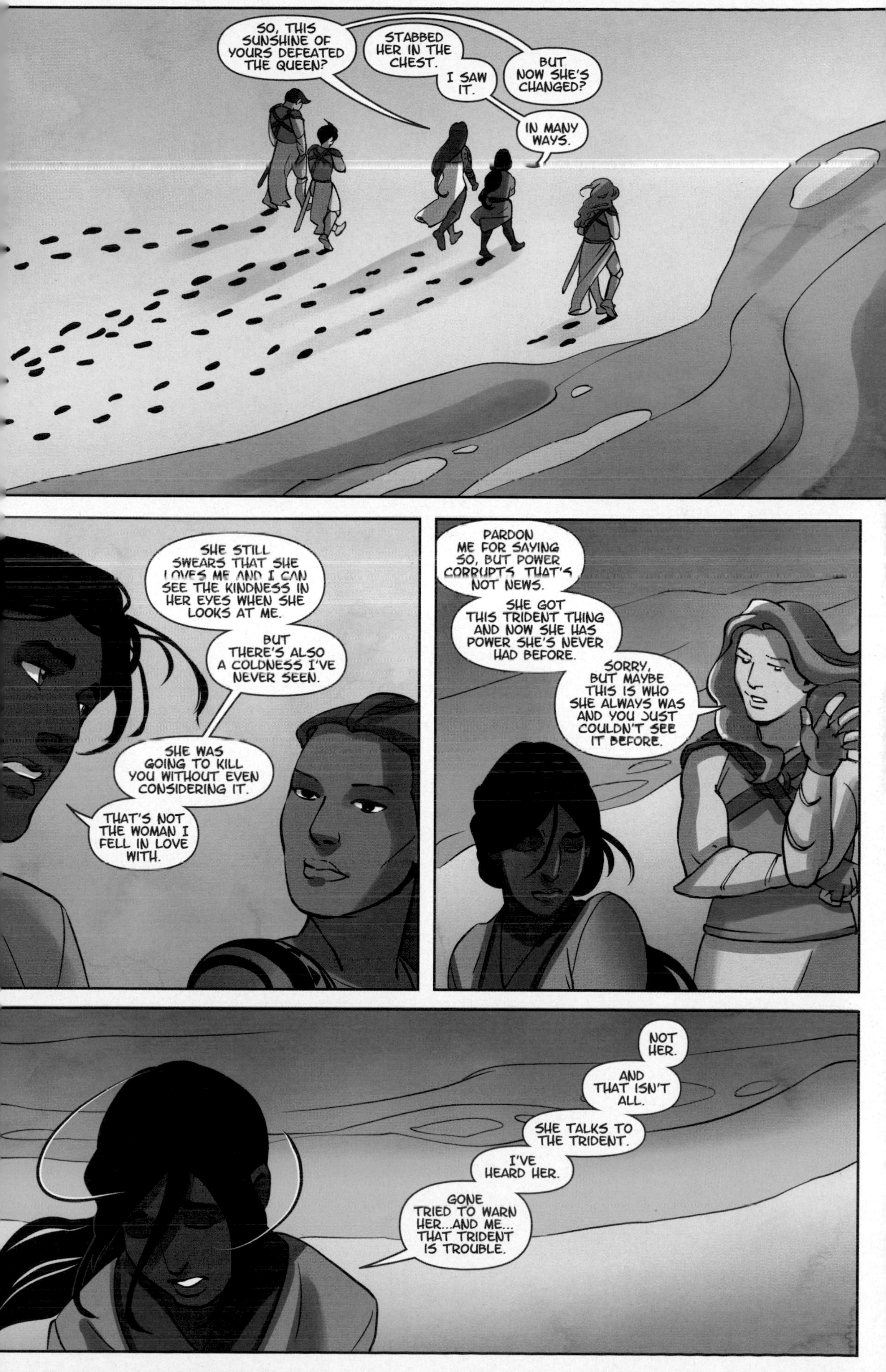
SO, THIS SUNSHINE OF YOURS DEFEATED THE QUEEN?
STABBED HER IN THE CHEST.
I SAW IT.
BUT NOW SHE'S CHANGED?
IN MANY WAYS.
SHE STILL SWEARS THAT SHE LOVES ME AND I CAN SEE THE KINDNESS IN HER EYES WHEN SHE LOOKS AT ME.
BUT THERE'S ALSO A COLDNESS I'VE NEVER SEEN.
SHE WAS GOING TO KILL YOU WITHOUT EVEN CONSIDERING IT.
THAT'S NOT THE WOMAN I FELL IN LOVE WITH.
PARDON ME FOR SAYING SO, BUT POWER CORRUPTS, THAT'S NOT NEWS.
SHE GOT THIS TRIDENT THING AND NOW SHE HAS POWER SHE'S NEVER HAD BEFORE.
SORRY, BUT MAYBE THIS IS WHO SHE ALWAYS WAS AND YOU JUST COULDN'T SEE IT BEFORE.
NOT HER.
AND THAT ISN'T ALL.
SHE TALKS TO THE TRIDENT.
I'VE HEARD HER.
GONE TRIED TO WARN HER...AND ME... THAT TRIDENT IS TROUBLE.

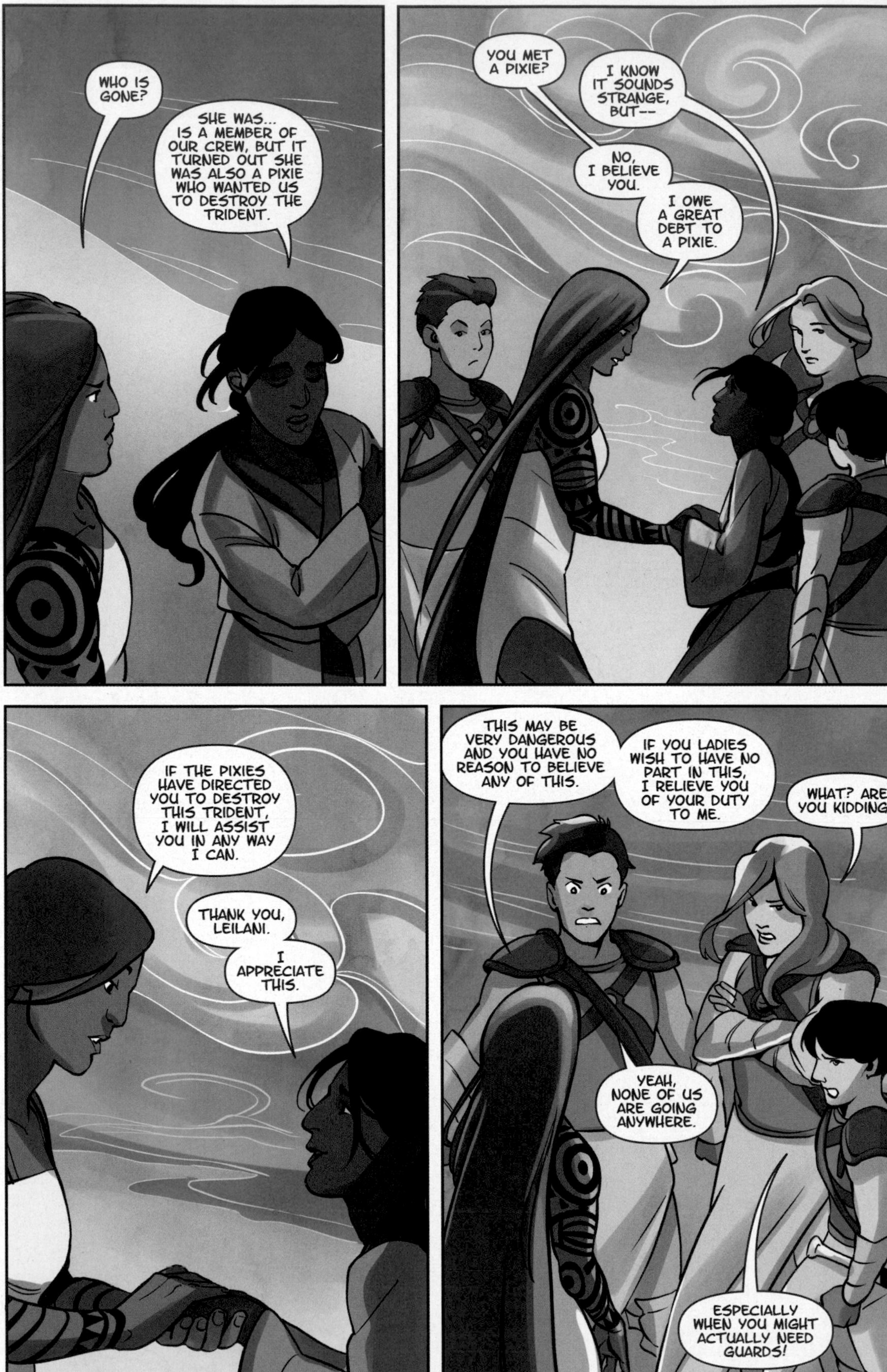
WHO IS GONE?
SHE WAS... IS A MEMBER OF OUR CREW, BUT IT TURNED OUT SHE WAS ALSO A PIXIE WHO WANTED US TO DESTROY THE TRIDENT.
YOU MET A PIXIE?
I KNOW IT SOUNDS STRANGE, BUT--
NO, I BELIEVE YOU.
I OWE A GREAT DEBT TO A PIXIE.
IF THE PIXIES HAVE DIRECTED YOU TO DESTROY THIS TRIDENT, I WILL ASSIST YOU IN ANY WAY I CAN.
THANK YOU, LEILANI.
I APPRECIATE THIS.
THIS MAY BE VERY DANGEROUS AND YOU HAVE NO REASON TO BELIEVE ANY OF THIS.
IF YOU LADIES WISH TO HAVE NO PART IN THIS, I RELIEVE YOU OF YOUR DUTY TO ME.
WHAT? ARE YOU KIDDING?
YEAH, NONE OF US ARE GOING ANYWHERE.
ESPECIALLY WHEN YOU MIGHT ACTUALLY NEED GUARDS!

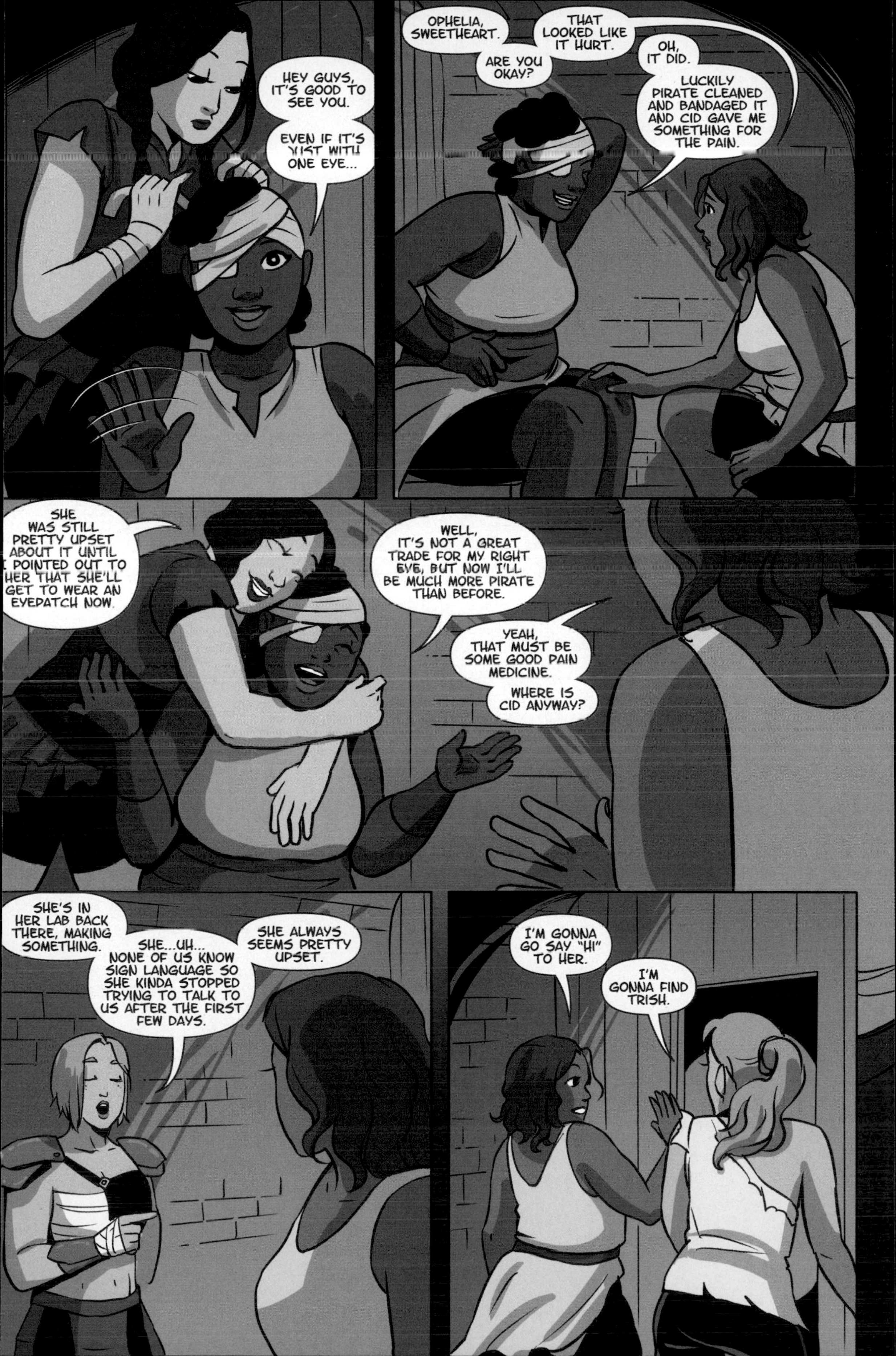
HEY GUYS, IT'S GOOD TO SEE YOU.
EVEN IF IT'S JUST WITH ONE EYE...
OPHELIA, SWEETHEART.
ARE YOU OKAY?
THAT LOOKED LIKE IT HURT.
OH, IT DID.
LUCKILY PIRATE CLEANED AND BANDAGED IT AND CID GAVE ME SOMETHING FOR THE PAIN.
SHE WAS STILL PRETTY UPSET ABOUT IT UNTIL I POINTED OUT TO HER THAT SHE'LL GET TO WEAR AN EYEPATCH NOW.
WELL, IT'S NOT A GREAT TRADE FOR MY RIGHT EYE, BUT NOW I'LL BE MUCH MORE PIRATE THAN BEFORE.
YEAH, THAT MUST BE SOME GOOD PAIN MEDICINE.
WHERE IS CID ANYWAY?
SHE'S IN HER LAB BACK THERE, MAKING SOMETHING.
SHE...UH... NONE OF US KNOW SIGN LANGUAGE SO SHE KINDA STOPPED TRYING TO TALK TO US AFTER THE FIRST FEW DAYS.
SHE ALWAYS SEEMS PRETTY UPSET.
I'M GONNA GO SAY "HI" TO HER.
I'M GONNA FIND TRISH.

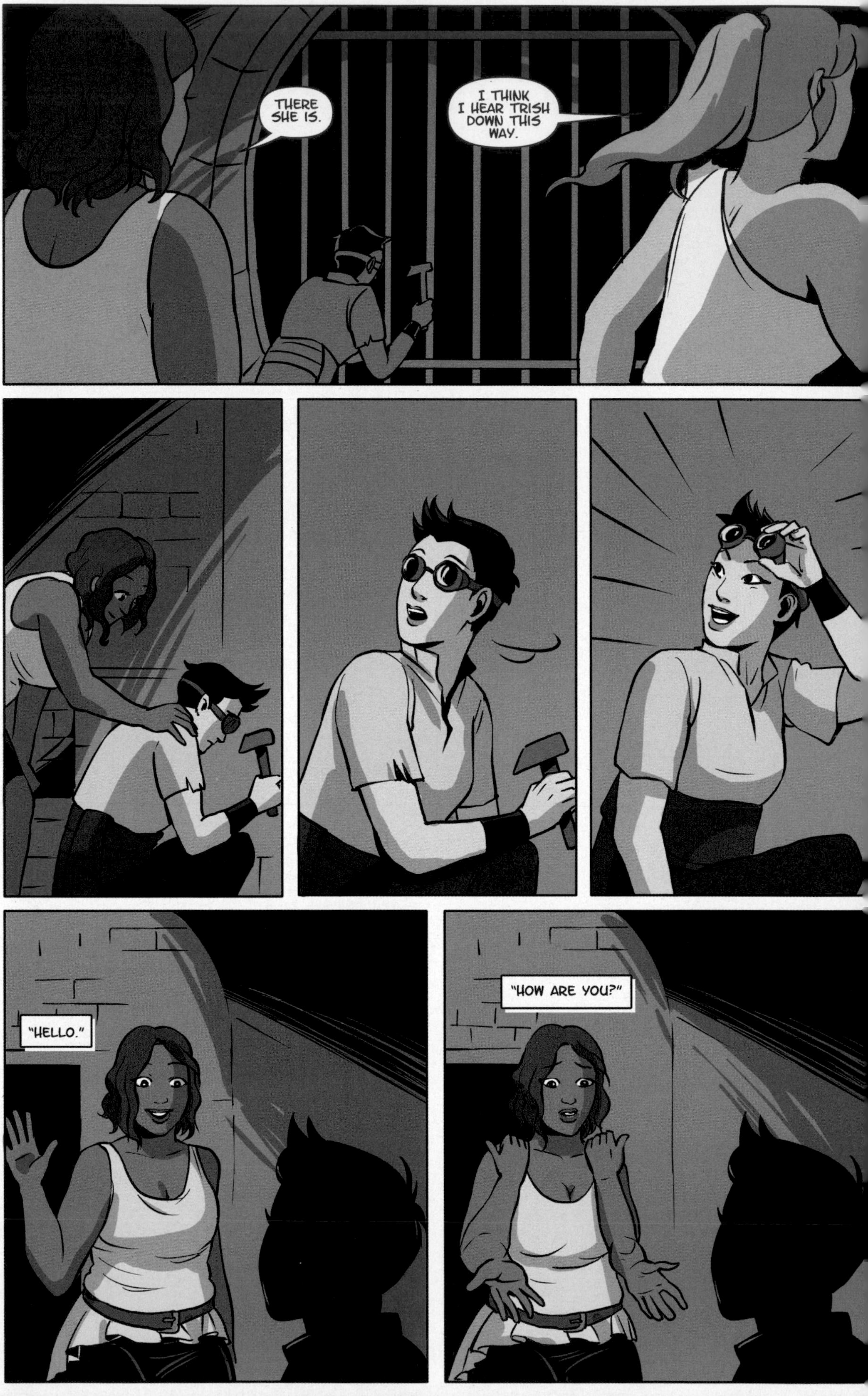
THERE SHE IS.
I THINK I HEAR TRISH DOWN THIS WAY.
"HELLO."
"HOW ARE YOU?"

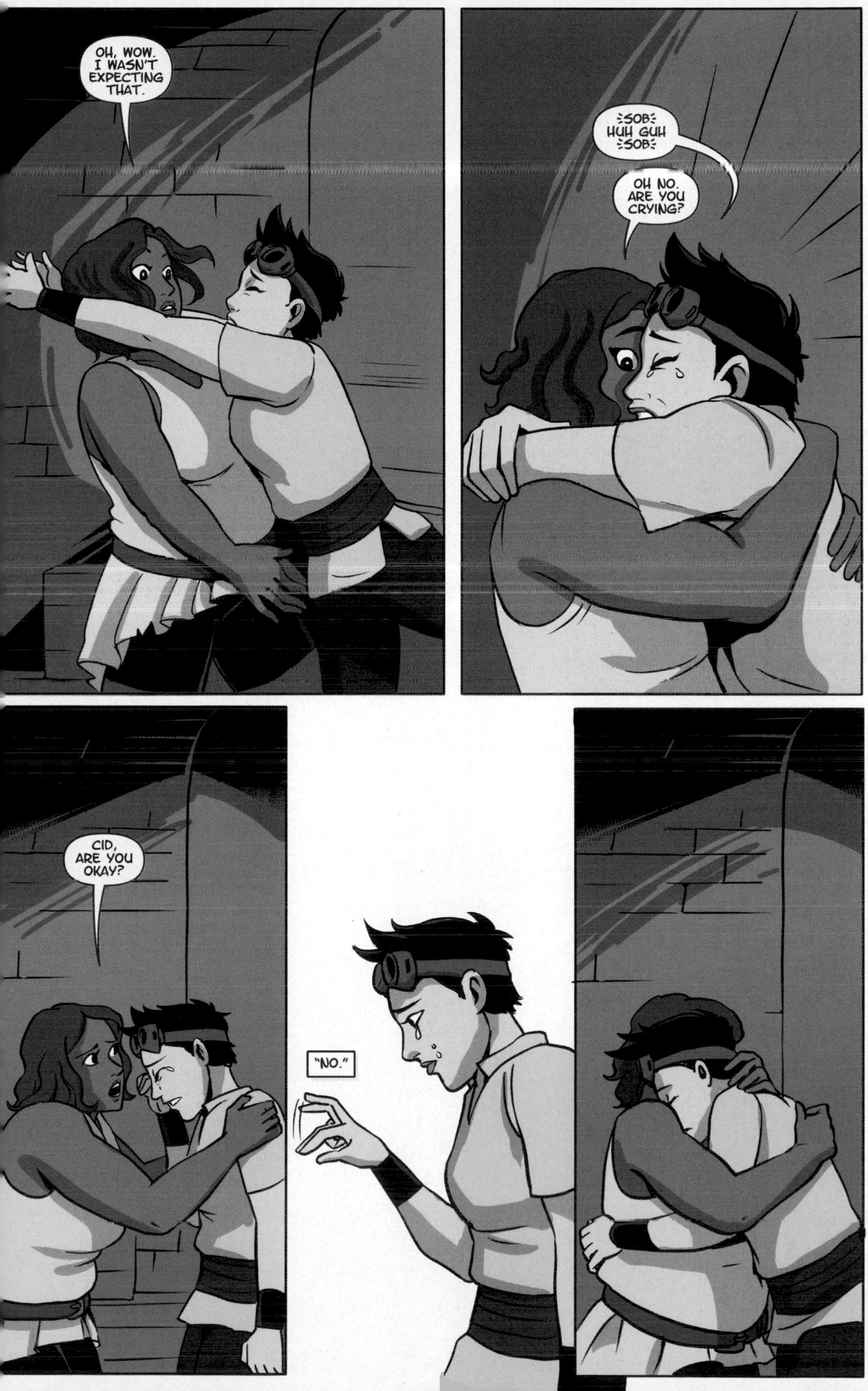
OH, WOW. I WASN'T EXPECTING THAT.
SOB HUH GUH SOB
OH NO. ARE YOU CRYING?
CID, ARE YOU OKAY?
"NO."

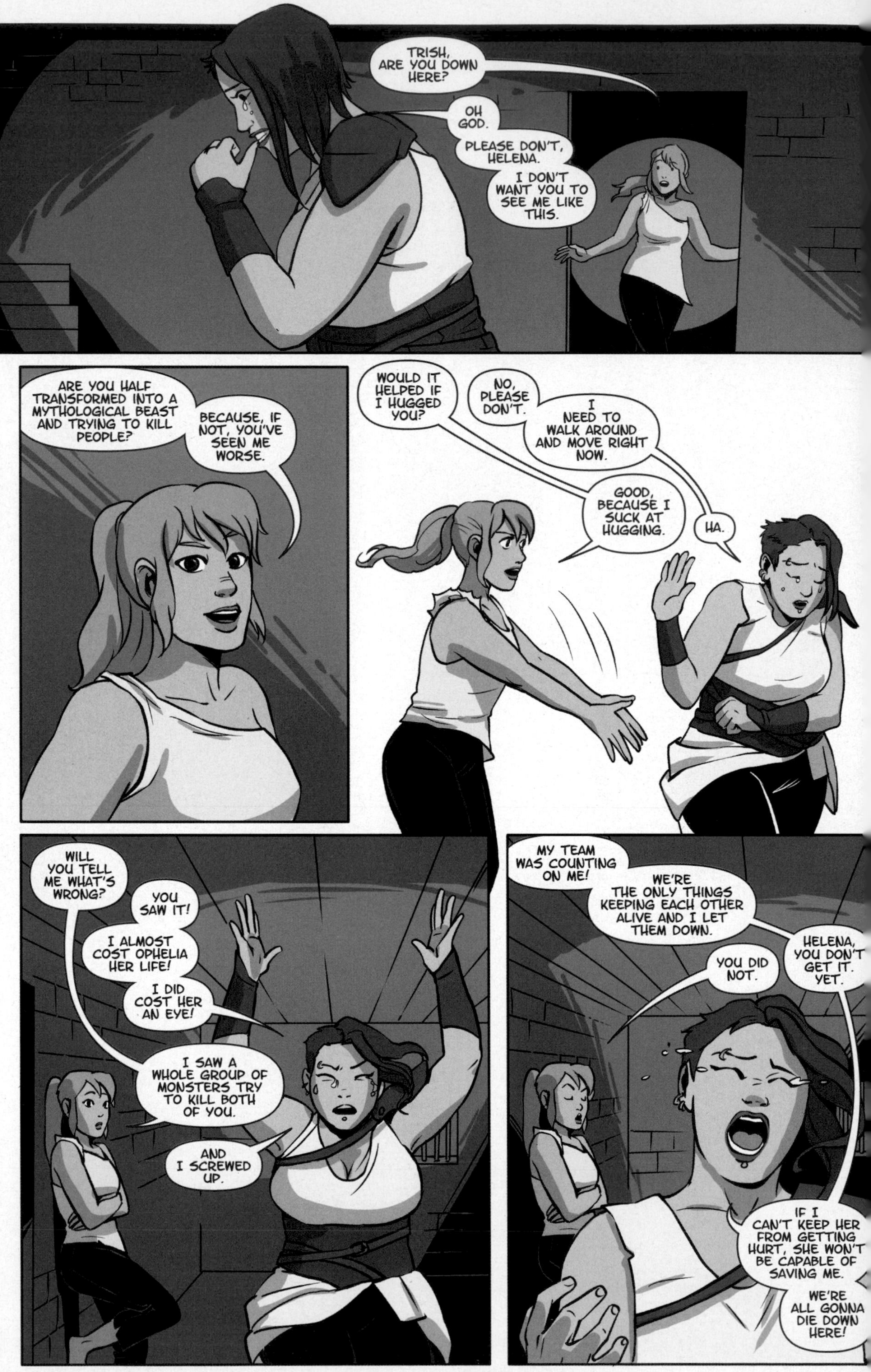

TRISH, ARE YOU DOWN HERE?
OH GOD.
PLEASE DON'T, HELENA.
I DON'T WANT YOU TO SEE ME LIKE THIS.
ARE YOU HALF TRANSFORMED INTO A MYTHOLOGICAL BEAST AND TRYING TO KILL PEOPLE?
BECAUSE, IF NOT, YOU'VE SEEN ME WORSE.
WOULD IT HELPED IF I HUGGED YOU?
NO, PLEASE DON'T.
I NEED TO WALK AROUND AND MOVE RIGHT NOW.
GOOD, BECAUSE I SUCK AT HUGGING.
HA.
WILL YOU TELL ME WHAT'S WRONG?
YOU SAW IT!
I ALMOST COST OPHELIA HER LIFE!
I DID COST HER AN EYE!
I SAW A WHOLE GROUP OF MONSTERS TRY TO KILL BOTH OF YOU.
AND I SCREWED UP.
MY TEAM WAS COUNTING ON ME!
WE'RE THE ONLY THINGS KEEPING EACH OTHER ALIVE AND I LET THEM DOWN.
YOU DID NOT.
HELENA, YOU DON'T GET IT. YET.
IF I CAN'T KEEP HER FROM GETTING HURT, SHE WON'T BE CAPABLE OF SAVING ME.
WE'RE ALL GONNA DIE DOWN HERE!

MELODY, YOU AND I MUST WORK TOGETHER TO DEFEAT THEM.

WE MUST USE OUR TEAMWORK TECHNIQUES.

OKAY, WE CAN DO THIS.

WHAT AM I SUPPOSED TO DO?

YOU TWO FIND A WAY TO GET RID OF THOSE BOUNTY HUNTERS.

GREAT, NOW I'M SUPPOSED TO FIGHT THE PSYCHOPATHS WE COULDN'T BEAT TOGETHER?

SHE SAID, "YOU TWO".

MY APOLOGIES FOR EXCLUDING YOU, OH SWORD MASTER JAYLA.

DO YOU HAVE A SECRET ATTACK YOU CAN USE TO TAKE THEM DOWN?

ME, NO. BUT I HAVE ONE FOR YOU.

HOLD YOUR SWORD OUT.

OKAY, I'M GONNA BEAT THEM BY HAVING A WET SWORD?

THE OPPOSITE, ACTUALLY.

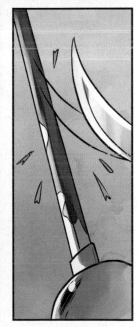

OOH!

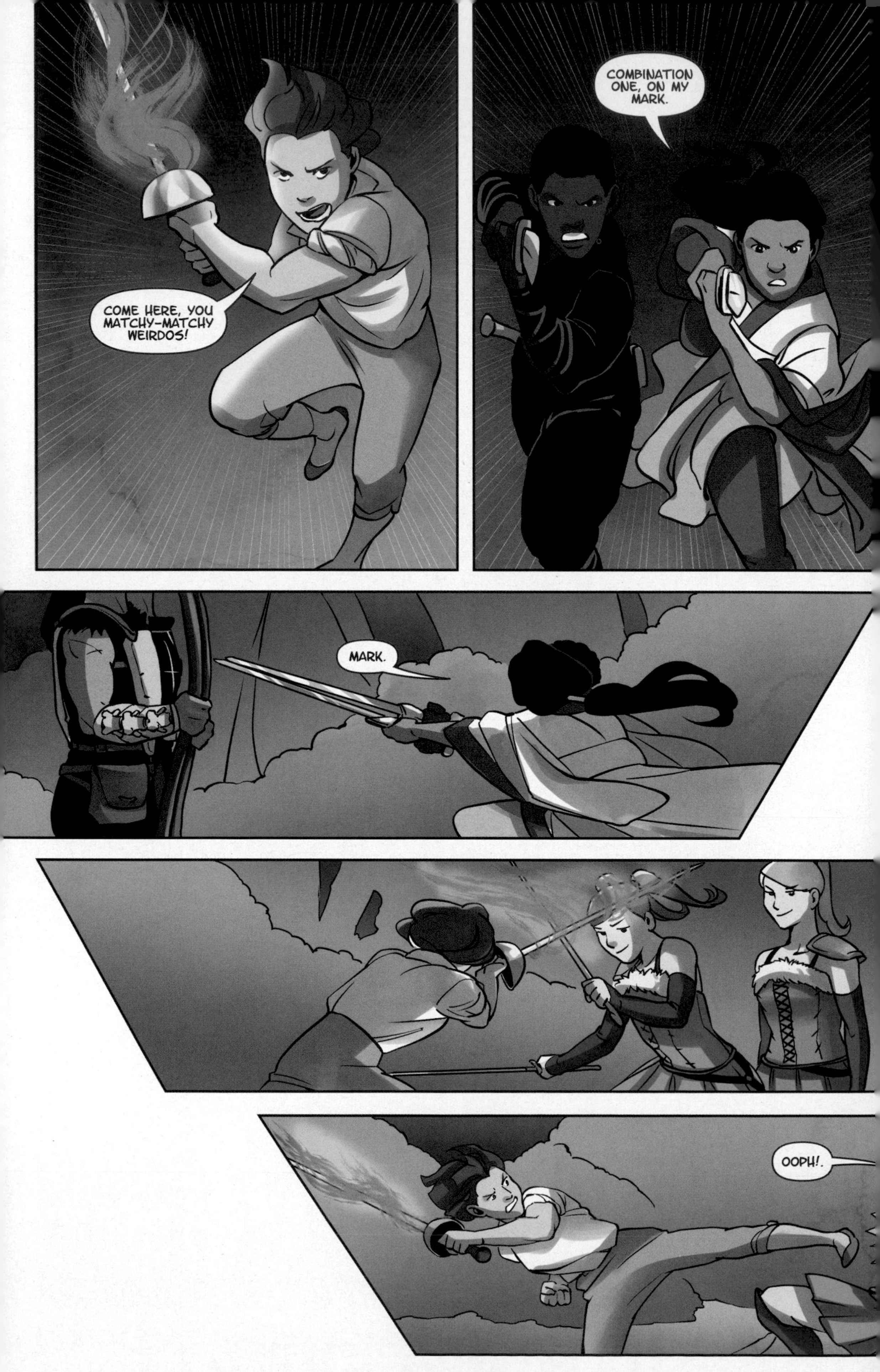
COME HERE, YOU MATCHY-MATCHY WEIRDOS!
COMBINATION ONE, ON MY MARK.
MARK.
OOPH!.

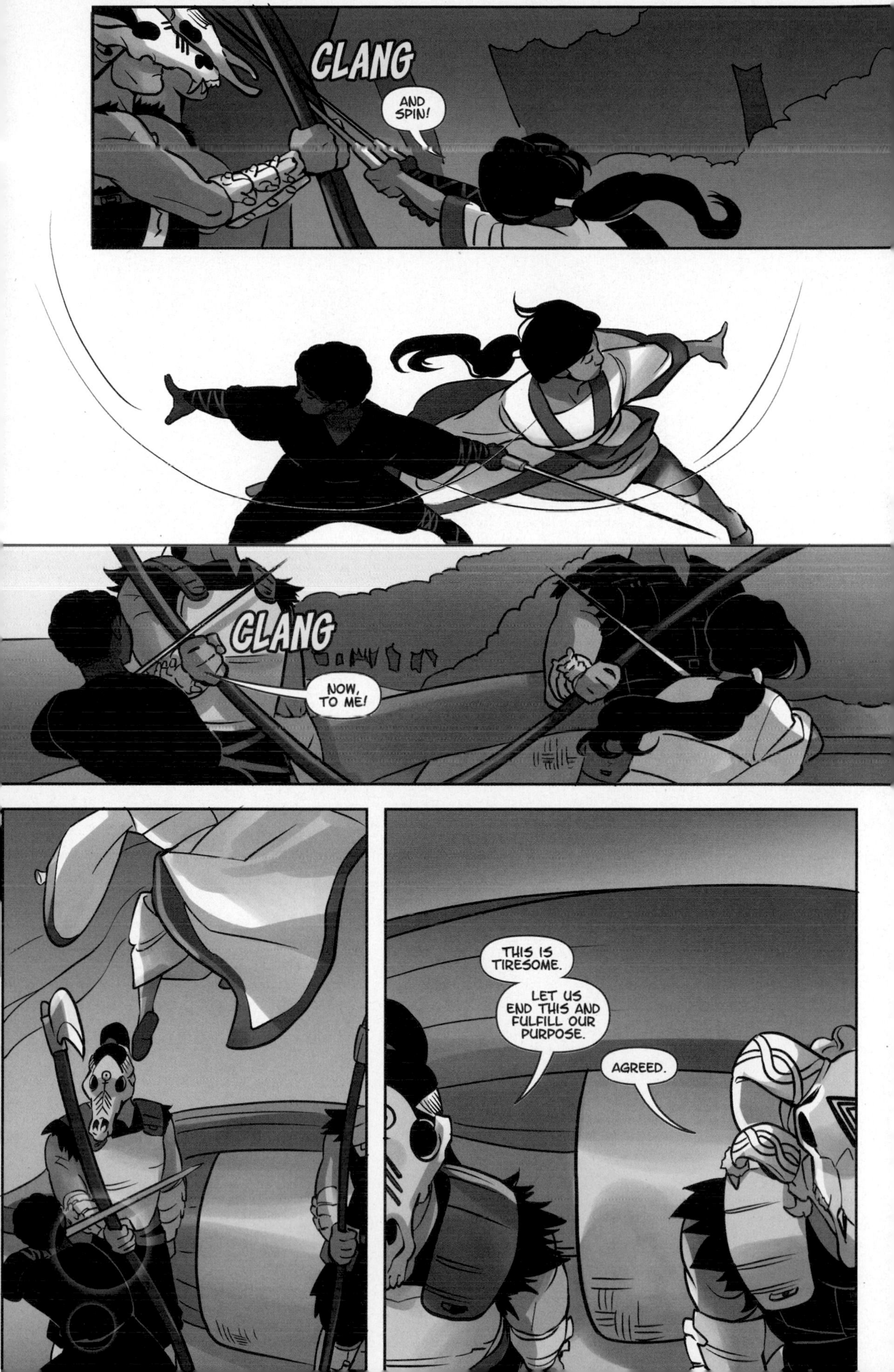
CLANG
AND SPIN!
CLANG
NOW, TO ME!
THIS IS TIRESOME.
LET US END THIS AND FULFILL OUR PURPOSE.
AGREED.

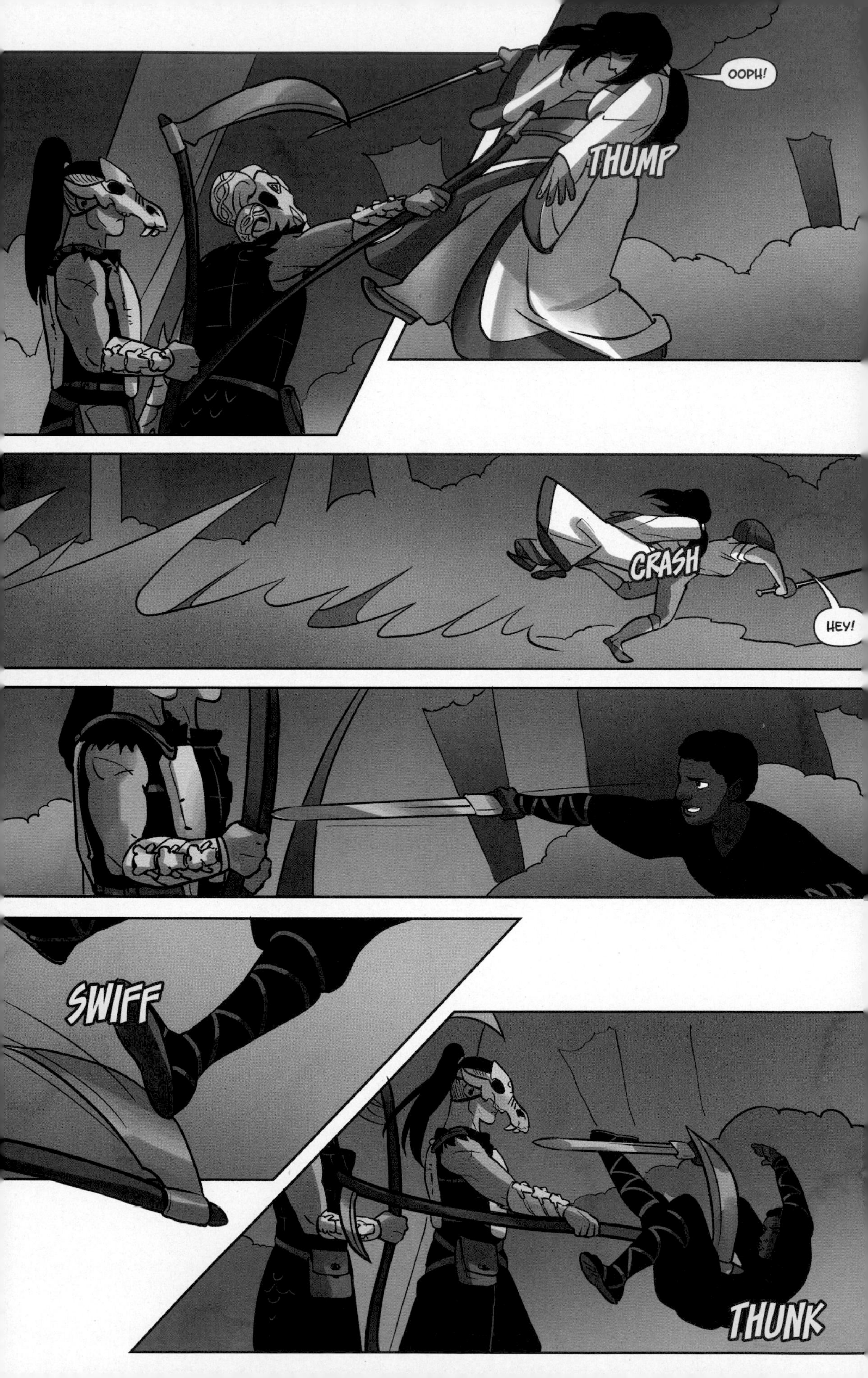
OOPH!
THUMP
CRASH
HEY!
SWIFF
THUNK

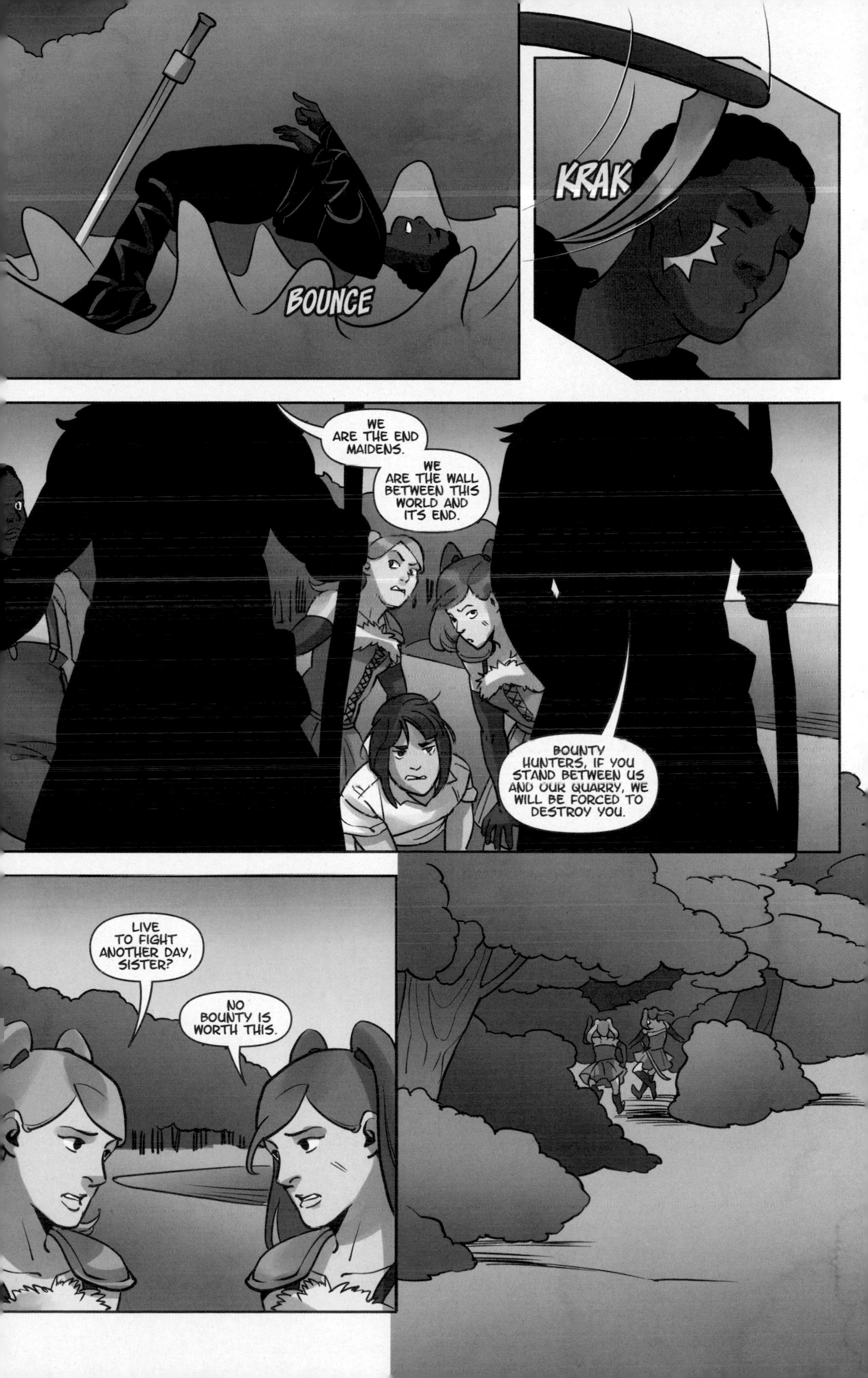
BOUNCE
KRAK
WE ARE THE END MAIDENS.
WE ARE THE WALL BETWEEN THIS WORLD AND ITS END.
BOUNTY HUNTERS, IF YOU STAND BETWEEN US AND OUR QUARRY, WE WILL BE FORCED TO DESTROY YOU.
LIVE TO FIGHT ANOTHER DAY, SISTER?
NO BOUNTY IS WORTH THIS.

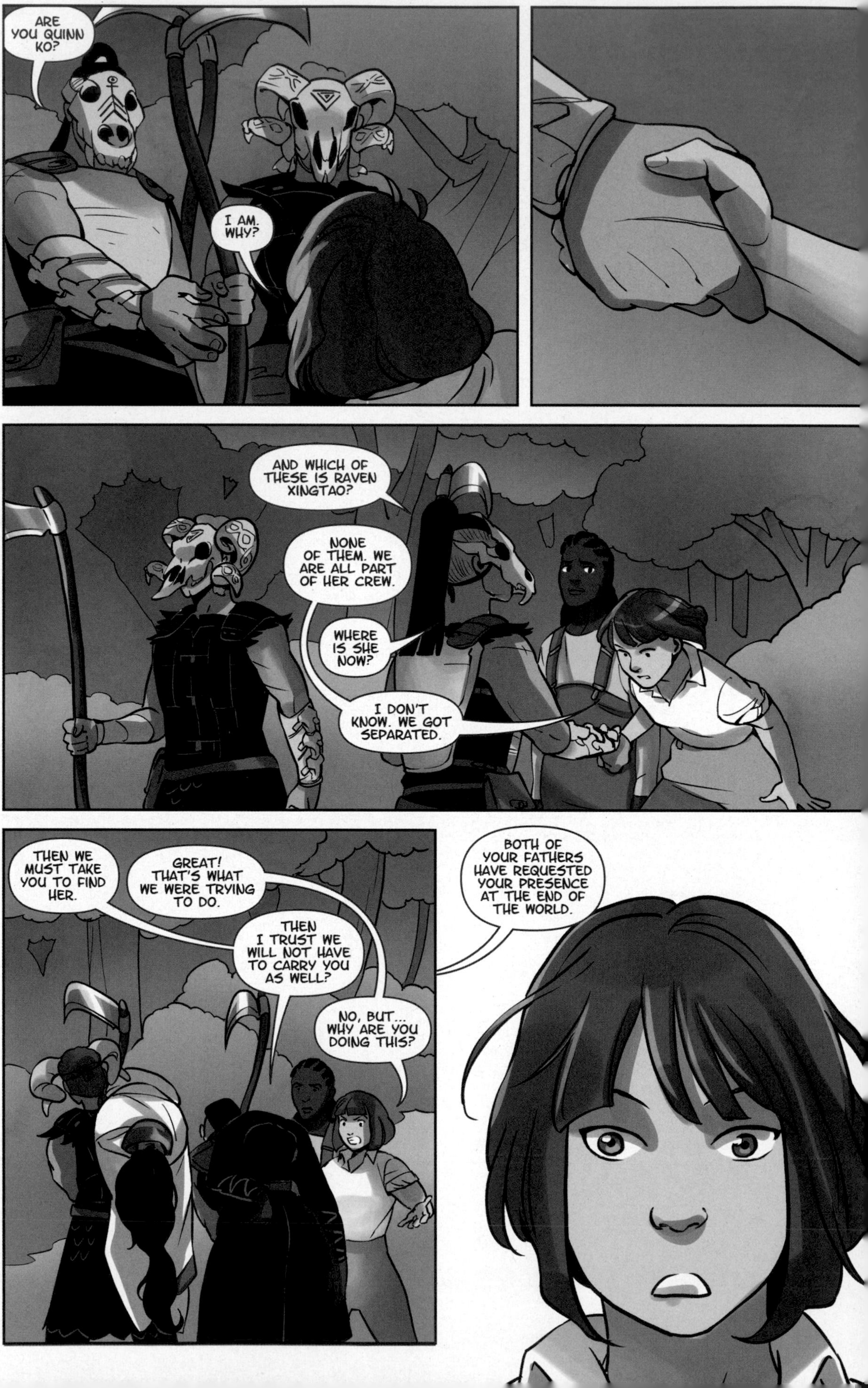
ARE YOU QUINN KO?
I AM. WHY?
AND WHICH OF THESE IS RAVEN XINGTAO?
NONE OF THEM. WE ARE ALL PART OF HER CREW.
WHERE IS SHE NOW?
I DON'T KNOW. WE GOT SEPARATED.
THEN WE MUST TAKE YOU TO FIND HER.
GREAT! THAT'S WHAT WE WERE TRYING TO DO.
THEN I TRUST WE WILL NOT HAVE TO CARRY YOU AS WELL?
NO, BUT... WHY ARE YOU DOING THIS?
BOTH OF YOUR FATHERS HAVE REQUESTED YOUR PRESENCE AT THE END OF THE WORLD.

Princeless

Raven: The Pirate Princess

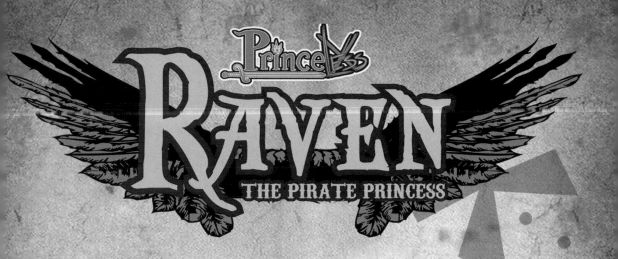

Year Three: Monsters of the Deep

Chapter Twelve: Ananda's Gambit

Written By: Jeremy Whitley

Pencils By:
(Pages 5-11, 17-24) Telênia Albuquerque
(Pages 1-4, 12-16) Xenia Pamfil

Inks By:
Pocket Owl

Colors By:
(Pages 5-11, 17-24) Valentina Pinto
(Pages 1-4, 12-16) Lexillo

Lettered By: Alex Scherkenbach

Cover By: Telênia Albuquerque

Bryan Seaton: Publisher - Vito Delsante: Editor In Chief
Jason Martin: Publisher-Danger Zone
Chad Cicconi: Deck Swabber

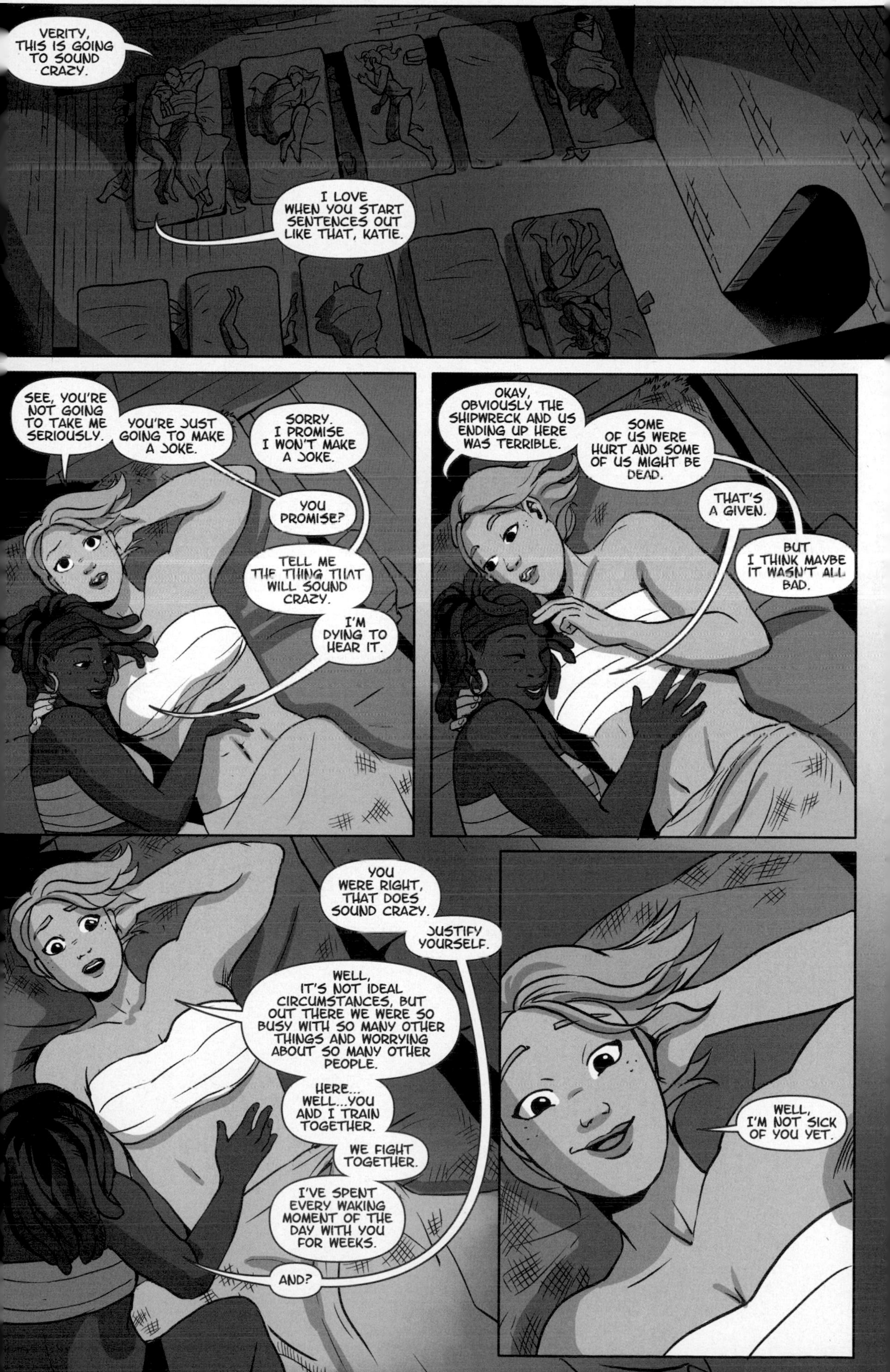
VERITY, THIS IS GOING TO SOUND CRAZY.
I LOVE WHEN YOU START SENTENCES OUT LIKE THAT, KATIE.
SEE, YOU'RE NOT GOING TO TAKE ME SERIOUSLY.
YOU'RE JUST GOING TO MAKE A JOKE.
SORRY. I PROMISE I WON'T MAKE A JOKE.
YOU PROMISE?
TELL ME THE THING THAT WILL SOUND CRAZY.
I'M DYING TO HEAR IT.
OKAY, OBVIOUSLY THE SHIPWRECK AND US ENDING UP HERE WAS TERRIBLE.
SOME OF US WERE HURT AND SOME OF US MIGHT BE DEAD.
THAT'S A GIVEN.
BUT I THINK MAYBE IT WASN'T ALL BAD.
YOU WERE RIGHT, THAT DOES SOUND CRAZY.
JUSTIFY YOURSELF.
WELL, IT'S NOT IDEAL CIRCUMSTANCES, BUT OUT THERE WE WERE SO BUSY WITH SO MANY OTHER THINGS AND WORRYING ABOUT SO MANY OTHER PEOPLE.
HERE... WELL...YOU AND I TRAIN TOGETHER.
WE FIGHT TOGETHER.
I'VE SPENT EVERY WAKING MOMENT OF THE DAY WITH YOU FOR WEEKS.
AND?
WELL, I'M NOT SICK OF YOU YET.

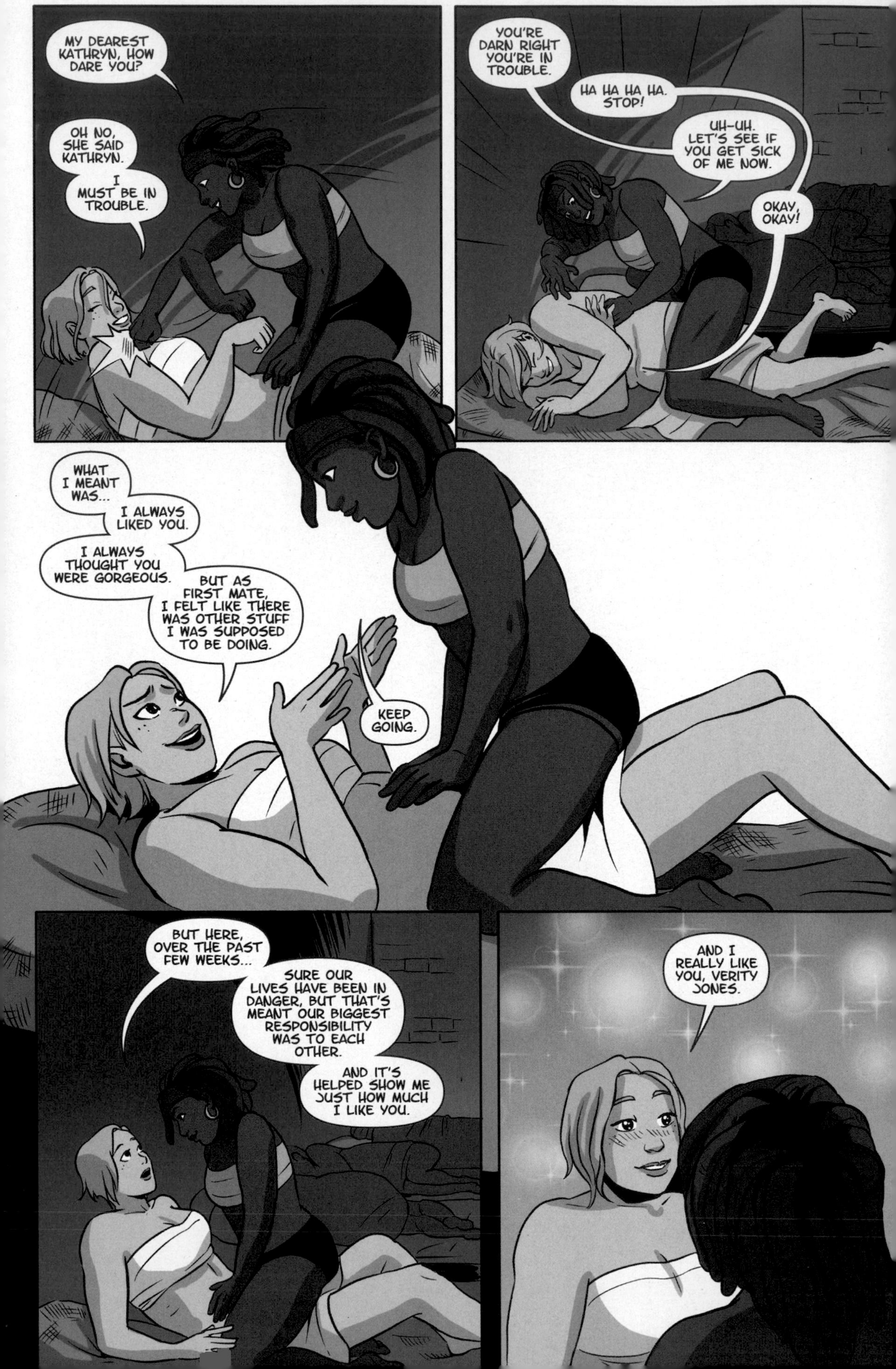
MY DEAREST KATHRYN, HOW DARE YOU?
OH NO, SHE SAID KATHRYN.
I MUST BE IN TROUBLE.
YOU'RE DARN RIGHT YOU'RE IN TROUBLE.
HA HA HA HA. STOP!
UH-UH. LET'S SEE IF YOU GET SICK OF ME NOW.
OKAY, OKAY!
WHAT I MEANT WAS...
I ALWAYS LIKED YOU.
I ALWAYS THOUGHT YOU WERE GORGEOUS.
BUT AS FIRST MATE, I FELT LIKE THERE WAS OTHER STUFF I WAS SUPPOSED TO BE DOING.
KEEP GOING.
BUT HERE, OVER THE PAST FEW WEEKS...
SURE OUR LIVES HAVE BEEN IN DANGER, BUT THAT'S MEANT OUR BIGGEST RESPONSIBILITY WAS TO EACH OTHER.
AND IT'S HELPED SHOW ME JUST HOW MUCH I LIKE YOU.
AND I REALLY LIKE YOU, VERITY JONES.

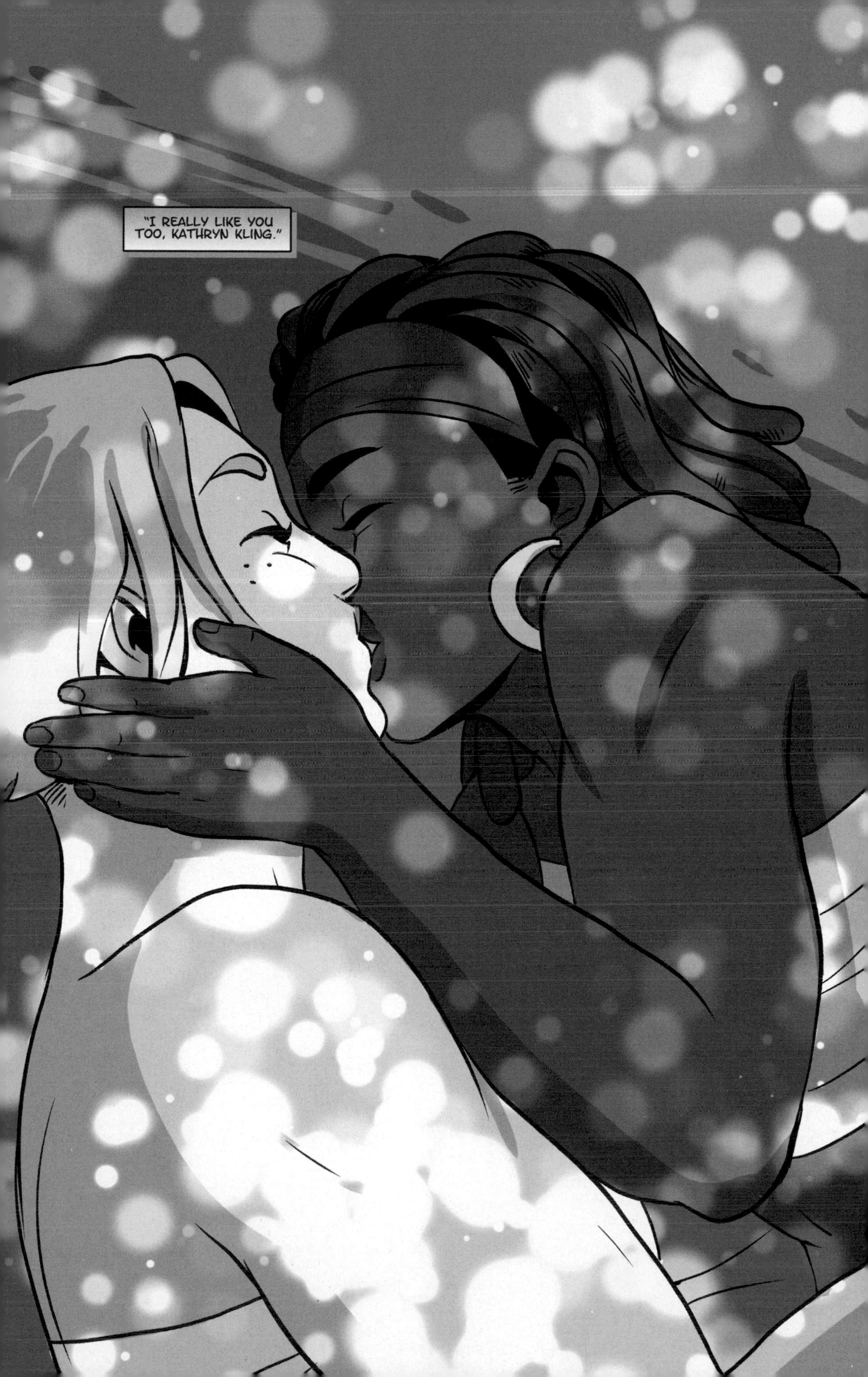
"I REALLY LIKE YOU TOO, KATHRYN KLING."

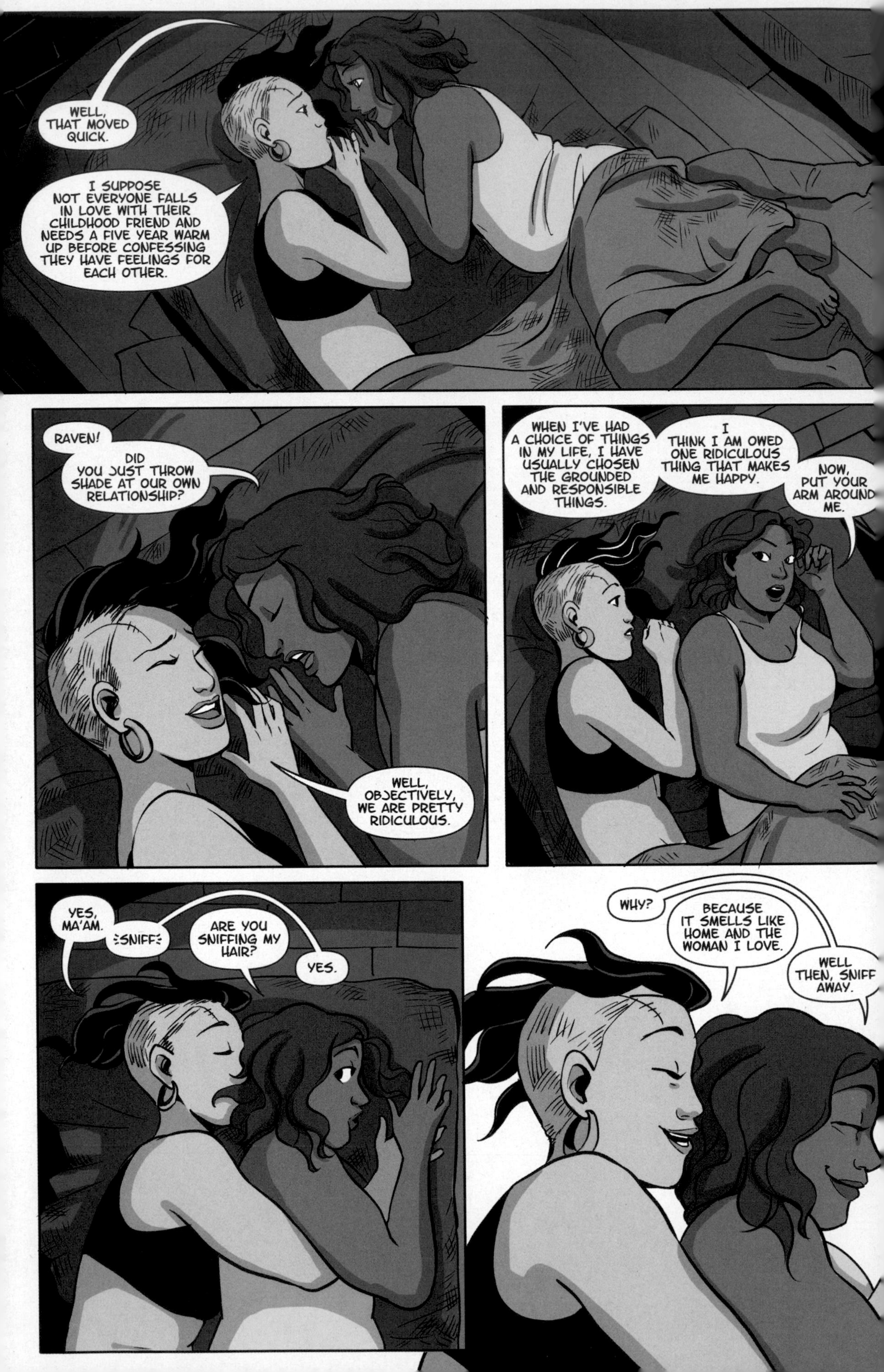
WELL, THAT MOVED QUICK.
I SUPPOSE NOT EVERYONE FALLS IN LOVE WITH THEIR CHILDHOOD FRIEND AND NEEDS A FIVE YEAR WARM UP BEFORE CONFESSING THEY HAVE FEELINGS FOR EACH OTHER.
RAVEN!
DID YOU JUST THROW SHADE AT OUR OWN RELATIONSHIP?
WELL, OBJECTIVELY, WE ARE PRETTY RIDICULOUS.
WHEN I'VE HAD A CHOICE OF THINGS IN MY LIFE, I HAVE USUALLY CHOSEN THE GROUNDED AND RESPONSIBLE THINGS.
I THINK I AM OWED ONE RIDICULOUS THING THAT MAKES ME HAPPY.
NOW, PUT YOUR ARM AROUND ME.
YES, MA'AM.
SNIFF
ARE YOU SNIFFING MY HAIR?
YES.
WHY?
BECAUSE IT SMELLS LIKE HOME AND THE WOMAN I LOVE.
WELL THEN, SNIFF AWAY.

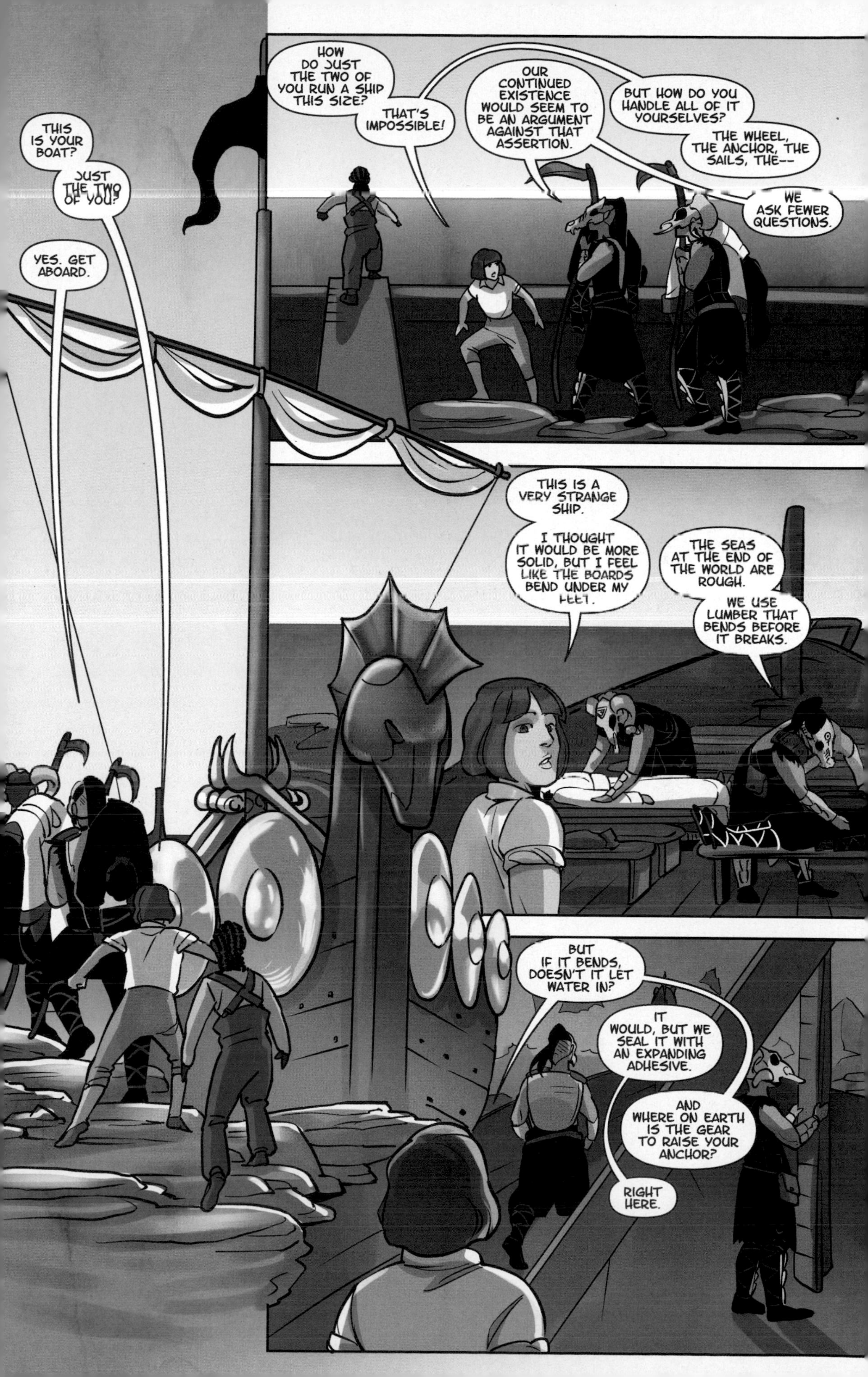
THIS IS YOUR BOAT?
JUST THE TWO OF YOU?
YES. GET ABOARD.
HOW DO JUST THE TWO OF YOU RUN A SHIP THIS SIZE?
THAT'S IMPOSSIBLE!
OUR CONTINUED EXISTENCE WOULD SEEM TO BE AN ARGUMENT AGAINST THAT ASSERTION.
BUT HOW DO YOU HANDLE ALL OF IT YOURSELVES?
THE WHEEL, THE ANCHOR, THE SAILS, THE--
WE ASK FEWER QUESTIONS.
THIS IS A VERY STRANGE SHIP.
I THOUGHT IT WOULD BE MORE SOLID, BUT I FEEL LIKE THE BOARDS BEND UNDER MY FEET.
THE SEAS AT THE END OF THE WORLD ARE ROUGH.
WE USE LUMBER THAT BENDS BEFORE IT BREAKS.
BUT IF IT BENDS, DOESN'T IT LET WATER IN?
IT WOULD, BUT WE SEAL IT WITH AN EXPANDING ADHESIVE.
AND WHERE ON EARTH IS THE GEAR TO RAISE YOUR ANCHOR?
RIGHT HERE.

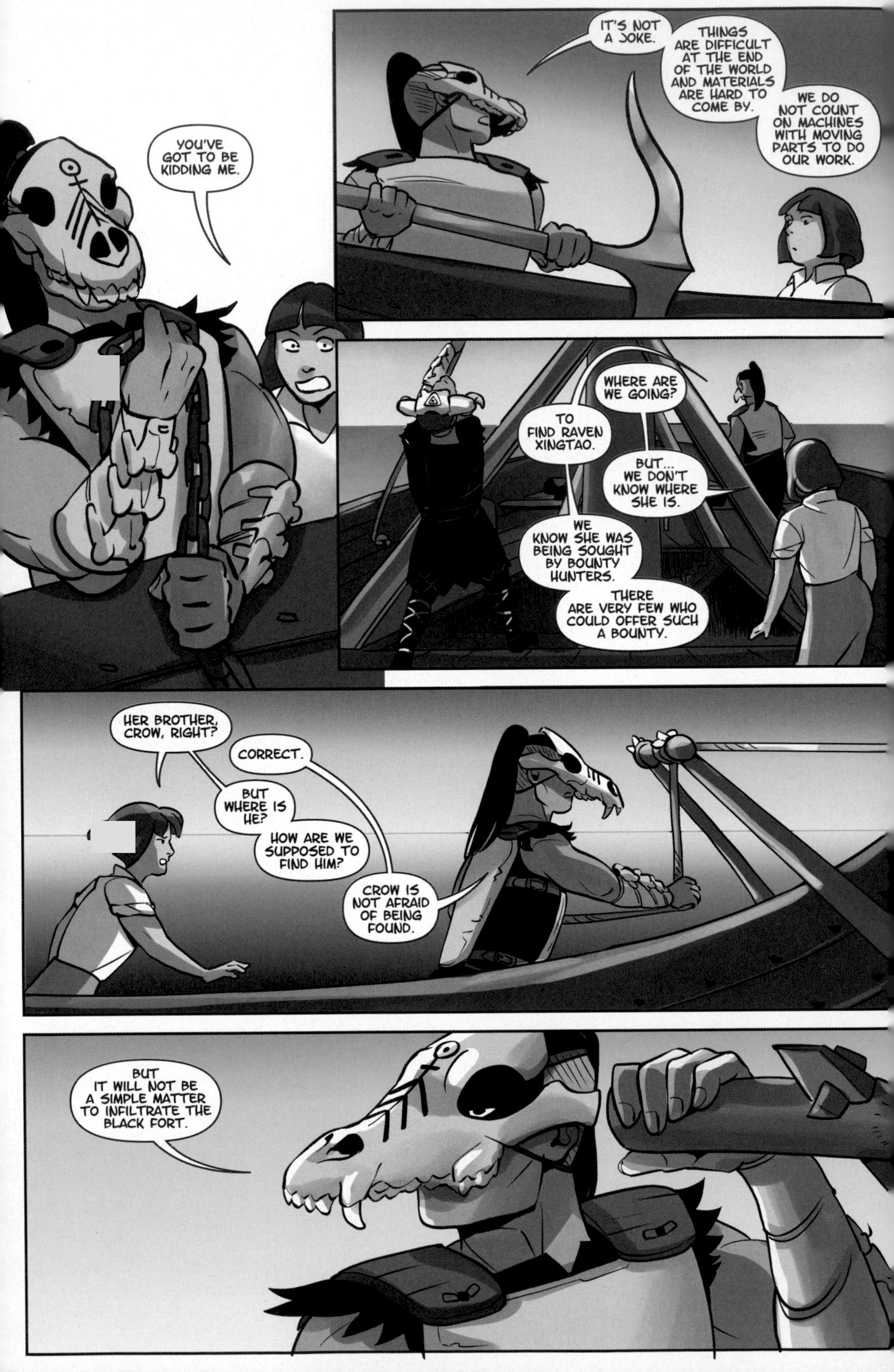
YOU'VE GOT TO BE KIDDING ME.
IT'S NOT A JOKE.
THINGS ARE DIFFICULT AT THE END OF THE WORLD AND MATERIALS ARE HARD TO COME BY.
WE DO NOT COUNT ON MACHINES WITH MOVING PARTS TO DO OUR WORK.
WHERE ARE WE GOING?
TO FIND RAVEN XINGTAO.
BUT... WE DON'T KNOW WHERE SHE IS.
WE KNOW SHE WAS BEING SOUGHT BY BOUNTY HUNTERS.
THERE ARE VERY FEW WHO COULD OFFER SUCH A BOUNTY.
HER BROTHER, CROW, RIGHT?
CORRECT.
BUT WHERE IS HE?
HOW ARE WE SUPPOSED TO FIND HIM?
CROW IS NOT AFRAID OF BEING FOUND.
BUT IT WILL NOT BE A SIMPLE MATTER TO INFILTRATE THE BLACK FORT.

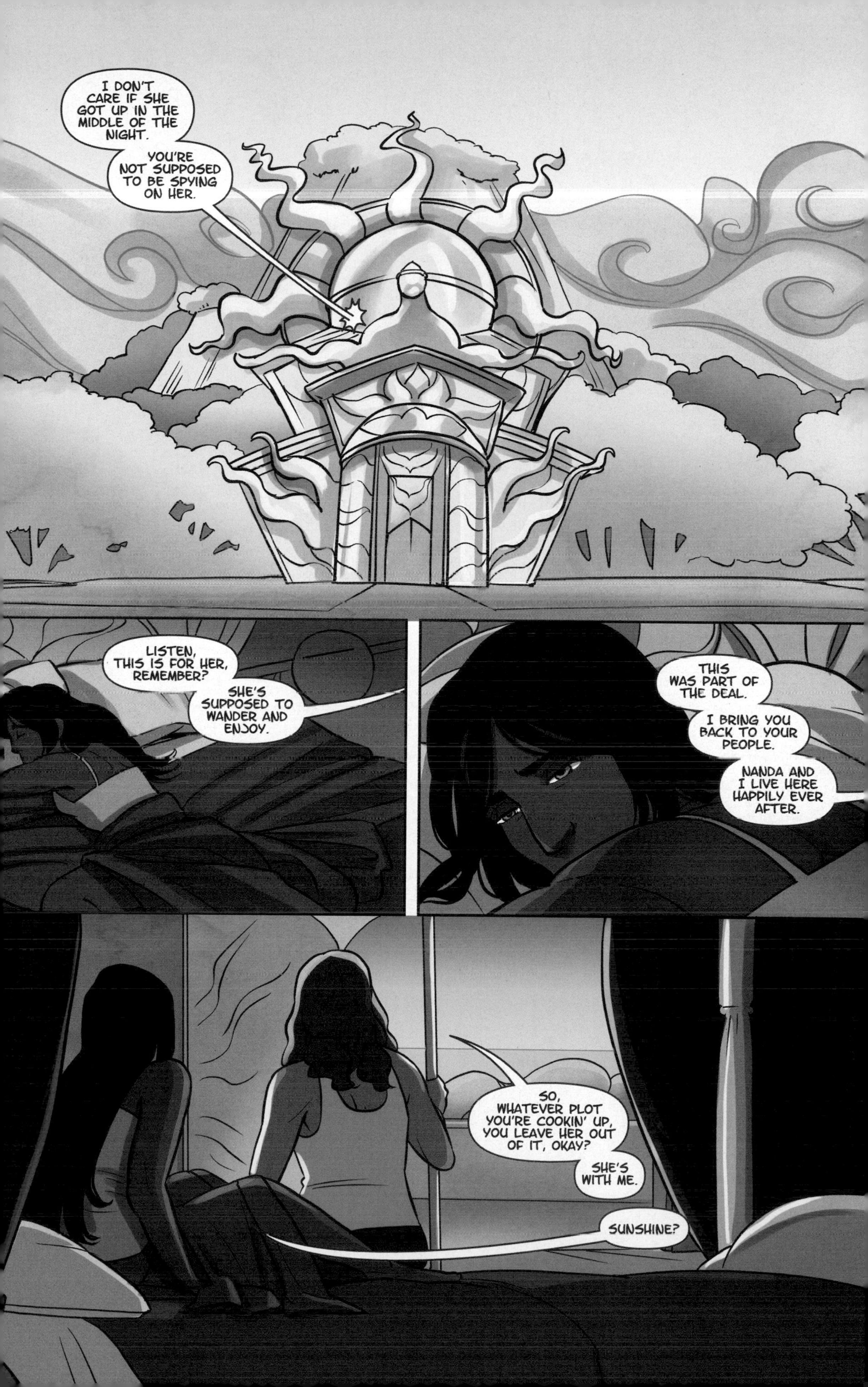
I DON'T CARE IF SHE GOT UP IN THE MIDDLE OF THE NIGHT.
YOU'RE NOT SUPPOSED TO BE SPYING ON HER.
LISTEN, THIS IS FOR HER, REMEMBER?
SHE'S SUPPOSED TO WANDER AND ENJOY.
THIS WAS PART OF THE DEAL.
I BRING YOU BACK TO YOUR PEOPLE.
NANDA AND I LIVE HERE HAPPILY EVER AFTER.
SO, WHATEVER PLOT YOU'RE COOKIN' UP, YOU LEAVE HER OUT OF IT, OKAY?
SHE'S WITH ME.
SUNSHINE?

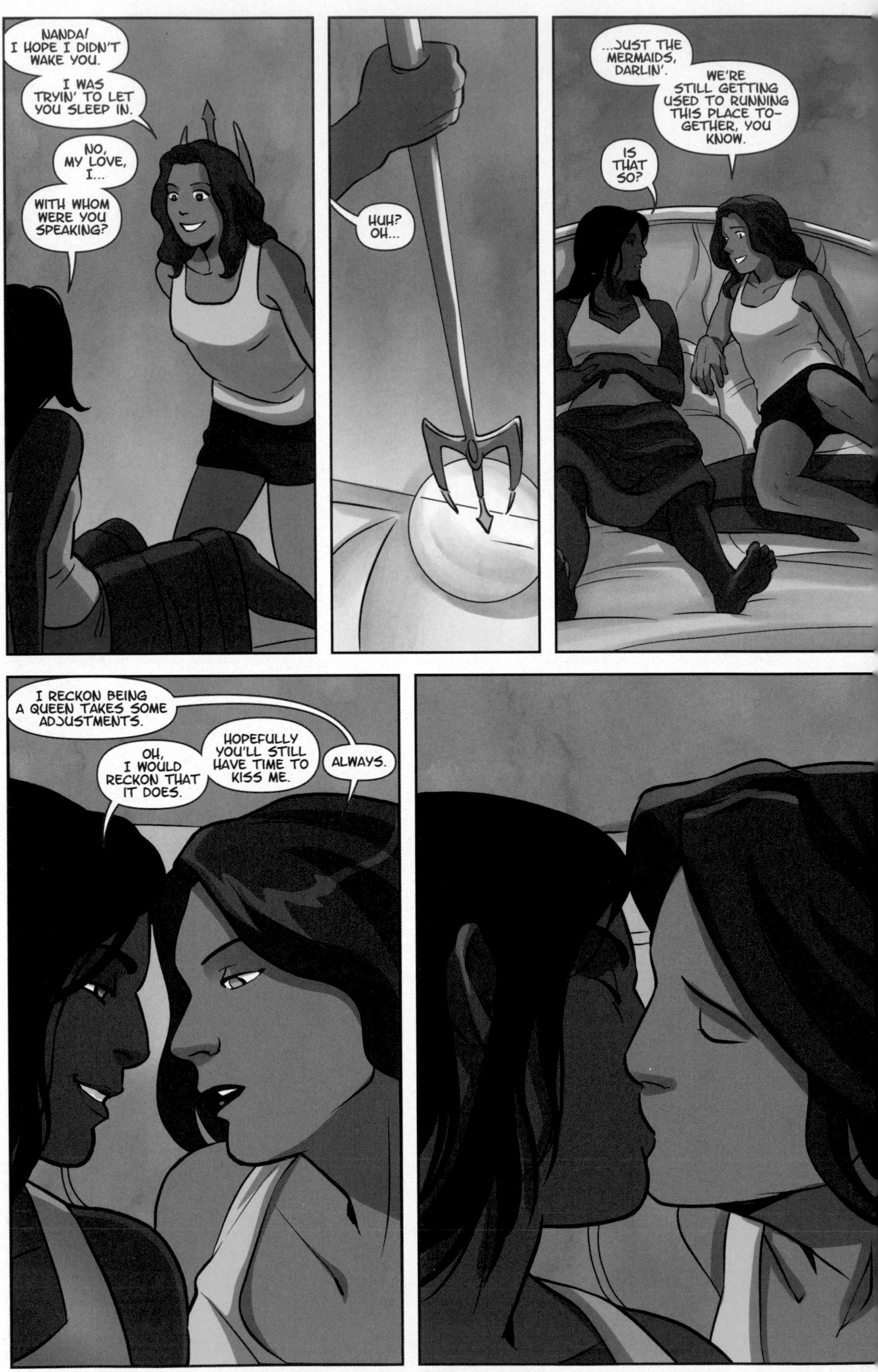
NANDA! I HOPE I DIDN'T WAKE YOU.
I WAS TRYIN' TO LET YOU SLEEP IN.
NO, MY LOVE, I...
WITH WHOM WERE YOU SPEAKING?
HUH? OH...
...JUST THE MERMAIDS, DARLIN'.
WE'RE STILL GETTING USED TO RUNNING THIS PLACE TO-GETHER, YOU KNOW.
IS THAT SO?
I RECKON BEING A QUEEN TAKES SOME ADJUSTMENTS.
OH, I WOULD RECKON THAT IT DOES.
HOPEFULLY YOU'LL STILL HAVE TIME TO KISS ME.
ALWAYS.

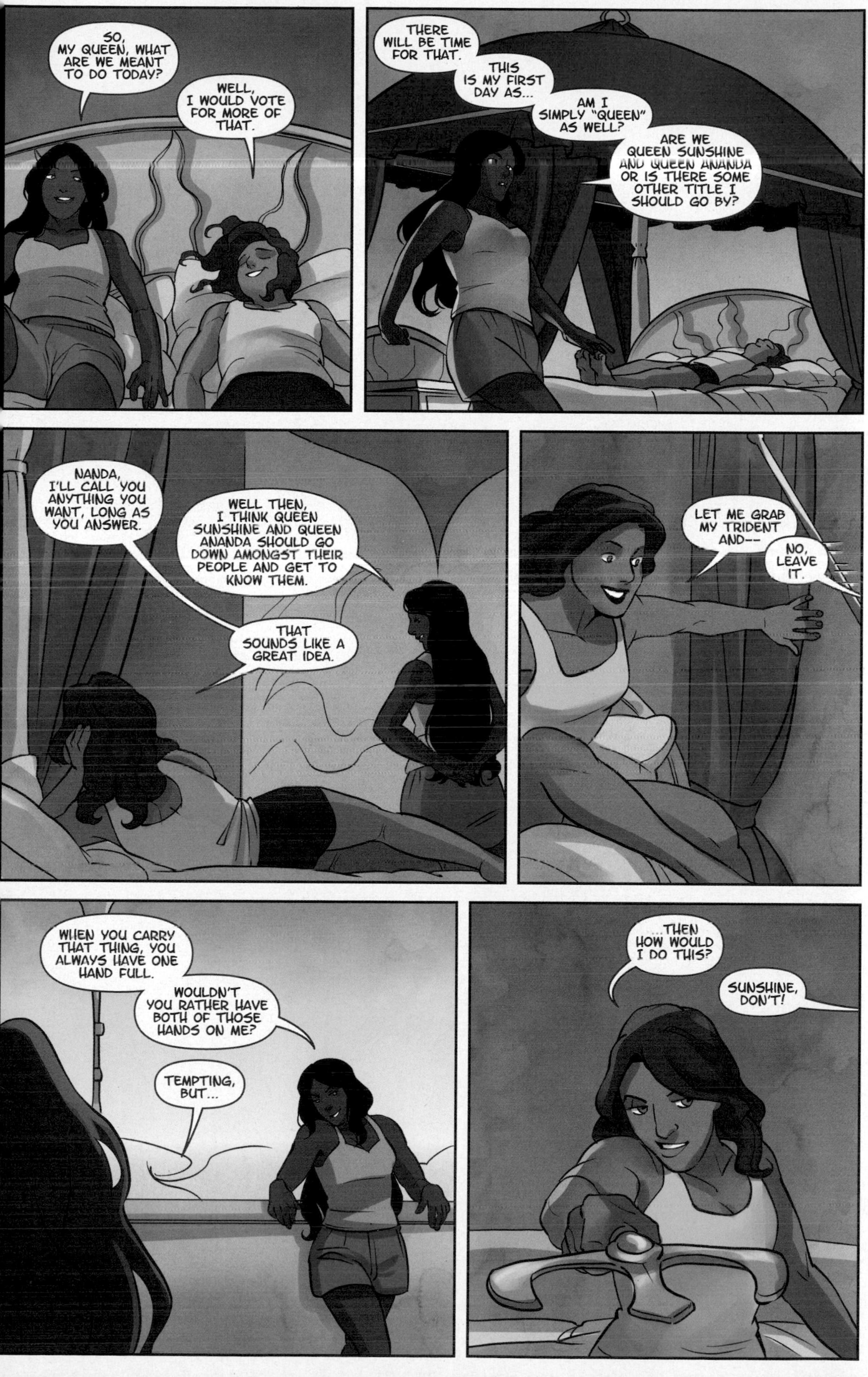
SO, MY QUEEN, WHAT ARE WE MEANT TO DO TODAY?
WELL, I WOULD VOTE FOR MORE OF THAT.
THERE WILL BE TIME FOR THAT.
THIS IS MY FIRST DAY AS...
AM I SIMPLY "QUEEN" AS WELL?
ARE WE QUEEN SUNSHINE AND QUEEN ANANDA OR IS THERE SOME OTHER TITLE I SHOULD GO BY?
NANDA, I'LL CALL YOU ANYTHING YOU WANT, LONG AS YOU ANSWER.
WELL THEN, I THINK QUEEN SUNSHINE AND QUEEN ANANDA SHOULD GO DOWN AMONGST THEIR PEOPLE AND GET TO KNOW THEM.
THAT SOUNDS LIKE A GREAT IDEA.
LET ME GRAB MY TRIDENT AND--
NO, LEAVE IT.
WHEN YOU CARRY THAT THING, YOU ALWAYS HAVE ONE HAND FULL.
WOULDN'T YOU RATHER HAVE BOTH OF THOSE HANDS ON ME?
TEMPTING, BUT...
...THEN HOW WOULD I DO THIS?
SUNSHINE, DON'T!

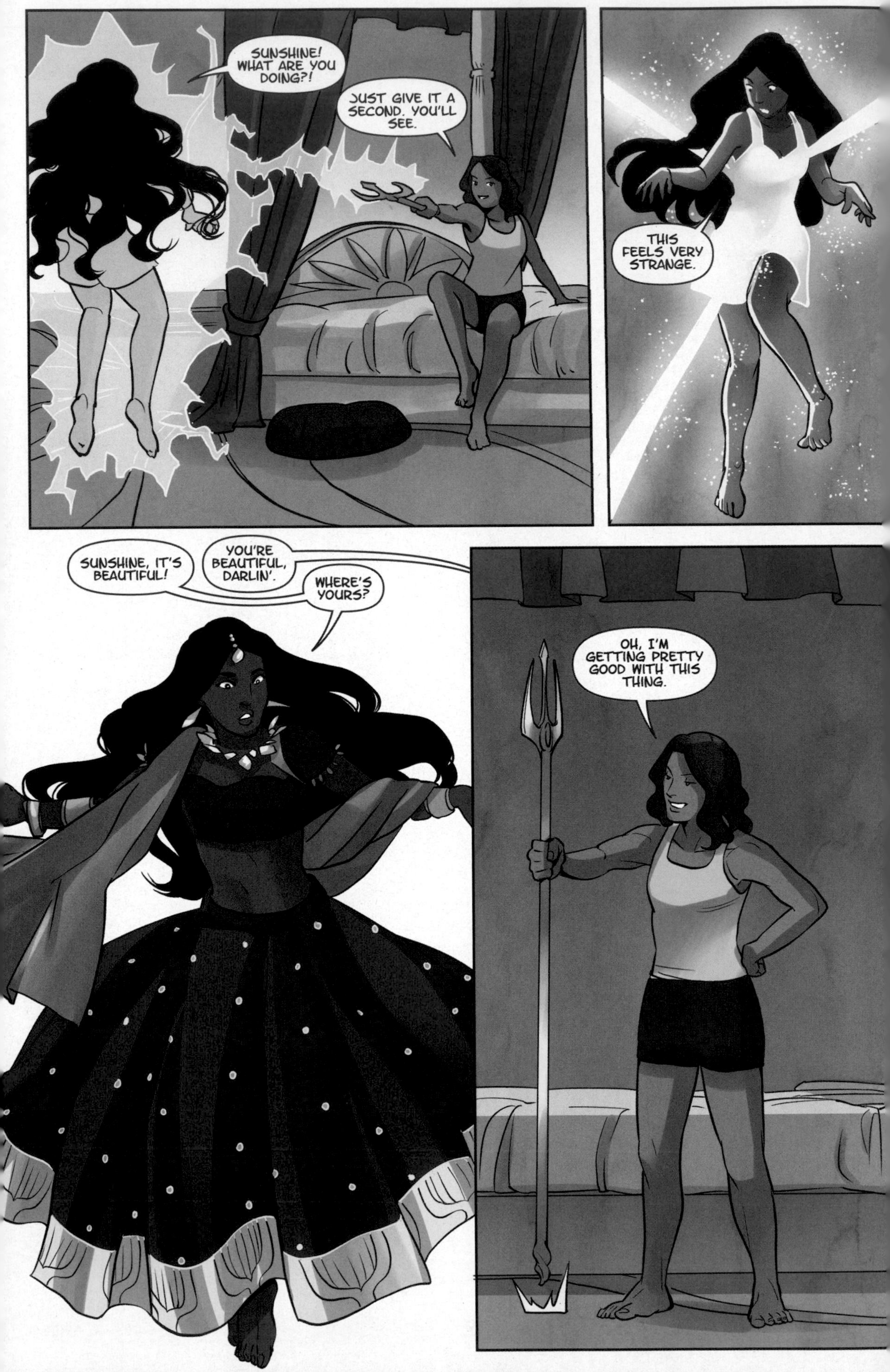
SUNSHINE! WHAT ARE YOU DOING?!
JUST GIVE IT A SECOND. YOU'LL SEE.
THIS FEELS VERY STRANGE.
SUNSHINE, IT'S BEAUTIFUL!
YOU'RE BEAUTIFUL, DARLIN'.
WHERE'S YOURS?
OH, I'M GETTING PRETTY GOOD WITH THIS THING.

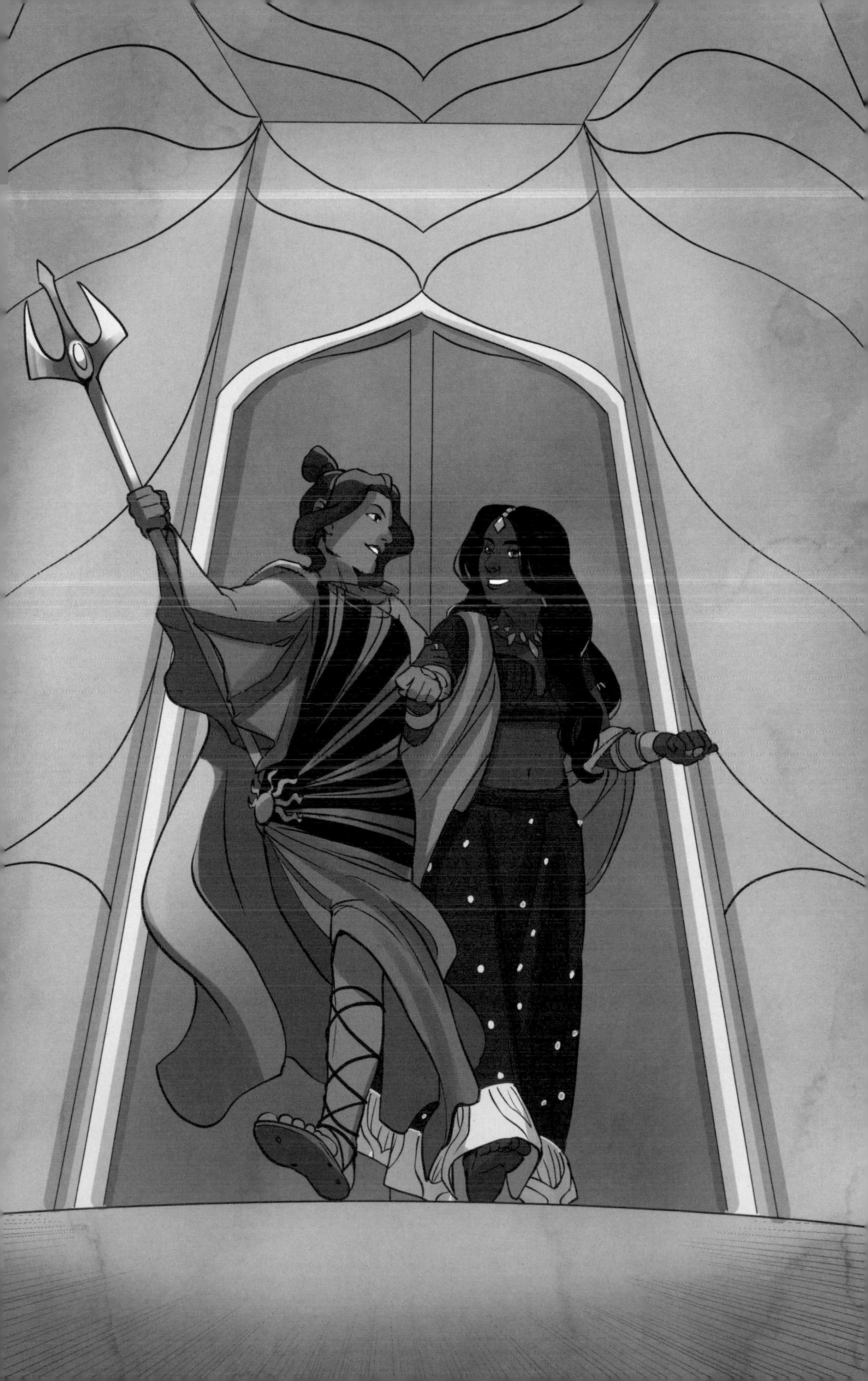

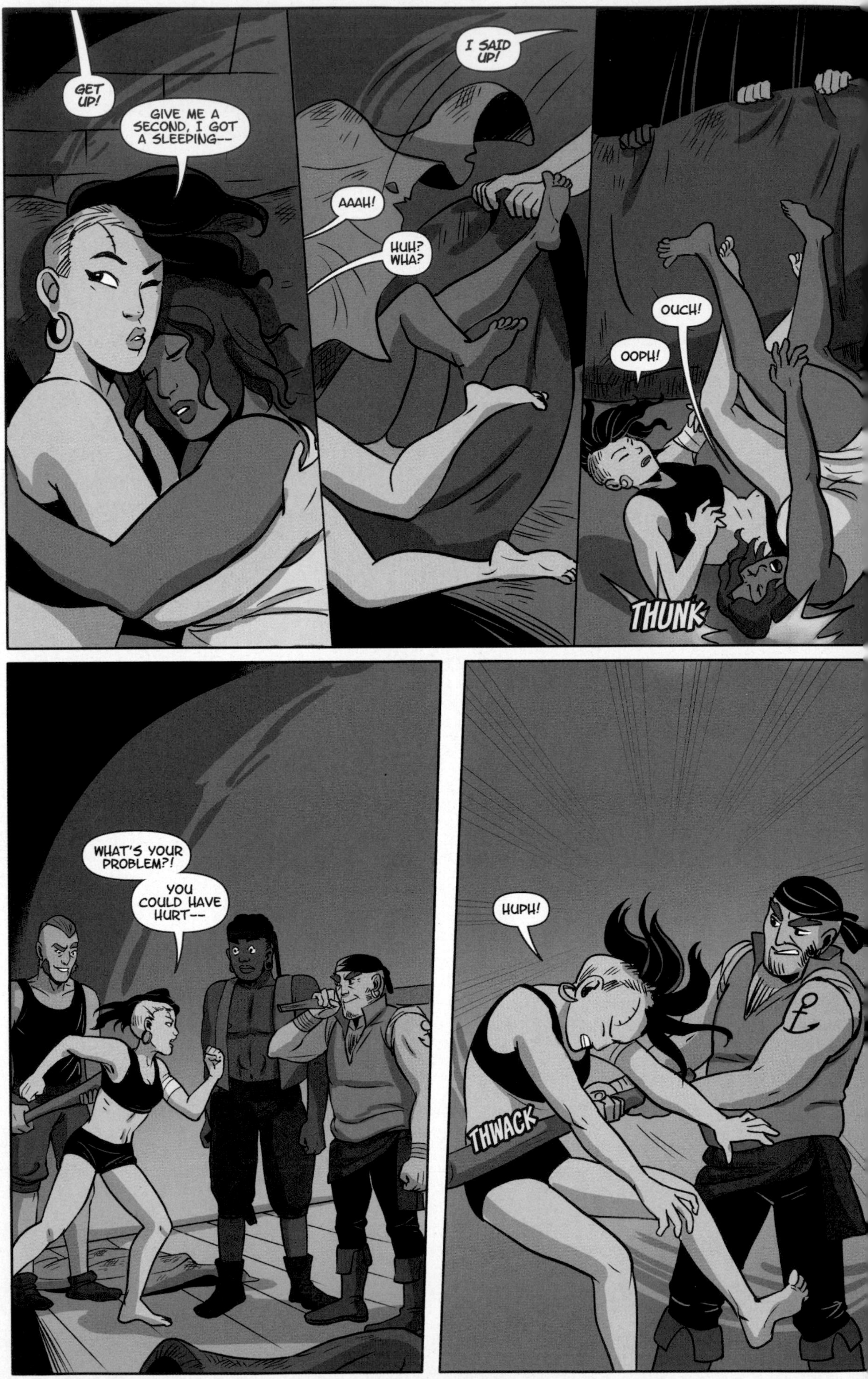
GET UP!
GIVE ME A SECOND, I GOT A SLEEPING--
I SAID UP!
AAAH!
HUH? WHA?
OUCH!
OOPH!
THUNK
WHAT'S YOUR PROBLEM?!
YOU COULD HAVE HURT--
HUPH!
THWACK

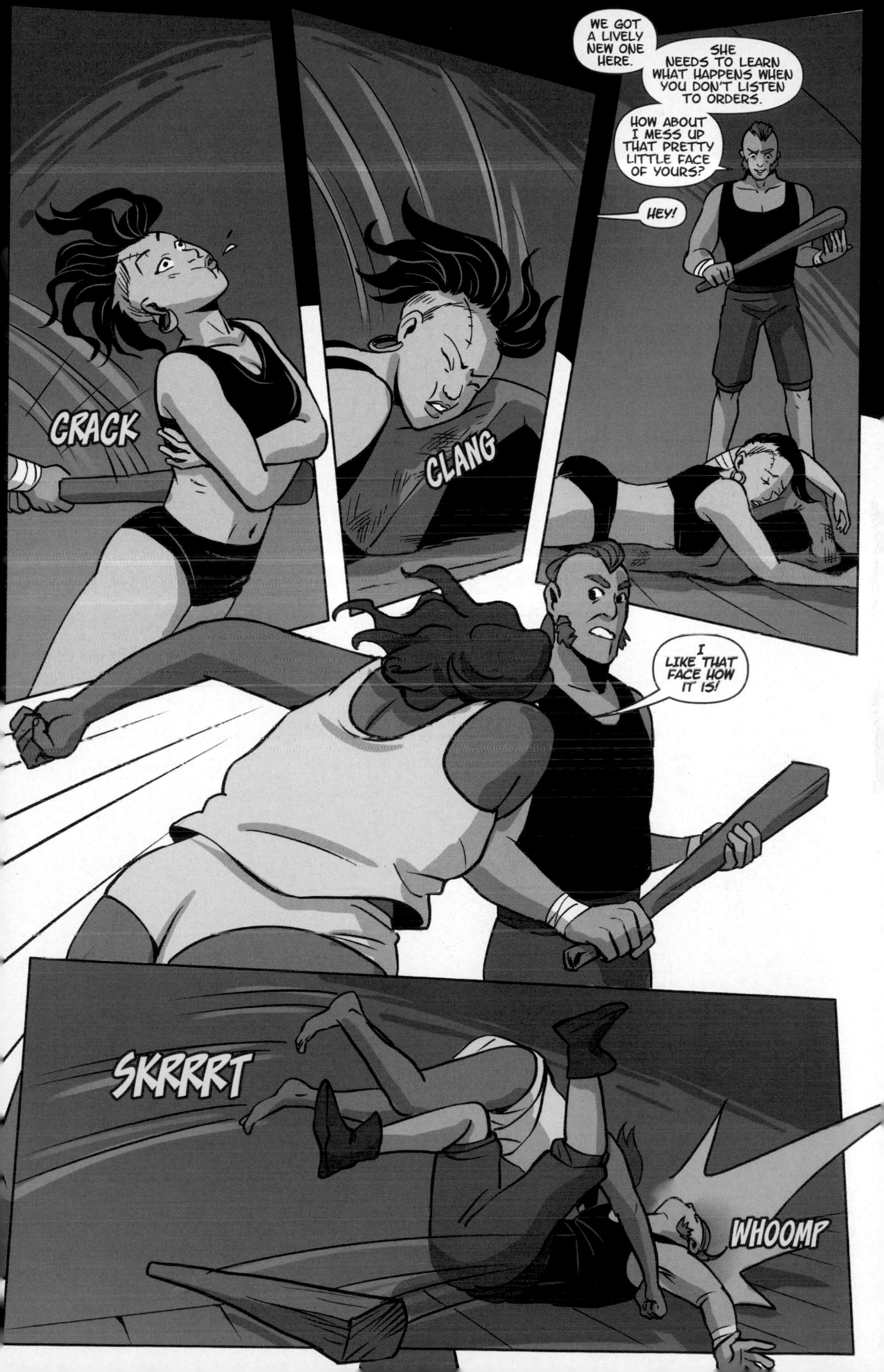
CRACK
CLANG
WE GOT A LIVELY NEW ONE HERE.
SHE NEEDS TO LEARN WHAT HAPPENS WHEN YOU DON'T LISTEN TO ORDERS.
HOW ABOUT I MESS UP THAT PRETTY LITTLE FACE OF YOURS?
HEY!
I LIKE THAT FACE HOW IT IS!
SKRRRT
WHOOMP

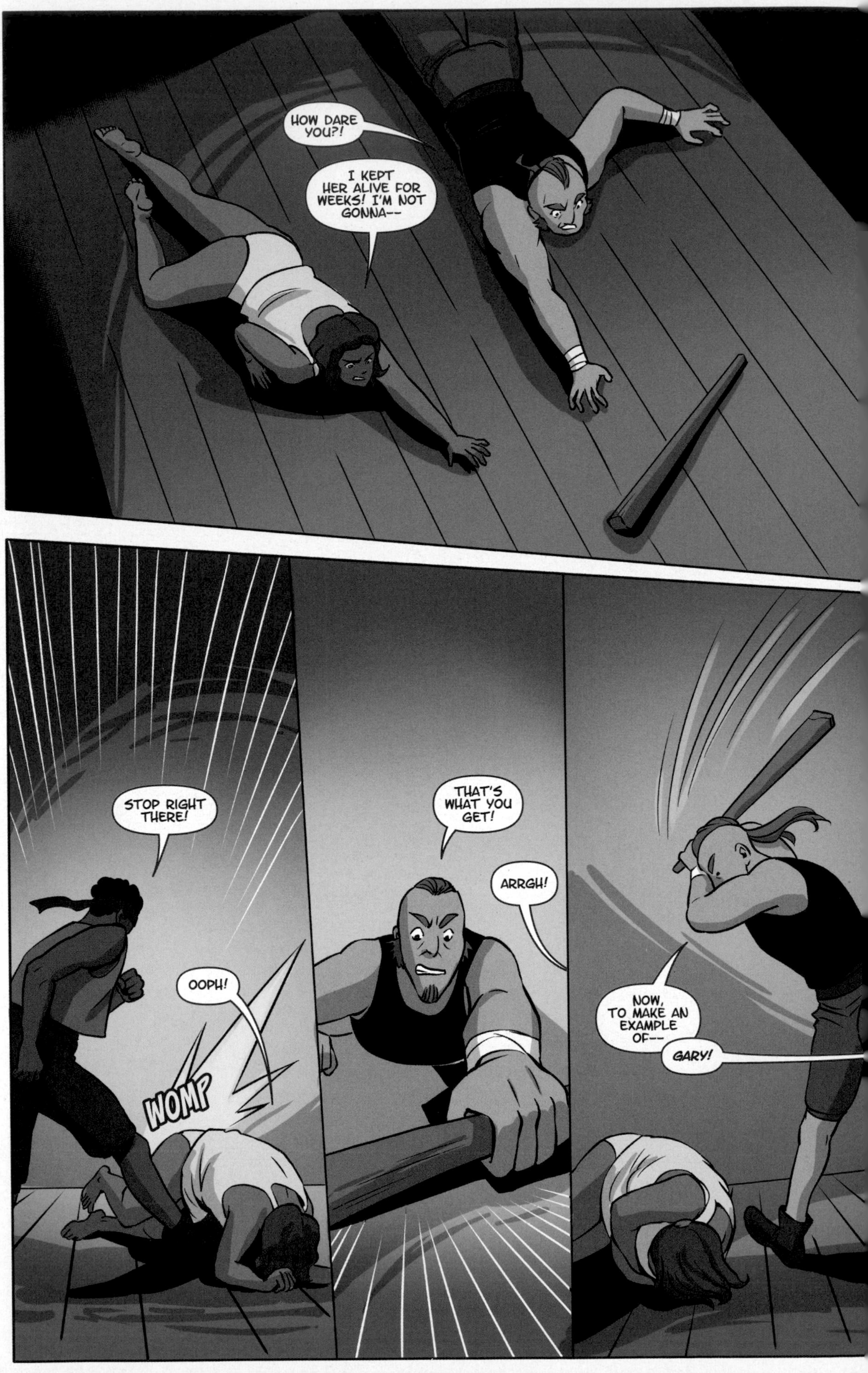
HOW DARE YOU?!
I KEPT HER ALIVE FOR WEEKS! I'M NOT GONNA--
STOP RIGHT THERE!
OOPH!
WOMP
THAT'S WHAT YOU GET!
ARRGH!
NOW, TO MAKE AN EXAMPLE OF--
GARY!

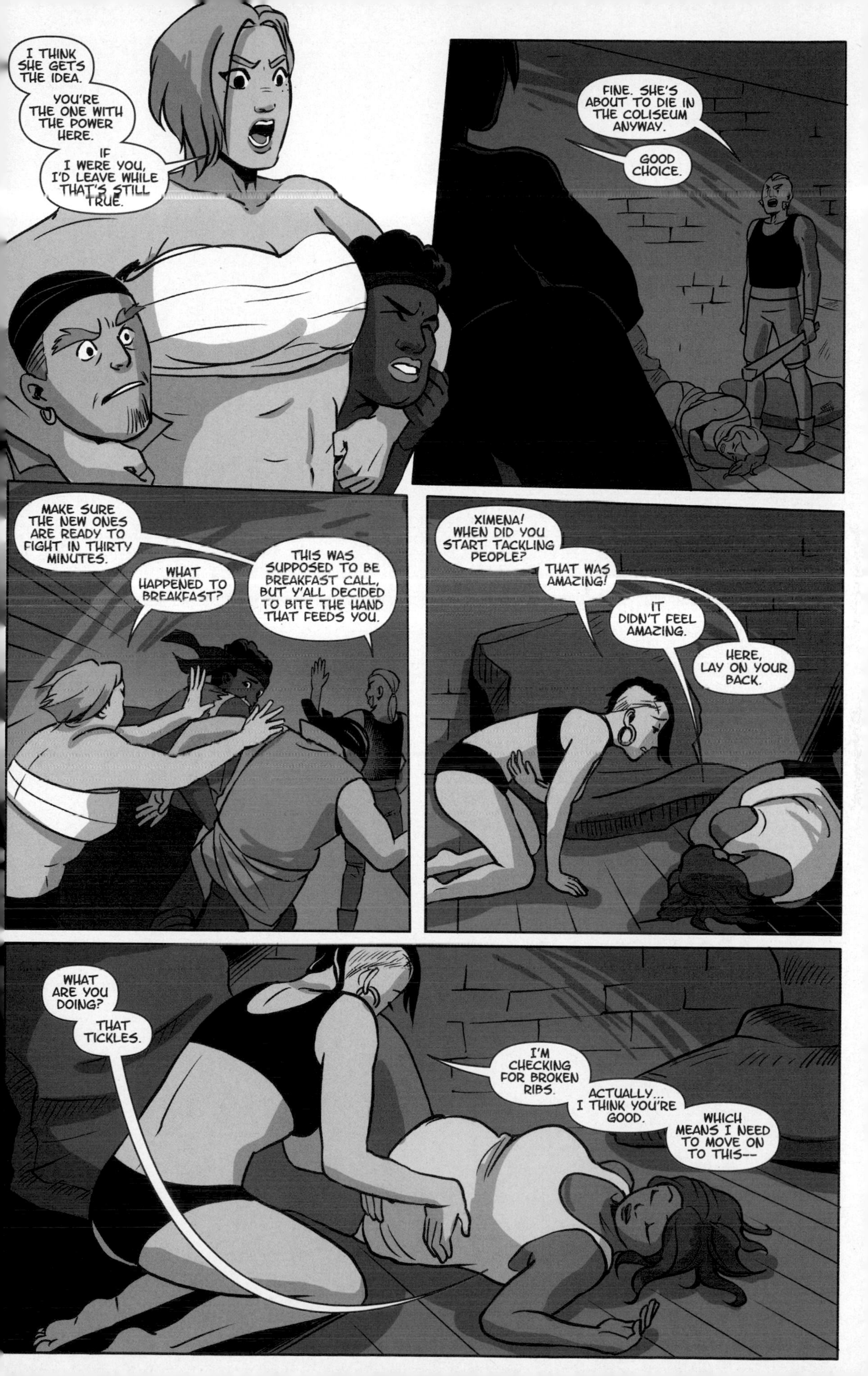
I THINK SHE GETS THE IDEA.
YOU'RE THE ONE WITH THE POWER HERE.
IF I WERE YOU, I'D LEAVE WHILE THAT'S STILL TRUE.
FINE. SHE'S ABOUT TO DIE IN THE COLISEUM ANYWAY.
GOOD CHOICE.
MAKE SURE THE NEW ONES ARE READY TO FIGHT IN THIRTY MINUTES.
WHAT HAPPENED TO BREAKFAST?
THIS WAS SUPPOSED TO BE BREAKFAST CALL, BUT Y'ALL DECIDED TO BITE THE HAND THAT FEEDS YOU.
XIMENA! WHEN DID YOU START TACKLING PEOPLE?
THAT WAS AMAZING!
IT DIDN'T FEEL AMAZING.
HERE, LAY ON YOUR BACK.
WHAT ARE YOU DOING?
THAT TICKLES.
I'M CHECKING FOR BROKEN RIBS.
ACTUALLY... I THINK YOU'RE GOOD.
WHICH MEANS I NEED TO MOVE ON TO THIS--

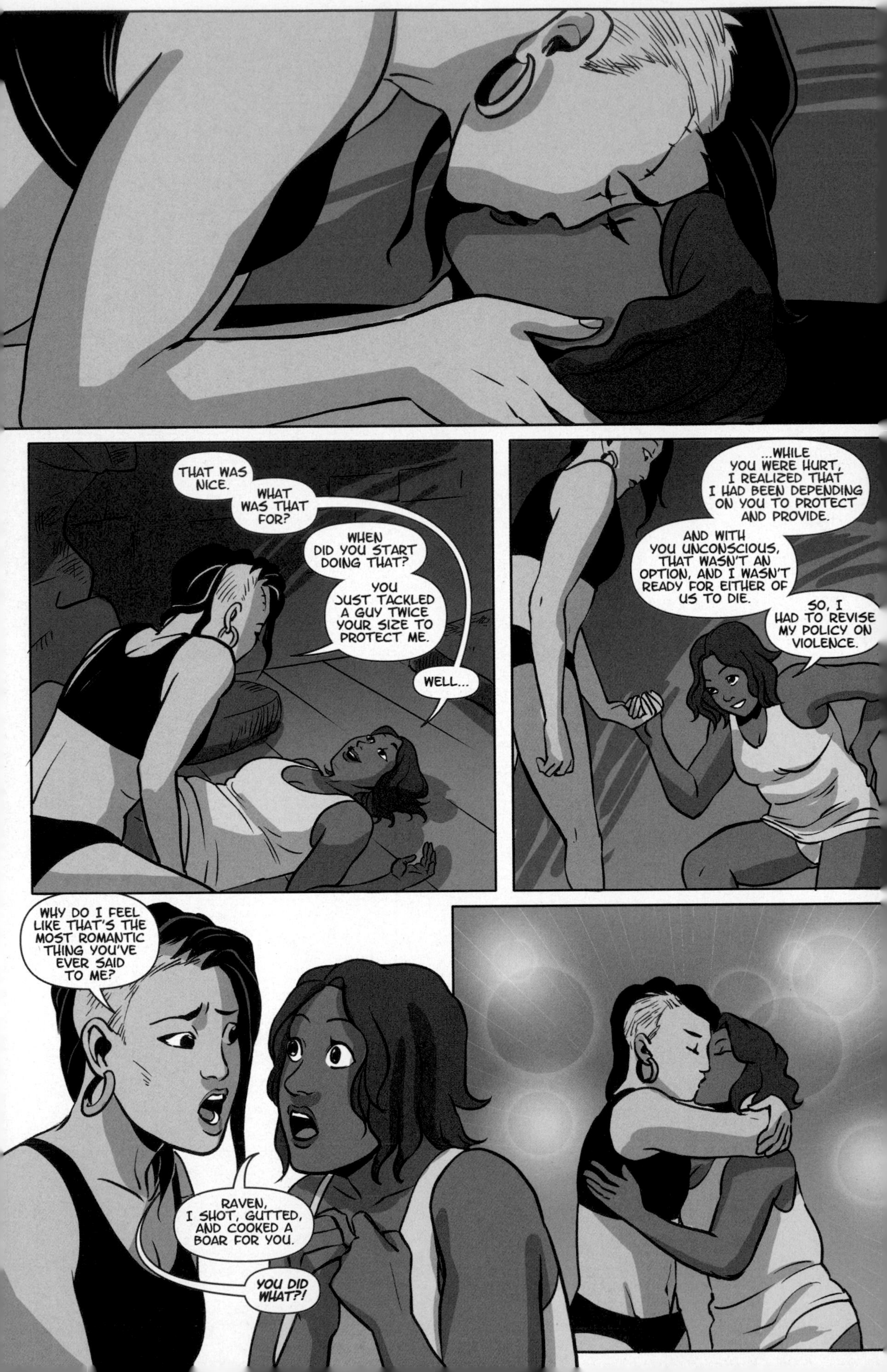
THAT WAS NICE.
WHAT WAS THAT FOR?
WHEN DID YOU START DOING THAT?
YOU JUST TACKLED A GUY TWICE YOUR SIZE TO PROTECT ME.
WELL...
...WHILE YOU WERE HURT, I REALIZED THAT I HAD BEEN DEPENDING ON YOU TO PROTECT AND PROVIDE.
AND WITH YOU UNCONSCIOUS, THAT WASN'T AN OPTION, AND I WASN'T READY FOR EITHER OF US TO DIE.
SO, I HAD TO REVISE MY POLICY ON VIOLENCE.
WHY DO I FEEL LIKE THAT'S THE MOST ROMANTIC THING YOU'VE EVER SAID TO ME?
RAVEN, I SHOT, GUTTED, AND COOKED A BOAR FOR YOU.
YOU DID WHAT?!

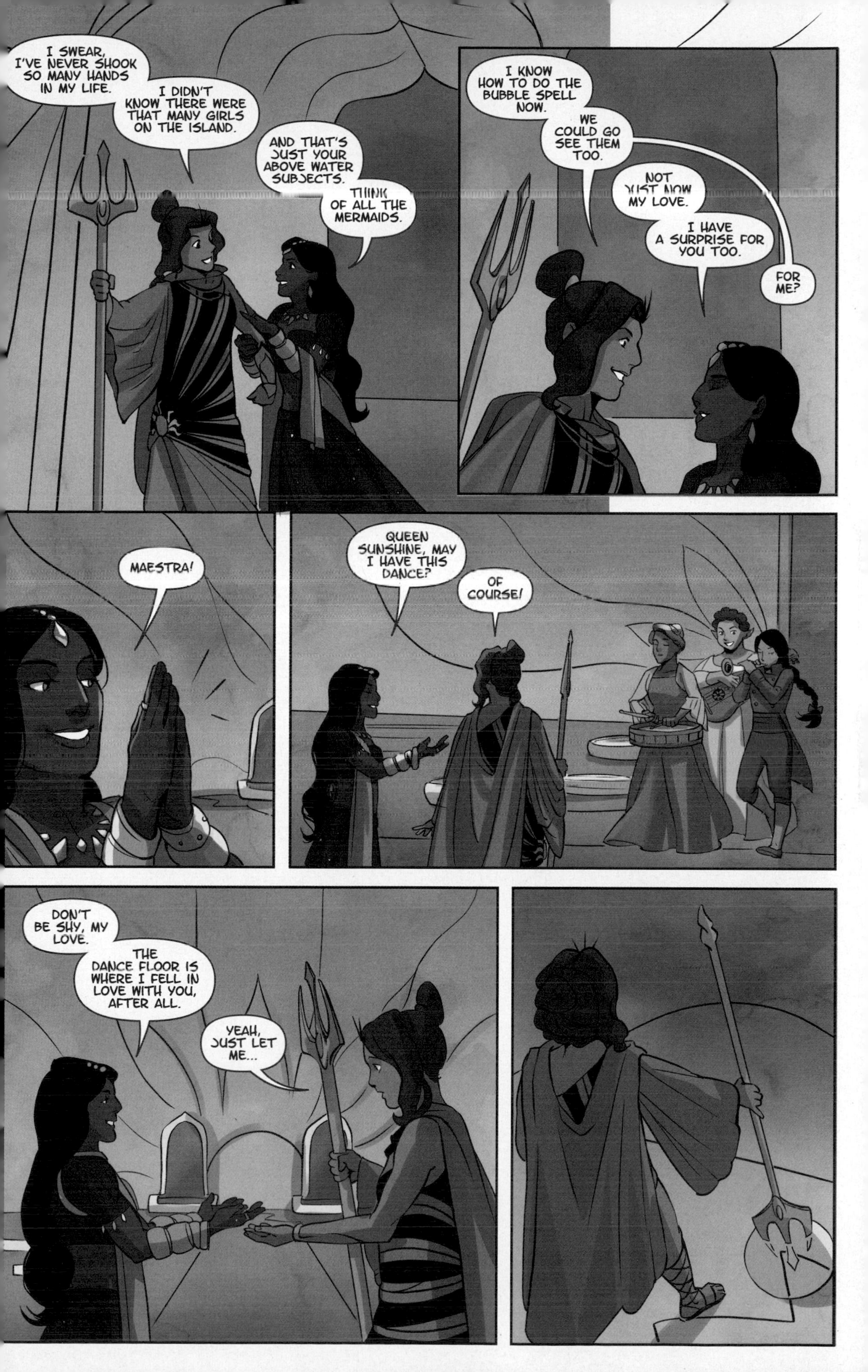
I SWEAR, I'VE NEVER SHOOK SO MANY HANDS IN MY LIFE.
I DIDN'T KNOW THERE WERE THAT MANY GIRLS ON THE ISLAND.
AND THAT'S JUST YOUR ABOVE WATER SUBJECTS.
THINK OF ALL THE MERMAIDS.
I KNOW HOW TO DO THE BUBBLE SPELL NOW.
WE COULD GO SEE THEM TOO.
NOT JUST NOW MY LOVE.
I HAVE A SURPRISE FOR YOU TOO.
FOR ME?
MAESTRA!
QUEEN SUNSHINE, MAY I HAVE THIS DANCE?
OF COURSE!
DON'T BE SHY, MY LOVE.
THE DANCE FLOOR IS WHERE I FELL IN LOVE WITH YOU, AFTER ALL.
YEAH, JUST LET ME...

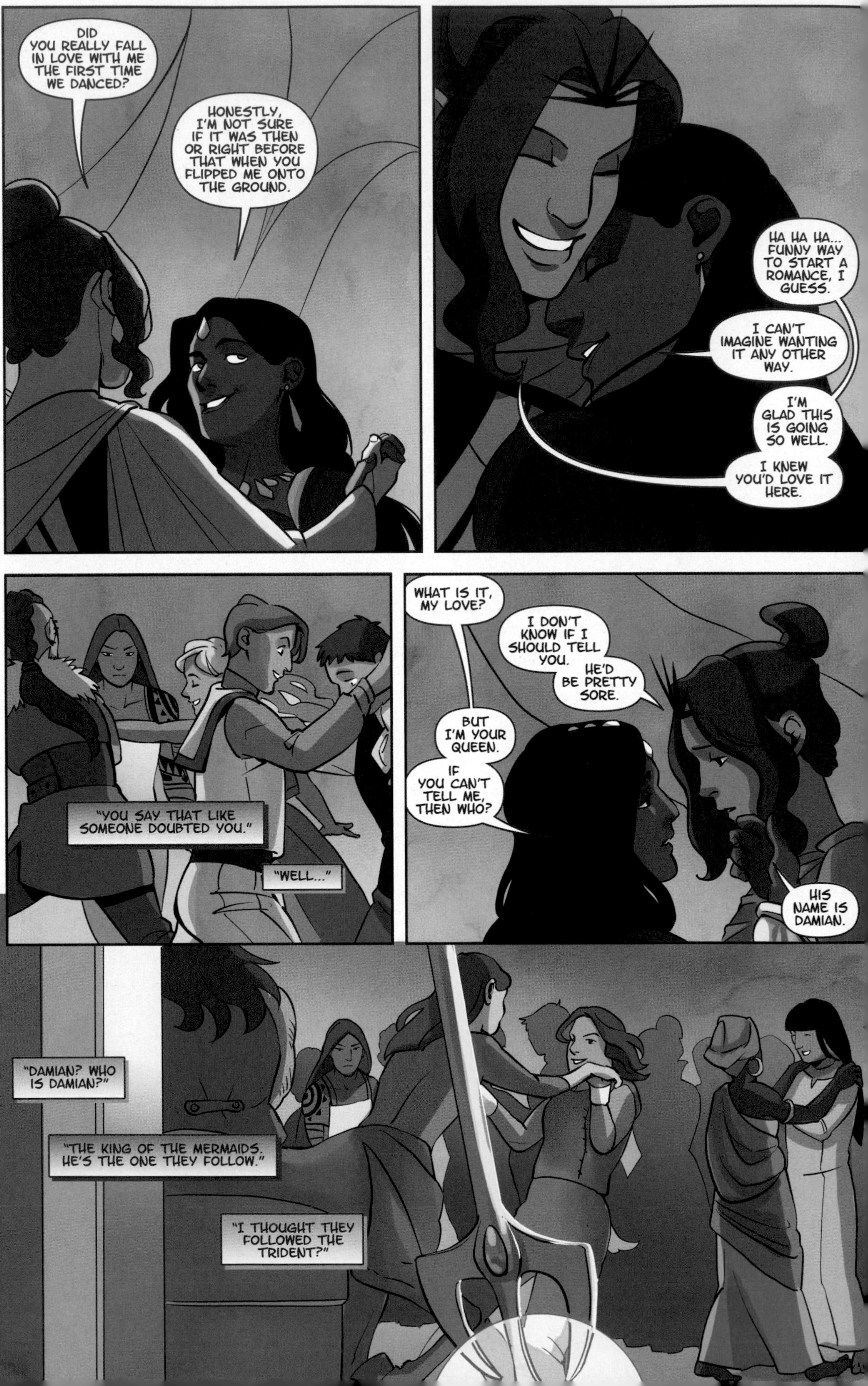
DID YOU REALLY FALL IN LOVE WITH ME THE FIRST TIME WE DANCED?
HONESTLY, I'M NOT SURE IF IT WAS THEN OR RIGHT BEFORE THAT WHEN YOU FLIPPED ME ONTO THE GROUND.
HA HA HA... FUNNY WAY TO START A ROMANCE, I GUESS.
I CAN'T IMAGINE WANTING IT ANY OTHER WAY.
I'M GLAD THIS IS GOING SO WELL.
I KNEW YOU'D LOVE IT HERE.
"YOU SAY THAT LIKE SOMEONE DOUBTED YOU."
"WELL..."
WHAT IS IT, MY LOVE?
I DON'T KNOW IF I SHOULD TELL YOU.
HE'D BE PRETTY SORE.
BUT I'M YOUR QUEEN.
IF YOU CAN'T TELL ME, THEN WHO?
HIS NAME IS DAMIAN.
"DAMIAN? WHO IS DAMIAN?"
"THE KING OF THE MERMAIDS. HE'S THE ONE THEY FOLLOW."
"I THOUGHT THEY FOLLOWED THE TRIDENT?"

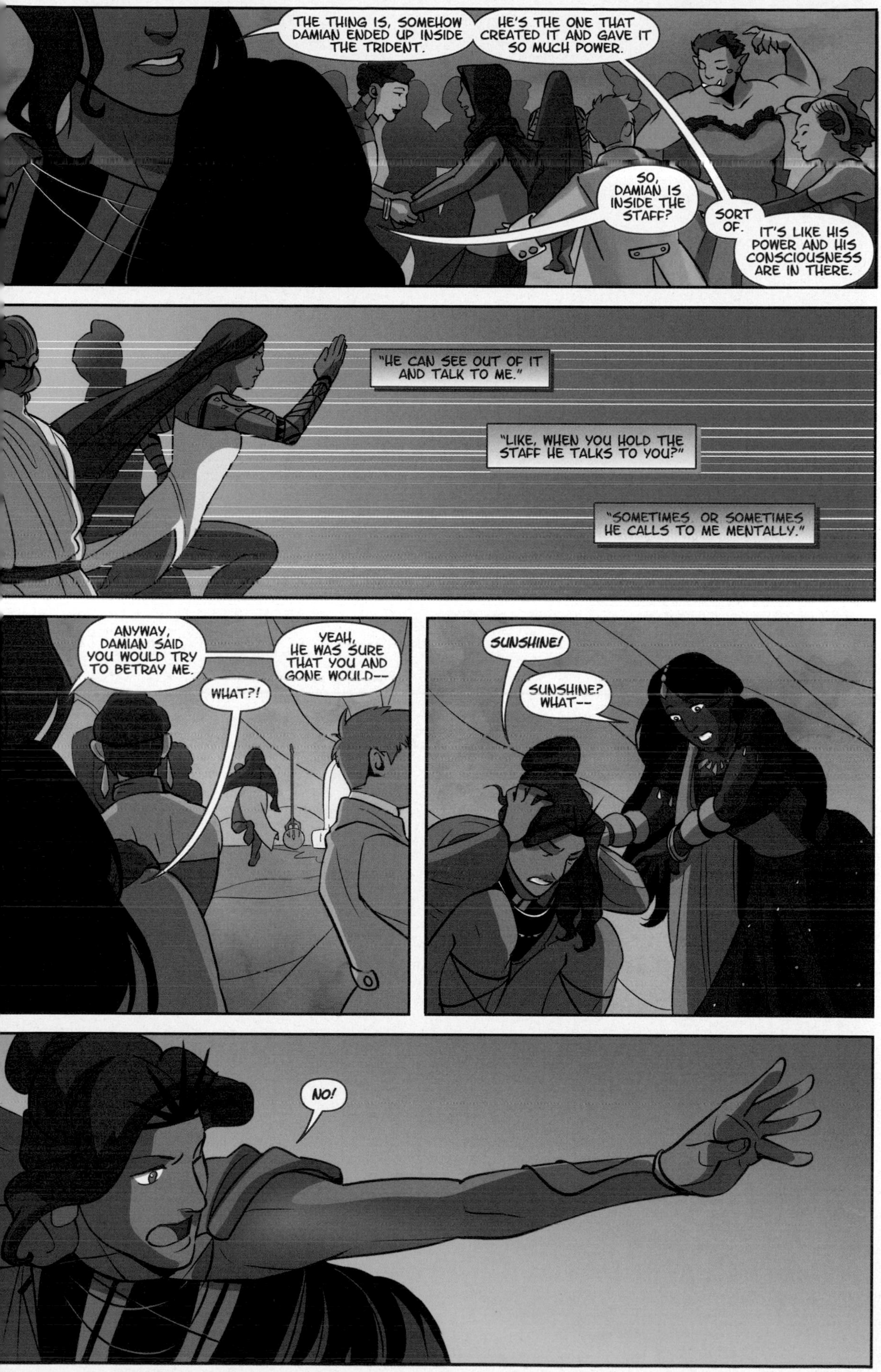
THE THING IS, SOMEHOW DAMIAN ENDED UP INSIDE THE TRIDENT.
HE'S THE ONE THAT CREATED IT AND GAVE IT SO MUCH POWER.
SO, DAMIAN IS INSIDE THE STAFF?
SORT OF.
IT'S LIKE HIS POWER AND HIS CONSCIOUSNESS ARE IN THERE.
"HE CAN SEE OUT OF IT AND TALK TO ME."
"LIKE, WHEN YOU HOLD THE STAFF HE TALKS TO YOU?"
"SOMETIMES. OR SOMETIMES HE CALLS TO ME MENTALLY."
ANYWAY, DAMIAN SAID YOU WOULD TRY TO BETRAY ME.
YEAH, HE WAS SURE THAT YOU AND GONE WOULD--
WHAT?!
SUNSHINE!
SUNSHINE? WHAT--
NO!

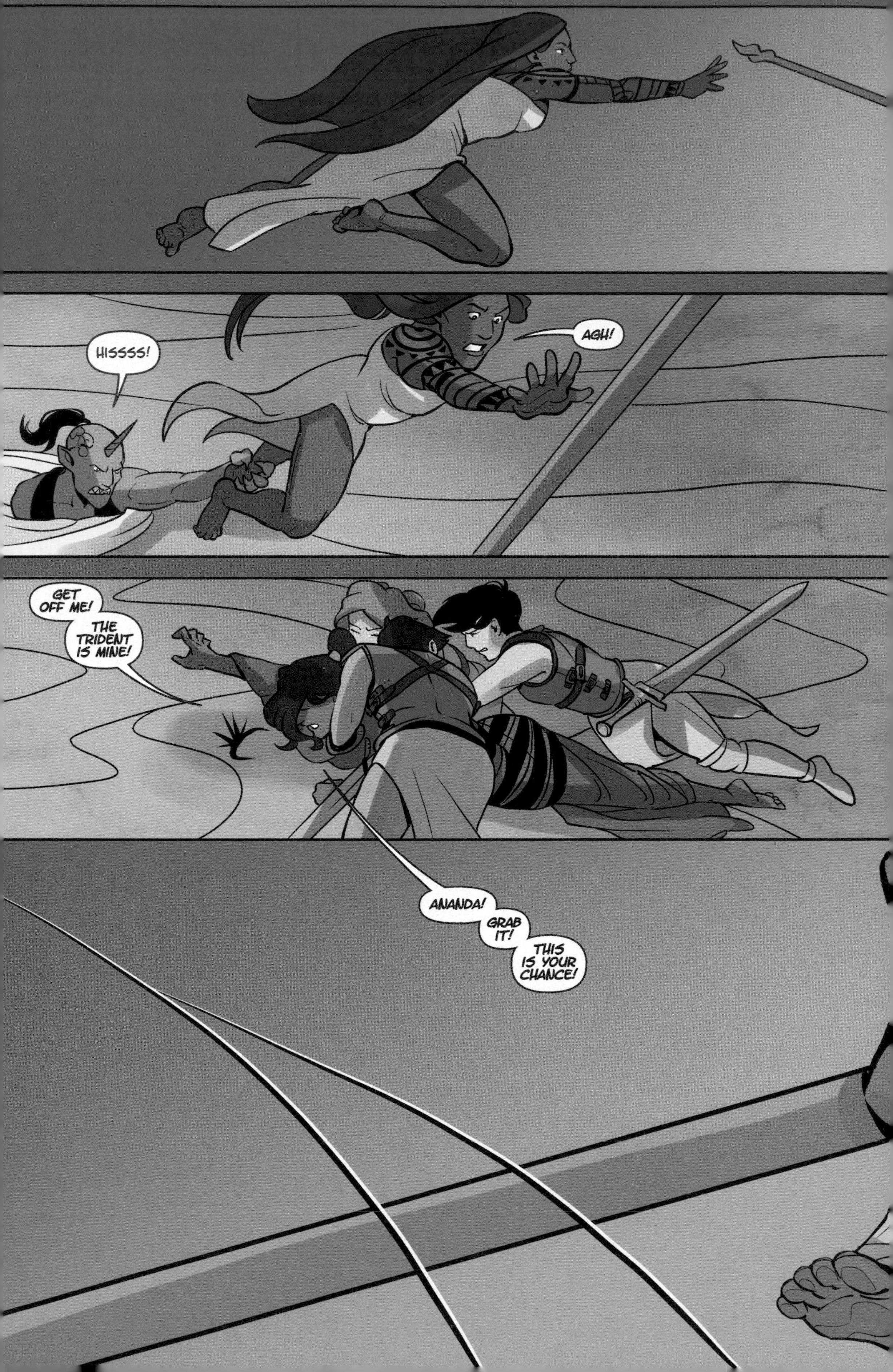
HISSSS!
AGH!
GET OFF ME!
THE TRIDENT IS MINE!
ANANDA!
GRAB IT!
THIS IS YOUR CHANCE!

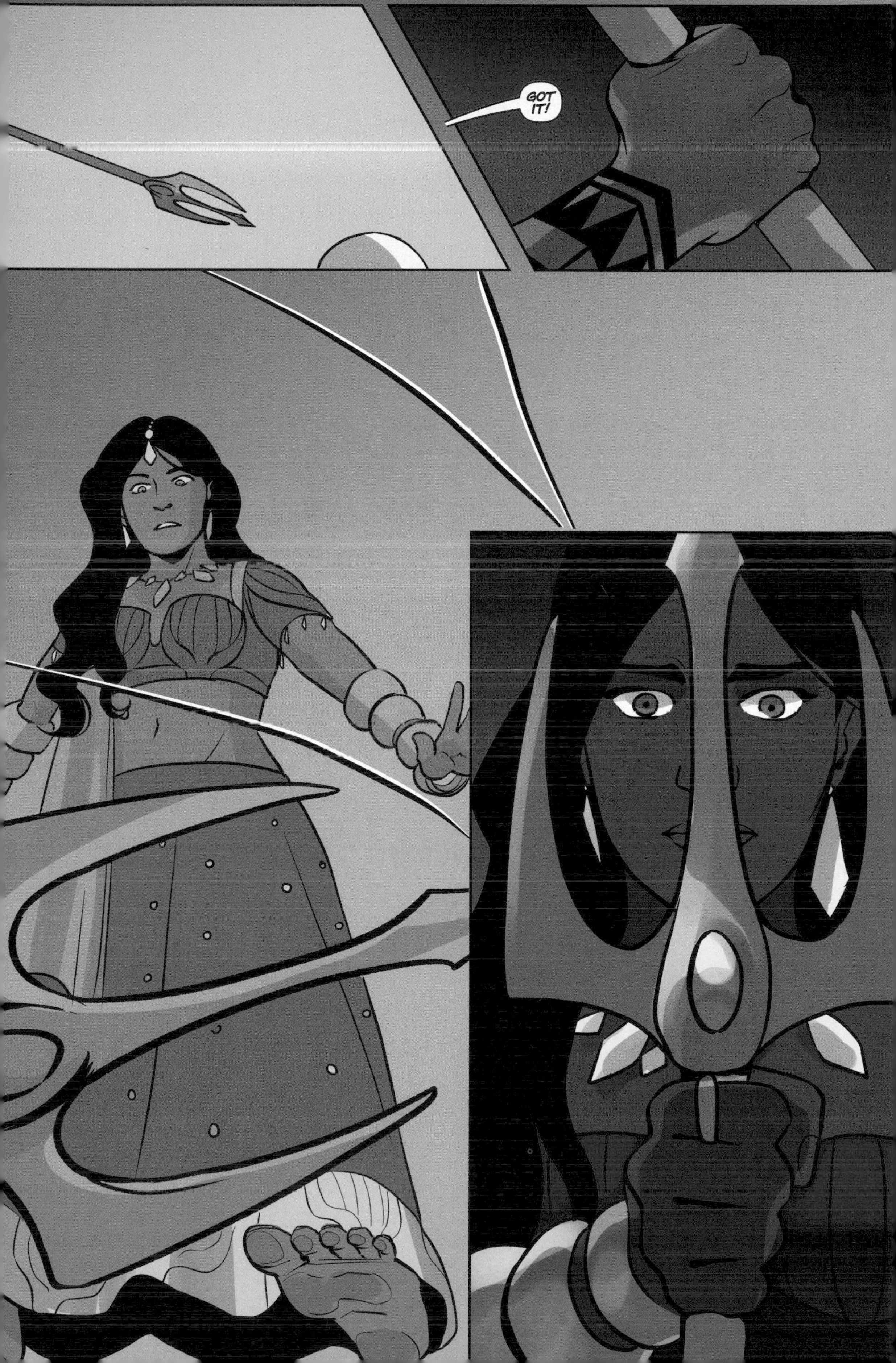
GOT IT!

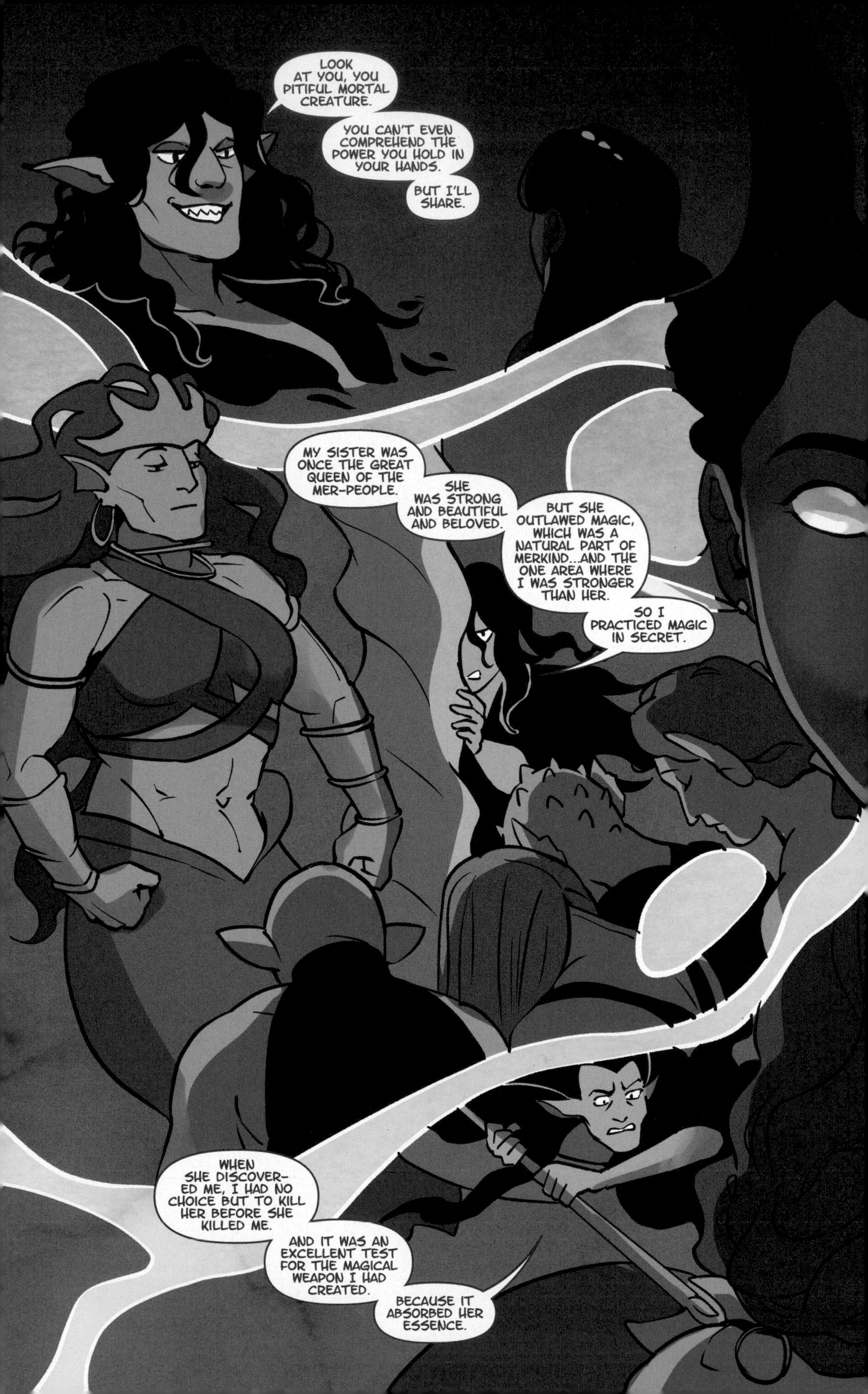
LOOK AT YOU, YOU PITIFUL MORTAL CREATURE.
YOU CAN'T EVEN COMPREHEND THE POWER YOU HOLD IN YOUR HANDS.
BUT I'LL SHARE.
MY SISTER WAS ONCE THE GREAT QUEEN OF THE MER-PEOPLE.
SHE WAS STRONG AND BEAUTIFUL AND BELOVED.
BUT SHE OUTLAWED MAGIC, WHICH WAS A NATURAL PART OF MERKIND...AND THE ONE AREA WHERE I WAS STRONGER THAN HER.
SO I PRACTICED MAGIC IN SECRET.
WHEN SHE DISCOVERED ME, I HAD NO CHOICE BUT TO KILL HER BEFORE SHE KILLED ME.
AND IT WAS AN EXCELLENT TEST FOR THE MAGICAL WEAPON I HAD CREATED.
BECAUSE IT ABSORBED HER ESSENCE.

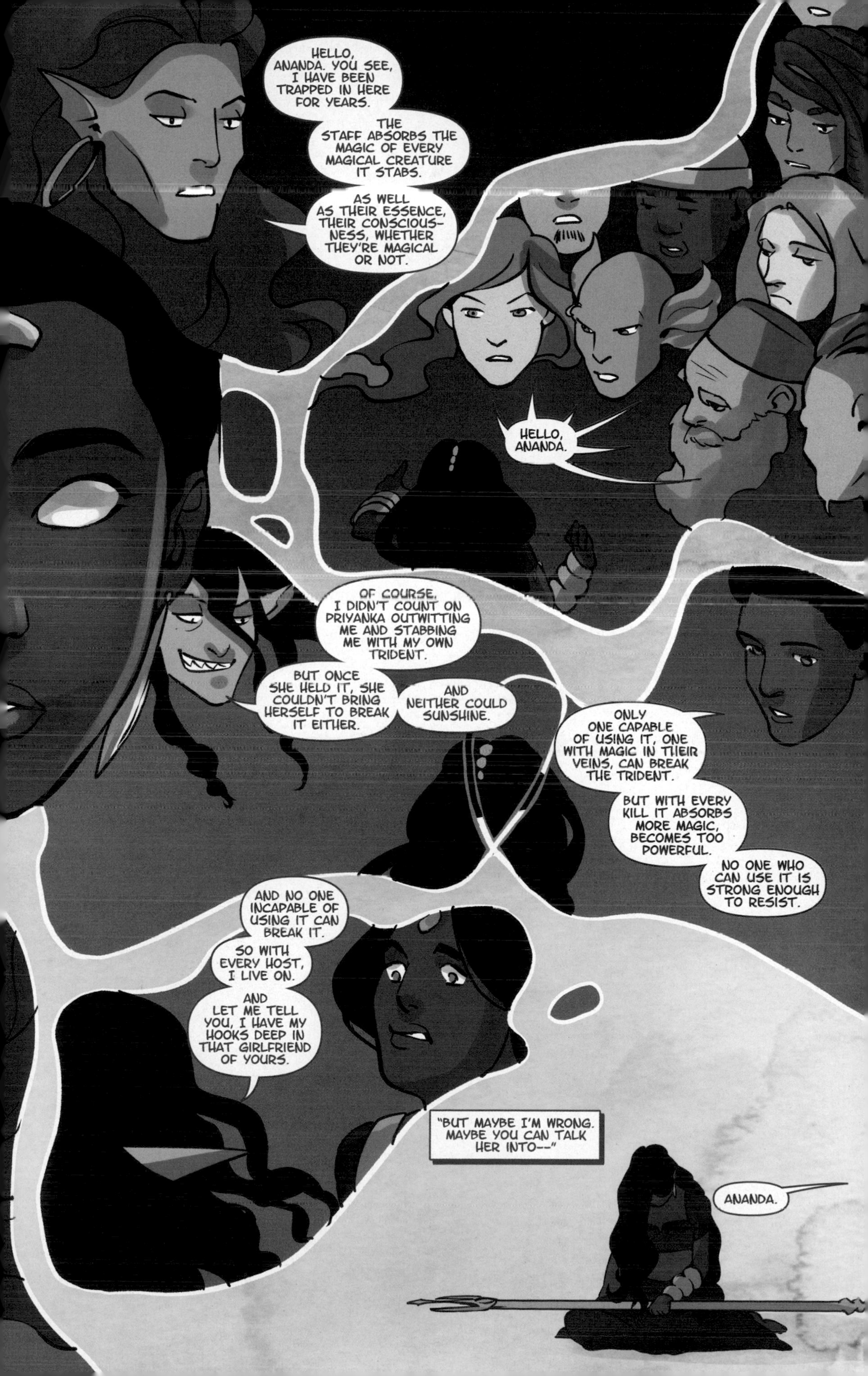
HELLO, ANANDA. YOU SEE, I HAVE BEEN TRAPPED IN HERE FOR YEARS.
THE STAFF ABSORBS THE MAGIC OF EVERY MAGICAL CREATURE IT STABS.
AS WELL AS THEIR ESSENCE, THEIR CONSCIOUS-NESS, WHETHER THEY'RE MAGICAL OR NOT.
HELLO, ANANDA.
OF COURSE, I DIDN'T COUNT ON PRIYANKA OUTWITTING ME AND STABBING ME WITH MY OWN TRIDENT.
BUT ONCE SHE HELD IT, SHE COULDN'T BRING HERSELF TO BREAK IT EITHER.
AND NEITHER COULD SUNSHINE.
ONLY ONE CAPABLE OF USING IT, ONE WITH MAGIC IN THEIR VEINS, CAN BREAK THE TRIDENT.
BUT WITH EVERY KILL IT ABSORBS MORE MAGIC, BECOMES TOO POWERFUL.
NO ONE WHO CAN USE IT IS STRONG ENOUGH TO RESIST.
AND NO ONE INCAPABLE OF USING IT CAN BREAK IT.
SO WITH EVERY HOST, I LIVE ON.
AND LET ME TELL YOU, I HAVE MY HOOKS DEEP IN THAT GIRLFRIEND OF YOURS.
"BUT MAYBE I'M WRONG. MAYBE YOU CAN TALK HER INTO--"
ANANDA.

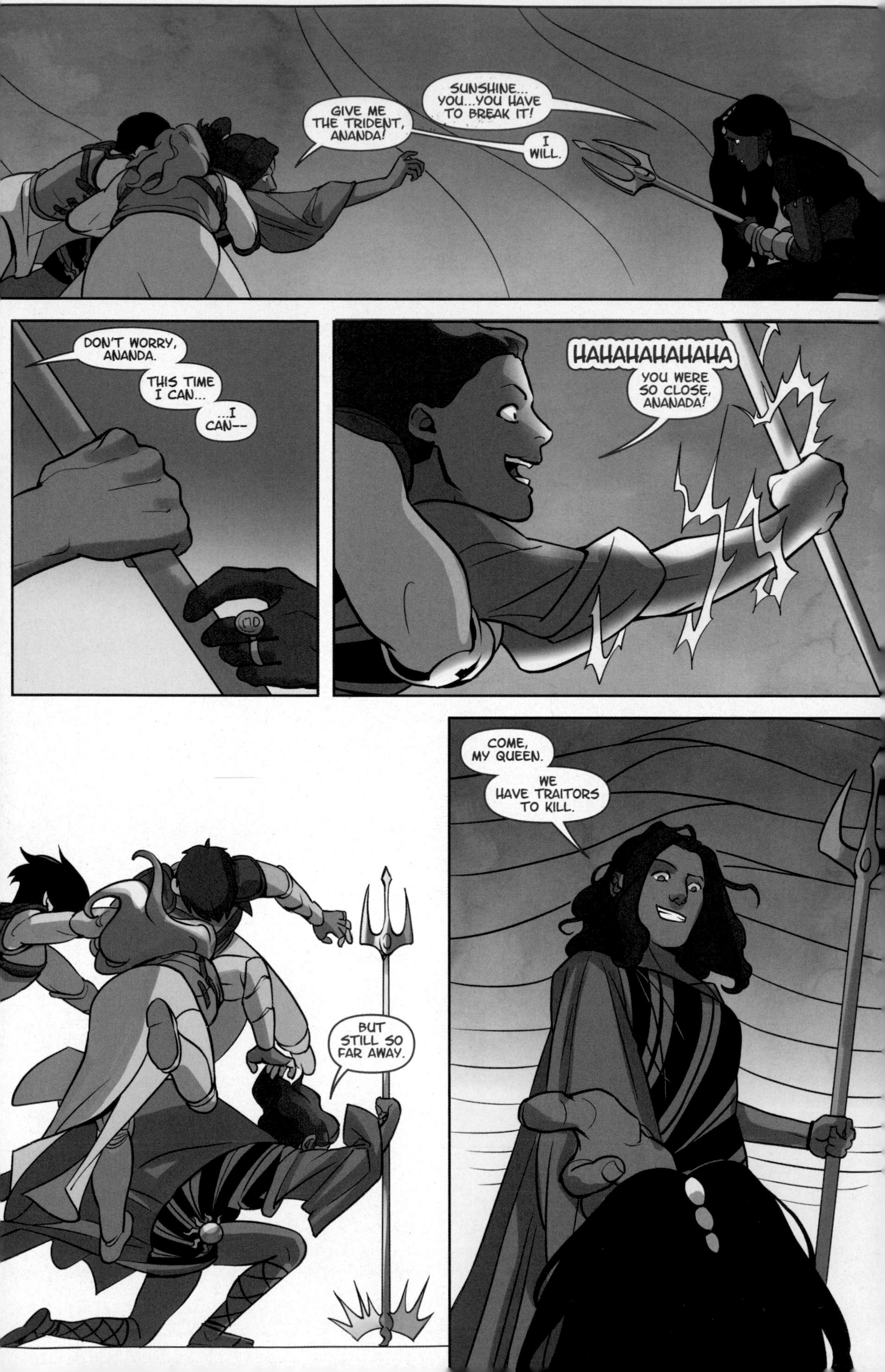
GIVE ME THE TRIDENT, ANANDA!
SUNSHINE... YOU...YOU HAVE TO BREAK IT!
I WILL.
DON'T WORRY, ANANDA.
THIS TIME I CAN...
...I CAN--
HAHAHAHAHAHA
YOU WERE SO CLOSE, ANANADA!
BUT STILL SO FAR AWAY.
COME, MY QUEEN.
WE HAVE TRAITORS TO KILL.